CLARION CALL

SEQUEL TO *RAVENSONG*

CAYLA FAY

SIMON & SCHUSTER BFYR

NEW YORK   LONDON   TORONTO   SYDNEY   NEW DELHI

SIMON & SCHUSTER BFYR

An imprint of Simon & Schuster Children's Publishing Division
1230 Avenue of the Americas, New York, New York 10020

SIMON & SCHUSTER BOOKS FOR YOUNG READERS
and related marks are trademarks of Simon & Schuster, LLC.
Simon & Schuster: Celebrating 100 Years of Publishing in 2024
For information about special discounts for bulk purchases, please contact
Simon & Schuster Special Sales at 1-866-506-1949 or business@simonandschuster.com.
The Simon & Schuster Speakers Bureau can bring authors to your live event.
For more information or to book an event, contact the Simon & Schuster Speakers Bureau at
1-866-248-3049 or visit our website at www.simonspeakers.com.
Interior design by Hilary Zarycky
The text for this book was set in Bell.
Manufactured in the United States of America
First Edition
2 4 6 8 10 9 7 5 3 1
Library of Congress Cataloging-in-Publication Data
Names: Fay, Cayla, author. | Fay, Cayla. Ravensong.
Title: Clarion call / Cayla Fay.
Description: New York City : Simon & Schuster Books for Young Readers, 2024. | Series:
Ravensong; book 2 | Audience: Ages 12 up. | Audience: Grades 7–9. | Summary: Having failed
to prevent her vengeful cousin from breaching the Veil, demi-god Neve attempts to prevent
more havoc and destruction in the mortal world while she also grapples with old memories,
a new family member's emergence, and the delicate balance between past, present, and an
uncertain future.
Identifiers: LCCN 2023034903 (print) | LCCN 2023034904 (ebook) |
ISBN 9781665905329 (hardcover) | ISBN 9781665905343 (ebook)
Subjects: CYAC: Mythology, Celtic—Fiction. | LGBTQ+ people—Fiction. | Fantasy. |
LCGFT: Fantasy fiction. | Novels.
Classification: LCC PZ7.1.F388 Cl 2024 (print) | LCC PZ7.1.F388 (ebook) | DDC [Fic]—dc23
LC record available at https://lccn.loc.gov/2023034903
LC ebook record available at https://lccn.loc.gov/2023034904

To Kelsey and Kristen,

the family I made along the way

CHAPTER ONE

No one would think that the girl bleeding out on the rocky beach was a god. They might think she was in some kind of horrible accident—a fall, maybe, from the high cliff above onto the shore below. Though that wouldn't explain why the blood pouring out of a massive wound in her midsection was a distinct, shimmering blue.

The funny thing was that they—the human observer unlucky enough to watch the elder Morgans, Mercy and Bay, with Alexandria Kuro's help, drag Neve's body through a swirling rift in the cliffside—would be right. Neve Morgan wasn't a god. She wasn't human, either, obviously. She was something else. Something worse. Something old and powerful and treacherous.

And now, the girl who wasn't a god was dying.

Except, no. She couldn't. She wasn't allowed.

"Neve Morgan, I love you, and that means you're not allowed to die!"

As she scraped up the last dregs of her strength, Neve held Alexandria's order close, as if she could use it as a shield.

It didn't do much about the blood pouring out of her middle

and clumping in the sand like so much spilled ink, or magically heal the gory, soupy mess of her torso, but Neve could pretend. It was something. It had to be something.

"You have to get out of here," Neve said. Tried to, anyway. What came out was more of a gurgle as a gout of frothy blood spilled out of her mouth, adding to the thin coating of viscera staining her skin.

"Don't try to talk," Alexandria urged, and Neve's focus snapped back to her. Even the muscles in her eyes ached as they fought to keep Alexandria in focus. "Neve, you're—"

Neve knew what she was. Alexandria didn't have to say it.

"I'm sorry," Alexandria whispered, bending to press her forehead against the matted bloody mess of Neve's hair. "I'm so sorry. I did this."

Neve's whole body shuddered, and something lit in her mangled chest. It felt like there was lightning in her veins, cauterizing her wounds every place it touched, because Alexandria was apologizing to her and that was bullshit. It wasn't Alexandria's fault—none of this was Alexandria's fault.

The ground shook beneath her, drawing Neve's attention back to the Gate, giving her a place to direct the new wellspring of fury. This wasn't Alexandria's fault, Neve thought again as she turned her attention to the Hellgate. To where Aodh—her fratricidal piece-of-shit cousin—was about to break free after a thousand years of trying, a thousand years of killing Neve and her sisters over and over and over again. Aodh, who had been haunting Alexandria for years, hunting the Morrigan for lifetimes, and who was about to walk out of the churning mess of magic that used to be the Gate.

After you forgot me, snarled Aodh's voice in the back of Neve's head. She'd been hearing it for months and only now knew where it had come from. *After you left me behind.*

Neve saw the horror dawning on Bay's face, felt Mercy's guilt shatter through her even as Mercy's expression froze over into glacial rage.

"I'm sorry," Neve tried to say, but there was too much blood where it wasn't supposed to be and it drowned the words before they could come out of her mouth.

She didn't want this.

What a stupid, selfish thing to think, especially in this moment, when everything was falling apart.

All Neve had wanted, all she had ever wanted, even before Alexandria, was to be like her sisters. To be their equal. To stand in the sun with them and not be left behind in the shadow of her own ignorance.

Now you know. It was probably her imagination that his voice was getting stronger now, louder, as if the volume was directly linked to his proximity to the Gate. *Is it everything you ever wanted?*

I didn't want this, Neve thought desperately, unsure of who she was trying to convince. Herself. Her sisters. Maybe her cousin, too, the version of him that existed within the scraps of her memories. But she'd realized it too late. Now the Gate was open, and the chain that had linked Neve and her sisters lifetime after lifetime had shattered. Neve could feel it, the aching loss of something that had been there for longer than she could remember. The pain should've been indistinct among the deluge from her other injuries as her nerves screamed and tore themselves to ragged pieces, but Neve could still feel that hurt in particular, even as the others ran together in a wash of blood and viscera and *painpainpainpain*.

"We have to shut it!"

Somehow, Alexandria's voice managed to cut through the noise and stimuli, dragging Neve unwillingly back to the nightmare she'd created.

There was blood on Alexandria's face that was not hers, on her shirt where Neve had clung to her, and on her hands where she'd helped drag Neve through the Gate.

Stupid, Neve thought. She didn't know if it was her voice or Aodh's anymore. They were blurring together in her head. *Should have just left me.*

"Hey, shut up," Alexandria said, her gaze snapping suddenly to Neve, who realized a beat too late that she'd spoken aloud. It might have been the blood loss, but in the haze of her dimming vision, Alexandria looked a little like she was glowing.

She also looked pissed.

"You don't get to talk like that, okay?" Alexandria said heatedly. "So shut up and focus on not dying."

Neve wasn't even sure she could manage that much, but Alexandria's attention had moved back to Mercy and Bay.

"How do we close it?" she asked, the severity in her voice giving way to naked desperation.

They didn't know.

Neve knew that without having to see the look that passed between her sisters. This was so beyond anything they had been raised to believe, beyond everything they had prepared for. It wasn't supposed to happen like this, none of it.

Neve watched as the look of hopelessness turned into something else. Normally, she could have understood the silent conversation that passed between her sisters in a matter of seconds, but Neve's mind was too blurry with pain and fear, and it happened too quickly for her to parse. But then tears spilled down Bay's cheeks, and Mercy gave a tiny, almost imperceptible nod.

They didn't say anything. They didn't even look back, but Neve felt her sisters' determination burn in her own chest. Adrenaline burst afresh, her body reacting to a decision they made without her. But before she could do anything—manage to stand, shout at them to stop—Mercy and Bay tore off down the beach.

"What are you—?" Alexandria yelled after them, but they were already gone.

Behind her, the waves pounded against the sharp sand that dug into Neve's knees and shins as she fought her way to her feet. Lightning split the sky, staving off the darkness of the storm long enough for Neve to see with perfect clarity the moment her sisters plunged back through the portal.

Like it was something hungry that had been sated, the churning bruise-purple maw of the Gate stilled. The instinctive part of Neve that knew magic, that felt it in her blood and all around her, quieted too.

Neve had been wrong before. There was enough strength left in her to scream. It wasn't a proper warscream, not even close, just a human sound of shock and panic that ripped out of her throat. Distantly, in the part of her that was still connected to her body, she felt the force dislodge something in her torso. Her insides felt more or less liquified, sloshing around in the punctured mess of flesh that was the rest of her body.

Then the Gate was still and Neve was screaming because what the hell else was she supposed to do? Her sisters were gone. They had *left*; they had left her behind.

It couldn't have been more than a minute—though it felt like much, much longer—when Neve's voice quit on her again.

Without the sound of her own scream echoing in her ears, Neve could hear frantic voices somewhere behind her. She recognized them, categorized them as safe, and let them fade to the background as the whole of her remaining focus narrowed on the place where her sisters had been swallowed up by the Gate. She couldn't look away.

Thunder rolled overhead, and the storm that had been threatening finally broke.

"Neve—*Neve!*"

She heard the voice calling her name and dismissed it, letting it fall into the ringing in her ears that might have been a symptom of head trauma or a panic attack or both.

Stabbing her sword into the sand like it was the world's pointiest walking stick, Neve staggered toward the Gate. She moved at a glacial pace, barely able to force her legs to hold her. Every step made her nerves scream in agony and shred themselves anew, but Neve wasn't in her body at the moment. She was somewhere above and to the left of it, a guiding force. The only thing that felt real was the ringing in her ears and the certainty that she needed to keep moving, she needed to follow Mercy and Bay.

"Stop." The part of her that was aware of her body, whatever bit of herself that was still in the driver's seat, felt the pressure of a hand on her arm. Gentle at first and then firm. Halting her progress. "Neve, you have to stop!"

"No." The voice that clawed its way out of her throat didn't sound like hers. It was barely a croak, halfway choked with blood. "They're in there. I have to get them. . . . I have to—"

"You can't!" Alexandria's face solidified somewhat in Neve's vision, despite her best efforts not to see anything but the Gate in front of her. "Neve, stop. Please, you're killing yourself."

Tears cut clean tracks down the grime and blood on Alexandria's face, and Neve was sorry for it. She was also completely out of her fucking mind.

"Open it," Neve rasped.

"What?"

"You did it before," Neve rambled. She wasn't entirely sure the words were making it out of her mouth, and if they were, there was a nonzero chance they were the wrong ones, but the look of horror on Alexandria's face indicated that she understood what Neve was asking.

"I can't." Alexandria shook her head. She looked like she wanted to step away, put distance between them, but gritted her teeth and stayed put.

"You did," Neve insisted. "You already did once. Do it again."

"I—"

"They're in there," Neve said raggedly. She thought she might be crying, but she couldn't tell if the wetness on her cheeks was from blood or tears. "Please, you have to. I can't . . . I—please. Alexandria, please," Neve begged.

"I don't know if it will work," Alexandria said. "I don't know . . . I don't know anything."

Neve didn't care. Alexandria was the key; Aodh had said so himself. She'd opened the Gate from the inside, and Neve had seen how the things within it had been drawn to her, even when the Gate was otherwise quiet.

She thought of the monster that had emerged from the Gate on a different night, during a different storm, when Alexandria had pressed her hand against the stone.

Neve looked at Alexandria with renewed desperation. Neve couldn't do this on her own—she didn't think she could do this at all. It had taken five humans and a centuries-old spell to open the Gate from their side *specifically* because Neve couldn't open it on her own.

"Please," Neve asked again.

Her mouth pressing into a thin, miserable line, Alexandria squared her shoulders. She stepped within arm's reach of the Gate, which had gone nearly dormant and looked like an ordinary stone wall again, but the spell didn't rekindle. The portal didn't spring back to life.

"No," Neve said. She shook her head and even that small motion sent pain rattling down her spine. The burst of panic and adrenaline that had kept her upright this long was fading.

Mercy and Bay were gone. Just gone. Neve couldn't feel them anymore; there was just a hollow place behind her heart that felt like it was going to swallow her whole.

"Neve, I'm—" Alexandria started before she cut herself off with a scream.

Neve didn't have any forewarning. One minute the Gate was very nearly closed, her metaphysical awareness of it dwindling to almost nothing, and the next it sprang back to seething life. The force of it nearly bowled her over, but Neve clenched her hands around the hilt of her sword and managed to keep her feet.

Alexandria shouted something, or tried to, before a single pale hand tore itself free of the sludgy swirl of the portal.

Without thinking, Neve lunged forward, forgoing her sword altogether to grab at the hand. She clasped it tight between both of her own and pulled as hard as she could. She could feel the spell recoiling, whether from her presence or because the Gate wanted to keep its prize, she wasn't sure. It didn't matter. With strength she did not have to spare, Neve pulled.

She could feel the Gate fighting against her. It was winning. She wasn't strong enough.

She was going to lose them.

"On three!" Alexandria shouted, clasping her hands over Neve's. "One . . . two . . . !"

They pulled together for a second that dragged out into infinity, until Neve was sure the Gate was going to close on them again. But then she felt the tiniest bit of give.

She and Alexandria pulled, inch by inexorable inch, until the Gate's polarity seemed to flip completely and the force they fought against vanished.

Neve collapsed into an ungainly pile of limbs, blood flooding out of her body afresh as her wounds were jarred by the fall.

"Oh no," Alexandria said with horror in her voice, a second before Neve's vision cleared enough to see that the person they'd pulled out of the Gate wasn't Bay or Mercy.

Aodh stood shakily, one hand thrown out to the now-solid portal for balance. The gloating triumph in his face faded as he looked back at the Gate, which had closed decisively behind him.

"What did you do?" Aodh demanded, his voice pitched high. If Neve hadn't known better, she might have thought that he was scared. She couldn't fathom why; he'd gotten what he wanted.

Before Neve could pull her wits back together into some semblance of rational thought—or at the very least, manage to drown out the high-pitched screaming inside her head—a blast like lightning exploded a hair's breadth away from Aodh's head.

"Get the hell away from them."

Neve knew the look of Aoife's magic and recognized the unyielding steel of Maeve's voice, but neither was a comfort.

The expression on Aodh's face calcified into a sneer, his gray eyes flashing as he took in the newcomers. Calculating his odds. Neve recognized the look because she'd worn it herself a hundred times.

With one last look at the Gate, Aodh snarled and ran. Part of Neve wanted to scream for someone to go after him, to insist that he not get away. The rest of her was just screaming, a high, terrible noise that rang through her blood, her bones, through the terrible empty space in her chest.

"Neve." She blinked and Clara's face swam before her own. "Neve, baby, what happened?"

It was only then Neve realized the keening noise wasn't just inside her head but coming out of her mouth as well, a wordless, pathetic whine.

"They're gone." The words coagulated on her tongue. She wasn't sure how she was still conscious. She wasn't sure of anything except the numb, creeping horror that had taken root behind her heart. Neve's blurred, white-wreathed gaze slid behind Clara as if she weren't there and fixed on the last place she'd seen Bay and Mercy before they vanished. "They're gone."

CHAPTER TWO

S he lived. Neve wished she could say that it was on purpose. That it was through stubbornness and willpower that her battered body didn't give out on her—that Neve had insisted her heart keep pumping—but it wasn't. She should've died, but she couldn't seem to manage it.

And wasn't that just the throughline of her life? Her lives, her lifetimes. That Neve seemed destined to die, destined to meet a premature end, only to keep on going despite the staggering odds. Lifetime after lifetime of wringing a few more hours, days, years out of life when she should have been dead and gone long ago. Neve somehow, no matter how improbably, kept on living.

Living hurt. Neve thought she'd known that before— she'd been injured enough times—but this was different. All of her hurt, from her torn skin and muscles all the way down to her organs, the veins and capillaries that carried her blood. Her *bones* hurt.

That was the thing about limping on even when the last fight should have killed you, and the one before that, and the one before that. It didn't come for free. Not even close.

Predictably, the first hazy times she'd swum back to consciousness, there hadn't been much *but* the pain. It was only the third or fourth time, when Neve woke up and actually stayed awake, that she noticed the quiet.

The convent, despite its austere exterior, was rarely silent. The metal catwalks that connected in tangled crisscrosses on the upper floors creaked. The windowpanes shook and juddered in the wind. The stones themselves made noise sometimes, the tiniest scraping sounds as they settled even farther against each other, holding fast despite centuries of weather wearing them down.

That wasn't what was missing, Neve thought as she tried to get her body to act like a body instead of a miserable miasma of pain, standing on shaky legs that seemed reluctant to take her weight. She could hear all those sounds, the background noise of her childhood. It was something else, something missing that she couldn't place but still nagged at her, a splinter in the back of her mind.

It was also a distraction from everything she was refusing to think about.

So, with one arm wrapped over her chest alongside the swaths of bandages keeping the stitched-up mess of her torso intact, Neve limped through the high-ceilinged, echoing halls she'd known her entire life.

In the weird stillness, the convent felt too much like the

mirror version she'd visited behind the Veil. That convent had been quiet too, and cold and angry. It hated her and Neve had felt it. The memory made her shudder and she quickly turned her thoughts away from the Veil. It was too close to the Gate for comfort, and Neve couldn't think about that without thinking about—

She needed some air.

Outside it was freezing, the icy breeze off the ocean stinging every bit of skin it could reach. Neve breathed shallowly through her nose, careful not to overburden her lungs, which had taken the brunt of the damage. They still ached despite her efforts, but the frigid air was bracing, even if it did make her chest hurt.

Neve tipped her head back, the stitches on her neck straining under their bandages as she did so. The sky was completely dark above her as clouds obscured the light from the moon and stars. Maybe that was why it took her so long to realize that, though she was only a few feet from the big tree where they roosted, she hadn't heard the ravens once.

"Poe?" she called, wincing at the sandpaper rasp of the word as it tore out of her throat.

No response.

"Poe," Neve tried again, louder this time, even though it hurt. Still nothing.

She wasn't sure how she knew he was gone. That all of

them were gone, the three ravens who were reborn with the Morrigan every new lifetime. She just did, with a staggering certainty that made her heart feel like it was breaking all over again.

That was it, then. The chain *was* broken. There were no more ravens. No more lives. No more chances.

It was the last domino to fall, and Neve felt the numbness she'd been clinging to since she woke up shatter into a million pieces. She fell to her knees, her arms wrapped around herself in a pathetic parody of a hug. Great, heaving sobs wrenched from her throat, making her chest ache and throb, but Neve didn't care.

Poe was gone. Her sisters were gone. The bedrock of her world had crumbled away, and Neve was alone.

For as long as Neve could remember, time had not been her friend. It dragged, hours seeming to take up much more space than their allotted sixty minutes. The more she wished it would spur forward, the more it seemed to slow just to spite her, especially once her eighteenth birthday had loomed on the horizon. How many times had Neve wished that time would go just a little bit faster, urging herself toward the day when she would finally turn eighteen and shed her remaining humanity?

Now time slipped around her like she was a stone in a river, passing over without making much of an impression. Days skipped forward and out of sight, until Neve stopped bothering to keep track.

Absently, Neve rubbed the knot of scar tissue that had formed above her breastbone, a gnarled reminder of where Aodh's sword had pierced her sternum. It was a miracle he hadn't nicked her aorta. It was a miracle that the damage the blade had done to her left lung wasn't worse and she hadn't drowned in her own blood and fluids. It was a miracle the additional stress she'd put on her lungs after coming back through the Gate hadn't caused them to collapse altogether. It was a miracle, it was a miracle, it was a miracle.

It didn't feel like a miracle. It just hurt.

"It's cold out tonight."

Neve didn't turn toward Daughter Maeve's voice. This was expected now, an established element of the routine they'd created since the night Neve found the ravens missing, once her survival became more certain than a snowball's chance in hell.

"Are you going to try to stop me?" Neve asked. Speaking didn't hurt as much anymore, but her voice hadn't recovered. It had always been low, tending toward a monotone that gave her a bored, detached affect. Now, though, words rasped through her lips, coming out soft and harsh, as if each syllable had been scraped through stone.

"Neve." Once, the tiredness in Daughter Maeve's voice

might have been enough to make Neve pause. Even without looking, Neve could picture the expression on her oldest guardian's face: gray eyebrows pinched together, deepening the furrow already carved there from lifetimes of raising Neve and her sisters, and her eyes, already ancient in an otherwise unremarkably middle-aged face, showing the weight of every single one of those years. Once, Neve would have felt sorry for putting that look on Maeve's face and might have reconsidered, might have course-corrected.

But Daughter Maeve had spent the last thousand years lying to her, lying to all of them, so Neve pushed the instinctive stab of guilt to the very back of her mind. Maeve didn't get to make Neve feel guilty about anything, not anymore.

Neve's silence must have spoken for itself, because Maeve sighed. "There's a blanket by the door," she said. The stairs creaked beneath her feet as she left without another word.

Neve took the blanket. The night was frigid, though she barely felt it. She'd always run warm on account of her preternatural metabolism, but now she felt like a walking furnace, feverish from the combination of her own body heat and the alarming regimen of medicine she was forced to choke down every morning to encourage her organs to heal.

It had snowed recently, a light dusting that left the grass crunchy and frostbitten and made the pebbly sand glitter in the pale light from the moon overhead. Neve's breath puffed out in little clouds as she walked the familiar route out of the convent and back down to the Gate.

It was as still and unyielding as it had been every other time she'd come down here, which had been almost every night since she was well enough to walk on her own. The Daughters had tried to put up a fuss, but they wouldn't stop her by force and that was the only thing that might have worked. Now it was the same exchange every night, usually with Maeve, but occasionally Clara or Aoife swapped in for flavor.

Like she had every other night, Neve pressed her palm into the center of where the portal would have been if the Gate were active, straining to feel something—anything. The briefest flash of intuition in her gut that meant Bay and Mercy were close, that they were waiting for her on the other side. But like every time before, there was nothing. Nothing stirred. It was just stone.

Neve couldn't open the Gate anyway. Even before, she and her sisters didn't have the ability to come through on their own. Now, though, it wasn't opening for anything. During one of her brief stints of consciousness before she'd managed to wake up and stay awake for more than a few minutes, Neve had groped for her phone, trying unsuccessfully to plug in her human friends' numbers. Tameka, Simon, Michael, Ilma, and Puck, the five humans who had dragged Neve unwillingly into their circle of friends and had become more important to her than Neve thought possible. They had opened the Gate for her the first time, when Aoife revealed that Neve couldn't do it herself. But, Clara had told her when Neve was still groggy and half-insensate, the Gate hadn't opened for them. They'd tried, just like Alexandria had tried, but it hadn't budged.

Neve tried not to think of it as a mouth, something that had swallowed her sisters and was unwilling to give up its meal, despite being prodded.

Like it had been waiting for her to notice, crouched on the edge of her awareness, the place in Neve's chest where her sisters' presences used to be yawned open. It was numb, a distinct lack of something that should have been there and had always been there before. A star that had collapsed into a black hole and was going to devour her from the inside out.

It should have hurt. It didn't. Neve didn't know if that was worse.

This is your fault. The voice in her head used to be Aodh's, but more and more, it was beginning to sound like her own. *You did this. They left to protect you.*

Neve knew that. Of course she did; how could she not? She hadn't been able to fight. She'd been hurt and useless like she always was, and her sisters had traded themselves away to keep her safe.

A chill that had nothing to do with the temperature settled behind her heart. Neve had the sense that, with enough time, she might not even notice the absence, the lack, the cold. She gritted her teeth, mentally probing at the space like it was a toothache, trying to find the exact shape of it. Trying to elicit some kind of reaction, even if it hurt. It should have hurt. Neve wished so very badly that it hurt.

She woke up aching, her wish from the night before granted, though not for the reason she would have liked.

Neve groaned and blinked in weak winter sunlight. She hadn't been aware of falling asleep. Despite her exhaustion, Neve couldn't bear the thought of trudging back up to the convent, where the Daughters were doubtless still awake and waiting for her. She didn't want to see them. And she was so tired. It had made the most sense, then, to sit with her back to the Gate, the blanket wrapped tightly around her shoulders. She would stay here, just in case something happened. If Bay and Mercy came back, Neve would be able to feel it.

"You can't keep doing this."

Neve startled fully awake, disturbing the fine dusting of snow she'd collected overnight.

Alexandria's face resolved above Neve, her pink rosebud mouth pressed into a thin line. Neve made a noise that didn't quite commit to being a word, and Alexandria's frown deepened.

"You're going to freeze to death," Alexandria said when Neve didn't make any more attempts at speaking. Mostly because, according to her internal clock, it was ass o'clock in the morning, and she was tired.

But she was also waiting, almost in spite of herself. Holding her breath and reaching for any sensation from the Gate, hoping beyond hope that Alexandria's presence might stir something. It didn't. The Gate was as still and mockingly silent as before.

Neve shook her head to clear it and spied a colorful, pen-stained backpack slouching a few feet away, no doubt dropped there when Alexandria had seen Neve sleeping like a corpse by the Gate that had almost killed them both. Guilt gnawed at her insides.

"Did the Daughters send you?" Neve asked, wincing internally as her voice came out rough and accusatory. Alexandria's eyebrows, which had been furrowed, leaped toward her hairline.

"No, they didn't," she snapped. "Shockingly enough, they're not using me to spy on you."

"Then why . . . ?"

"You don't think I have enough reasons to be back here?" Alexandria asked. All the bluster evacuated from her voice at once, and it sounded as if she might cry. The sick, guilty feeling in Neve's stomach compounded. She was making things worse. As per usual.

Neve managed to scrape herself back up to her feet, the

still-healing wounds on her chest and shoulders complaining but not enough to keep her down.

"I'm sorry," Neve said. She held open her arms and wrapped them both in a blanket-hug. "I . . . I'm sorry."

For a moment, with the blanket keeping them warm and Alexandria so close that Neve could feel her heart beating, Neve actually felt okay. Then something occurred to her that she should have thought of at the outset.

"Why do you have your backpack?"

Alexandria stiffened slightly, and Neve knew she wasn't going to like the answer.

"School starts back up today," Alexandria muttered. She didn't try to push away, but Neve could feel her beginning to fidget and stepped away first, leaving the blanket around Alexandria's shoulders. She needed it more than Neve did, though Neve was already beginning to shiver a little.

"No," Neve said flatly.

Alexandria's eyes sparked, and she crossed her arms over her chest. The effect was only slightly lessened by the presence of the blanket wrapped snugly around her body. "No?" Alexandria repeated. "Just no?"

Neve cast about for a better answer, despite the fact that "no" was really all she had at the moment.

Neither of them had talked about going back to school—mostly because Neve assumed they were both smart enough to know that it was a bad idea, but also because Neve knew that if Alexandria disagreed, Neve didn't have a prayer of convincing her otherwise. Which, if the look on Alexandria's face was any indication, was exactly what was happening.

"It's not safe," Neve said lamely, doing her best to pull herself back together long enough to form a coherent, maybe halfway-convincing argument.

"Try again," Alexandria said, shaking her head. "I'm not putting my whole life on hold because it's not safe."

Why not? Neve wanted to ask. *Her* life was on hold. More than on hold. Neve's life, the life she'd always known, was over. As far as Neve was concerned, everything from before was dead and gone, immolated the second her sisters had passed through the Gate and not come back out.

"Why bother?" Neve asked, her rasping new voice making the question sound even more lifeless and pathetic. "I just . . . monsters are real. I'm one of them. My cousin is loose and my sisters are gone and your parents are dead, so who cares about school?"

Alexandria's eyes went hard and flinty, her mouth opening with some fiery retort before it closed again more slowly. "My parents are dead," she repeated. Neve shuddered, feeling horrible for bringing it up. That had been a low blow and she knew it. "But I'm not. And neither are you."

Neve opened her mouth, trying to will an argument to

appear on her tongue, but Alexandria cut in before she could cobble a sentence together. "Are you going to try to stop me?" she asked, parroting the same question Neve had asked Daughter Maeve hours earlier, though Alexandria couldn't know about that.

Neve could stop Alexandria from going. Her stomach twisted at the thought. Obviously, it was physically possible, but Neve would never, and Alexandria clearly knew it.

When Neve didn't answer, Alexandria just nodded as if she'd expected as much. "So I'm going. You should go home. Get out of the cold before you give yourself hypothermia, if you haven't already."

Neve watched Alexandria walk away for exactly seventeen seconds before she tipped her head back to look at the uncaring gray sky. She ground the heels of her hands into her eye sockets, letting out a long stream of curses that would've had Daughter Aoife swatting her backside with a wooden spoon.

"Damn it, fine," Neve said at last, marching toward Alexandria, her long legs eating up the distance between them.

Alexandria's eyes cut to Neve and narrowed into suspicious slits. "What are you doing?"

"School," Neve said. There was a whining bite to her voice, and she was only a little embarrassed, too occupied with the prospect of going back to class this morning when she'd never really expected to step foot in Newgrange Harbor High School again. "Apparently."

"Don't you need your backpack? Or a change of clothes?"

"Nah."

Alexandria shifted her weight from foot to foot anxiously. "You don't think you should check in with the Daughters?"

Neve's pissy mood soured further. "Well, they already lost my sisters," she said, trying for flippant and missing the mark. "If I disappear, at least they have the satisfaction of going three for three."

"Neve . . ."

"Come on, Alexandria, like the library," Neve said, cutting her off before Alexandria could suggest something insane, like speaking more than a sentence to the Daughters. "Don't want you to be late."

CHAPTER THREE

Neve had regrets. Several lifetimes' worth of them, in fact, but this morning she was regretting the stubborn decision to follow Alexandria and not just let the whole thing go.

She probably still could, if she really wanted to. Ask Alexandria to let her out of the car and trudge home with her tail between her legs. But Neve wasn't that much of a coward—not yet at least—and despite Alexandria's blasé attitude, Aodh was still running around Newgrange Harbor.

He hadn't shown his face yet and the Daughters hadn't been able to find him, though not for lack of trying. As far as Neve understood, and as far as she was willing to listen to anything they said to her at this point, Daughter Aoife had been doing sweeps of the town, but it was slow going. Mostly because he seemed to know how to hide from her, the absolute bastard, but also because Aoife's magic was finite and she couldn't just lay down a seeking spell in one go. Searching in quadrants was safer, though if Clara's new worry lines were any indication, Aoife was still stretching herself too thin. Not that Neve noticed. Or cared.

The thought of Aodh running around loose and unaccounted for made Neve twitch, and she knew that if there weren't a massive Bay-and-Mercy-sized cavern where her heart should be, she would be an entire wreck. But there was, and as it turned out, Neve just didn't have room to house that much misery within her. She was full up.

The part of her that wasn't utterly occupied with coping with her sisters' loss wondered idly about where he was and if he had heard about her survival and planned on coming back to finish the job.

Neve didn't think she cared. She had turned that worry over in her mind, waiting for the accompanying spike of fear to rise up and steal the breath from her lungs, but nothing came. Bay and Mercy were gone and Neve had no idea how to get them back. Or if it was even possible. With that in mind, what the hell did she care if Aodh returned? He'd have a hard time cutting her heart out of her chest this time, considering that it had vanished behind the Gate with her sisters.

A tiny, miserable, wretched part of her almost wished he would do it already. At least then she wouldn't have to deal with the growing emptiness, the shocking, icy cold every time she remembered her sisters were missing. Neve might have forgone Aoife's fancy magic searching methods altogether and gone to seek him out herself, if not for Alexandria.

Alexandria, who was still here, who was still vulnerable,

and who was currently making nervous conversation that Neve was not absorbing in the slightest. Who had insisted on going to school, where she would be totally unprotected if Aodh came looking for her.

Who pulled him out of the Gate. The thought rose up unbidden and Neve's breath caught, turning into a painful wheeze. *She's the one who can open it. You weren't making any progress until she got involved.* Neve shook her head, pushing down hard on the surge of anger that accompanied those thoughts. She didn't blame Alexandria for what happened. She didn't. Alexandria wasn't responsible; she was a casualty of the lifetimes' worth of lies Neve had been living.

It wasn't Alexandria's fault. Neve told herself that over and over, until the ugly, anger-hot feeling in her stomach began to dissipate. It took longer than she would have liked, and when it was gone, Neve just felt cold and horrible.

She shook herself again, holding on tight to the flashes of pain as her ribs reacted badly to the movement, and cast about for a distraction. Something, anything else to think about.

"I should have looked up your schedule too. I'm sorry," Alexandria was saying, a little breathlessly. Like she was talking to fill the silence, instead of her usual cheerful info-dumping on whatever had popped into her brain. If Neve didn't know her better, she might not have noticed the difference. But Neve could hear the slight strain behind the words where Alexandria's discomfort bled through, the way her hands gripped the steering wheel tight enough for her knuckles to go white, instead of tapping her fingers to the radio or some unheard rhythm.

"Do you want me to leave?" Neve asked, something awful occurring to her.

Alexandria's stream of consciousness ended with an abrupt click of teeth, and her head snapped to look at Neve. "What?"

"I can . . ." Neve hedged, trying to hold herself still and make herself as small as possible in the passenger seat. "I'm scaring you."

Now that Neve was paying attention, she couldn't think of another reason for Alexandria's sudden tension, and she couldn't blame her either. Alexandria had spent her entire life being chased by monsters, only to find out that her would-be hero girlfriend not only had failed to protect her and her family but was also one of those monsters herself. Neve might actually be worse, because at least the creatures that wrenched themselves from the Gate had the honesty to look the part. Neve still wore a human face and had been pretending to be a god when she was anything but.

It made sense that Alexandria would want to keep her distance after the revelations behind the Veil.

Shit, was that why she had come this morning? To say

goodbye? And Neve had turned it into an argument about going to school, of all things, before inviting herself along when that was probably the exact last thing Alexandria wanted.

Neve hunched even lower into her seat, her shoulders drawn up around her ears. Her fingers twitched, reaching up to start absently braiding her hair—a self-soothing habit from as long as she could remember—before she clenched her fists by her sides. No sudden moves. She'd already done enough harm.

Neve watched Alexandria's face closely, trying to gauge her expression without luck. She'd gotten better at it after so many months of having Alexandria and the rest of her human friends in her life—oh. Neve hadn't thought about them. But her human friends probably wouldn't want anything to do with her either.

She was wondering if it was too much to ask that Alexandria tell them she said goodbye, and maybe that Neve was sorry, when Alexandria burst out laughing.

One hand leaped from the wheel to clap over her mouth, stifling the sound, and all thoughts of hasty goodbyes and apologies fled from Neve's thoughts in the face of complete and utter confusion.

"I'm sorry," Alexandria said after a moment. Her face had

gone a little pink. "I'm sorry. That's so inappropriate, but what are you even talking about?"

Well, now Neve was doubly confused.

"I thought . . . you seemed nervous and—"

"And you jumped to me being scared of you?" Alexandria asked so incredulously that when Neve hunched even farther into herself, it was from embarrassment, not an—apparently completely stupid—impulse to make herself look less dangerous.

"But I'm a monster," Neve muttered, eyes cast downward. "I'm the same thing that hurt you—I'm worse, because I didn't protect you."

Attention fixed on her hands, Neve didn't see Alexandria's expression change. She did, however, feel the car screech to a stop as Alexandria jerked the wheel and pulled them over to the side of the road.

"Hey." Alexandria's voice was harsh and Neve cringed a little. Alexandria reached out and gripped Neve's chin, gentler than she expected and kinder than she deserved. "Look at me. You're being stupid."

Neve jerked back. "What?"

"You need to cut this shit out," Alexandria said, making a wide gesture that encompassed the whole of Neve, which was less than helpful. "I'm not scared of you, one." Alexandria retracted her hand to begin ticking points off her fingers.

"You're not a monster, two. And three, you don't get to push me away and blow up your life because you feel guilty."

"That's not—" Neve said, wanting to curl in on herself even more now. The way Alexandria laid it all out like that, as if it was simple and totally obvious, made Neve feel flayed open, exposed.

A part of her, the same part that had shoved anger and blame onto Alexandria at the first opportunity, urged Neve to snap back and defend herself. She managed to get a leash on that impulse. Barely.

As if she could see the emotions warring on Neve's face— and who knew, maybe she could—Alexandria's expression softened, just a little.

"I'm sorry that this happening," she said, not unkindly. "And I love you. But . . ." Her voice wobbled, just the tiniest bit, and all at once Neve saw how hard Alexandria was fighting to keep it together. Which was a much saner explanation for her nervous chatter than suddenly flipping a switch and being afraid of Neve, no matter how reasonable it had felt while Neve's imagination was spiraling out of control.

"I'm sorry," Neve rasped, because she was, and what else was there to say?

Alexandria nodded sharply and pulled the car back onto the road. This time she didn't fill the silence with anxious talking. The silence wasn't comfortable, exactly, but it was better than before, even if Neve could feel the spiraling tension at the back of her mind. She shoved it down as best she could before reaching over and lacing her fingers through Alexandria's. Alexandria squeezed her hand tight, like she was using Neve as a lifeline and not the other way around.

Or maybe they were both just hanging on to each other, desperately clinging as they tried to float through the carnage their lives had dissolved into.

Honestly, Neve hated that Alexandria was here with her, because it meant that she was hurting, that she was in danger. But more than that, Neve was so, so grateful not to be alone.

Some of the calm she'd managed to wrangle by sheer bloody stubbornness began to fade as they drew closer to Newgrange Harbor High School. Neve really hadn't expected to come back here. There had been a stretch when she wasn't even sure whether she would survive until the end of winter break, let alone worry about the next semester.

Neve wondered if there was a natural mechanism to stifle feelings of guilt like there was for pain. Shock, adrenaline, enough magic to put down a bull elephant, all these things made pain manageable, at least temporarily. But as Neve contemplated seeing her friends again, guilt crawled up her throat, tasting of bile. She'd barely thought about them since she woke up, and even less once it became clear that she was going to live. They were supposed to be her friends, but Neve had just . . . forgotten. She hadn't even bothered to send a text. Not even a short one: *I lived.* Nothing.

In fact, now that she thought about it, Neve didn't even know where her phone was. The stupid thing was probably gathering dust in a forlorn corner someplace.

"I . . ." Neve started once Alexandria had parked in her usual spot at the front of the lot with the rest of the seniors. "Did you tell them?" she managed after swallowing hard, not bothering to specify who. "That I survived, I mean."

"I told them," Alexandria said softly, squeezing Neve's hand once more before letting go. It took a surprising amount of self-control for Neve not to reach for her again, seeking out comfort like a child.

"Thank you," Neve said in a half-relieved, half-humiliated rush. "I should have . . . I didn't think, I—" She started to apologize again when Alexandria waved a hand.

"You going to be okay?" Alexandria asked, squinting at Neve's face. "You look like you're going to be sick."

As it turned out, Neve had enough pride to force an eye roll at the question, as if Alexandria was being silly and smothering and Neve wasn't about twelve seconds away from jumping into the driver's seat and speeding off to avoid this confrontation.

"Obviously," Neve blustered.

There was no way Alexandria was convinced, but she didn't

35

call Neve on it. Small mercies. "Good. Now get out of my car."

Neve did as she was told and had only just closed the passenger side door when a weight collided with her. Not enough to even come close to knocking her over, but Neve's heart still jumped painfully, one hand going to the dagger at her waist before her brain caught up to what was happening.

"Jesus Christ," Alexandria swore loudly, slamming her hand against the car in surprise. "Ilma!"

It was then that Neve noticed the brightly patterned hijab at her chin.

"Don't ever do that again," Ilma said fiercely. Ilma's dark brown eyes were bright and intense, and this time it wasn't adrenaline that made Neve's heart lurch. She released her grip on the dagger in her coat pocket before wrapping Ilma in probably the world's most uncomfortable hug.

For what it was worth, Ilma didn't seem to mind. She just squeezed Neve tightly round the middle once more and stood back, swiping at her nose. Ilma glared at the familiar group of humans who'd arrived while Neve was distracted by being attack hugged, as if daring them to comment. No one did. Puck dropped their chin onto Ilma's shoulder.

Neve fought the urge to shrink herself again, to hunch and make herself less of a threat. Or maybe a smaller target; she wasn't sure. But she hadn't seen her friends since the beach, since everything had fallen apart. Somehow she'd forgotten to miss them, and now, seeing everyone safe and together, it almost felt like she was making up for lost time.

"What she said," Tameka said after a moment. The wobble in her voice betrayed her otherwise cool expression.

"Next time," Simon said, jabbing a finger at her, "answer your goddamn phone."

"And also," Michael added, giving Simon a sharp look. Neve had the sudden impression that there had been a conversation beforehand about how to handle this reunion and Simon had gone slightly off-script. "We're happy you're okay."

They all nodded, not quite in unison, looking slightly like bobbleheads that were bouncing out of sync.

"If there's anything we can do," Ilma said, her eyes still bright with what Neve thought might be unshed tears, "you just tell us, okay? We're here for you."

Neve somehow managed to mumble her thanks through the chorus of assent and promises that her friends would help any way they knew how, though the knowledge that there wasn't much they *could* do hung heavy around them. Neve was spared any additional humiliation by the morning bell calling any remaining students into the building for the start of the school day, and she filed in with the rest of her classmates like nothing at all had changed.

CHAPTER FOUR

Neve earned some odd looks throughout the day. Whether it was from her disheveled, clearly slept-in clothing or her absent backpack, she couldn't say, though no one was bold enough to actually say anything to her face. Neve could hear some of them whispering, but that was normal. It was sort of comforting, actually, a sliver of normalcy that she could cling to.

She made it through the first half of the day mostly without incident. Mostly. There had been the slight issue of running into one of the football players in the hallway on the way to third period—Neve hadn't been paying attention, kind of just floating along with Simon, Michael, and Tameka as they walked to class, when she collided with something solid enough to rattle her.

The immediate rage had been quickly chased away by pain as Neve's chest spasmed. She recognized the feeling of her rib jostling out of alignment, the head shifting in its socket with a grinding she could feel in her *teeth*. It didn't feel dislocated, thank the—thank something. But the pain was unexpected and intense enough to show on her face.

"Are you . . . ?" asked a voice beside her. Neve looked, recognizing one of the football boys—a senior, like her. She thought his name might be Harrison, but she wasn't sure and didn't really care. He must have been what—who—she'd run into.

"Watch where you're going," Neve snarled. Her voice, already uncomfortably different, came out a little strangled. She strode forward and the football player had the good sense to get out of her way before she collided with him again.

"Bitch," Neve heard him mutter under his breath when he thought she was out of earshot.

Neve almost turned around, almost gave in to the impulse to prolong the conflict and make it *much* worse, but she was a little busy jamming her rib back into place. The noise of the passing period was enough to cover her grunt of pain as she pressed the heel of her hand against her side and *pushed*. Simon was the closest to her, and while he almost certainly couldn't hear the sound of her rib popping back into alignment, he still looked slightly green, as if he guessed what she was doing and was trying not to throw up.

"I'm fine," Neve said, twisting slightly to make sure that nothing moved that wasn't supposed to. She needed to pay attention next time.

They need to learn to stay out of your way, snarled the mean little voice in the back of her head. *Relearn, since you let them forget in the first place.*

Neve gritted her teeth, tried to shake the voice away. Wisps of white fog curled in her peripheral vision and vanished when she tried to look at them more closely. They were memories, Neve knew. Tiny snippets that had escaped from the door in her head. The door Aodh had put a hole in, back behind the Veil. For a moment she held her breath, wondering if another memory was about to drag her under, but nothing came. She could almost pretend it was a trick of the light, some weird effect of sitting under the ugly glow of the school's fluorescent lightbulbs.

Thankfully, sixty-something minutes of sitting at a cramped desk and staring off into the middle distance was enough for her jostled rib to settle and the fog to fade. The pain was muted by the time the period was over. Though Simon still looked a little ill and kept shooting Neve worried glances when he thought she wasn't looking. Which was sweet, in a deeply annoying kind of way.

Besides that, though, everything was going okay. School was the same as always, boring and uneventful. Mr. Robinson had even managed to make a snide remark about Neve's lack of preparedness that made her want to dismantle his car and reassemble it on a roof somewhere.

Unfortunately, that left a lot of room for thinking, which had never really been Neve's strong suit.

She was twitchy, jumping at everything and looking for

threats around every corner. Which she had been before, to a certain extent, but now Neve had the wounds to show what happened if she let her guard down. Every scrape of chairs against the linoleum floor was a blade being freed from a sheath; every person getting up to throw something out was a potential attacker.

The word "paranoid" came to mind, though Neve would argue it wasn't paranoia when you were right and the proof had jammed a sword into your gut, like, two weeks ago.

The day trickled by with no ambush and no sign of Aodh, no matter how much Neve strained herself looking for him. Despite her worst fears, it really was kind of going okay. She had even laughed at a dumb joke Simon had made, the sound bubbling out of her and surprising everyone, especially herself. There had been a single, glorious moment when Neve could almost pretend that things were normal.

Then that moment ended as Neve remembered that her sisters were gone and nothing was the way it was supposed to be. And here she was, laughing at some throwaway comment, as if her sisters weren't trapped behind the Gate, as if Neve wasn't pissing her time away pretending to be a real girl when she should be doing something—anything—to get them back.

Neve wasn't sure what exactly set her off. It might have been the noise of the cafeteria, so much louder and more overwhelming than she expected, even though she'd only been out of school for a few weeks. With so many overlapping voices, Neve couldn't sift through them all. She couldn't pinpoint the ones that might indicate danger—if Aodh were in here somewhere, she wouldn't be able to hear him.

It might have been the sight of some freshman's carrot-red hair, which was brighter than her cousin's but close enough in color and length, that made Neve freeze up like her boots had rooted into the cafeteria floor.

Or it could have been none of those things. Neve might simply have overrun some arbitrary timer she hadn't been aware of, counting down to bug-the-hell-out o'clock. It didn't really matter, in the end. What mattered was that the walls were pressing in, and Neve was fairly certain something was going to leap out at her any second. Also, and probably most importantly, she couldn't breathe.

Out of nowhere, the noise of the cafeteria was drowned out by a high-pitched whining noise. Neve swatted at her ears, but it didn't do any good. The others were still talking among themselves, not noticing the slightly strangled expression on Neve's face, or how the air seemed to have gone thin all of a sudden. When had that happened? It was hot in the cafeteria, which should have been a good thing considering the near-freezing temperatures outside, but Neve could feel sweat dripping between her shoulder blades and everything was going a little bit fuzzy.

Then she was moving, her legs feeling wholly unconnected from the rest of her body as they pushed her from her seat and left the cafeteria at what could charitably be called a jog. Neve wasn't aware she'd decided to head for the teachers' bathroom—single-use, unisex, with a lock on the door—until the bolt slid home with a heavy metal click.

The tiled room made the whining in her ears echo. Neve's skin felt as though it were stretched too thin over her bones, her nerves taut and humming like plucked guitar strings. She wasn't entirely sure why her body had brought her here, until bile burned at the back of her throat. Then she had a moment to be grateful before lunging for the toilet and promptly vomiting her guts up.

By the time her digested breakfast had been flushed down the toilet, Neve was firmly seated back in her body and already wishing for the fuzzy disconnection as reality reasserted itself.

Really? she thought, laying her head against the cool tile wall of the bathroom. She couldn't go even a whole day without having a panic attack. *Well done, Morgan. Way to prove you're healing and adjusted.*

Never mind that Neve was neither of those things, not even close, but it stung that she couldn't even pretend.

To add insult to injury, and more injury to injury, the effort of expelling the contents of her stomach had aggravated her chest wound. Now blood mingled in the appetizing mix of bile and vomit on her tongue, and Neve winced as she yanked down the intentionally high collar of her sweater to see a blue stain growing on the bandage.

"Shit," Neve swore. Her voice came out ragged and pain lit up her nerves now that she could feel them again. Redoing the bandage took longer than it should have, her shaking hands making things more difficult, and Neve pretended it was dehydration from throwing up, not the aftereffects of having a full-blown meltdown in the middle of the day. She just felt lucky some part of her hindbrain retained enough sense to get her the hell out of there before she lost it.

When the new bandage was finally applied and the evidence torn up and flushed, Neve pulled her sweater back on and assessed the damage.

The girl who peered back at her in the mirror looked like hammered shit. The wisps of greasy red hair that had escaped her messy ponytail framed a face that was thinner than it should have been. Her cheekbones stood out prominently under her sallow, blotchy skin, and her jaw, which had always been hard and jutting, looked like it was about to burst free of her flesh. The purple bags under her eyes looked bruised, like she'd recently been punched in the face, and beneath the clothes that now hung a little too loosely on her frame, Neve knew that she'd lost weight, lost muscle. What remained of her, this thin, wretched shade, was frailer than Neve could remember being, her skin knit together with scar tissue that had formed because her wounds were bad enough that even her accelerated healing struggled to keep up.

The strain of putting herself back together, the magic and the energy to keep her body alive while it did its best to quit on her, made Neve feel as though some part of herself had been lost in the attempt. Sacrificed, cannibalized, in order to keep her breathing just a little bit longer.

Something flickered in the corner of her vision, and for a second Neve's reflection distorted, rippling like disturbed water. The girl that looked back at her in that moment sneered, her lip curling over her teeth. She looked like Neve, or like Neve should have looked: strong and square-jawed, red-haired with a mess of matching freckles, but her expression was haughty and cold, like she was disgusted with what she was seeing.

Neve staggered, taking an involuntary step back. She blinked white spots out of her vision, mentally cursing the fluorescent lights in here, but when she looked back in the mirror, the strange reflection was gone. Neve looked like herself again, like she'd been through hell and not all of her had come back out. Like she'd lost an integral piece of herself— *two* integral pieces—along the way.

Neve closed her eyes and leaned her forehead against the glass. That much, she thought, was true.

CHAPTER FIVE

The words "I'm fine" were beginning to turn into mush in Neve's mouth before the day was up. Despite the less-than-subtle exit from the cafeteria, she thought she'd managed to pull herself together okay. But that didn't stop her friends from treating her like something about to explode or shatter into a million pieces. Maybe both at the same time.

That's me, Neve thought to herself bitterly when Michael shot her yet *another* worried glance. *A dirty bomb*. Before, she might have tried for a smile to make Michael feel at ease, but the effort was more than she could manage at the moment. Her throat hurt. Her chest hurt. All of her hurt.

Neve was so, so tired of hurting.

It's okay. It's okay. It's okay. How many times did she have to say that to make it true? What was the magic number she had to hit for the world to warp beneath her desperate desire for things to just, for once, *actually* be okay?

"Are you—?" Alexandria started once they were in the car together. The sudden lack of noise hit Neve like a blow and she sagged in the passenger seat of Alexandria's car, feeling like a popped balloon.

"Please don't ask," Neve cut in. She ground the heels of her hands into her eye sockets until lights danced on the back of her eyelids.

"Well, because you said 'please.'"

Neve cracked one eye open, her girlfriend instincts tingling at Alexandria's tone. "What?" she asked. Too blunt, probably, but Neve didn't do subtlety on the best of days, especially not when her nerves felt as taut as piano wire.

"You shouldn't have come in today," Alexandria said, staring straight ahead. Her knuckles were white from gripping the steering wheel.

Neve sighed and sank lower. She pulled her hood over her unwashed hair and wondered if disappearing into it would make this conversation stop. Probably not.

"*You* came in," Neve said after a long, expectant silence that was only punctuated by the rattle of Alexandria's engine. Her car really was a piece of shit.

"I," Alexandria said, in the tight-lipped way of someone trying to sort out their words carefully before they said them, "didn't almost die two weeks ago." *And my sisters aren't missing.* Neve didn't know if she was imagining the addition, but it made her breath catch slightly.

"You were kidnapped and held hostage by my batshit cousin," Neve replied as reasonably as she could manage, which wasn't much. "And we all could've died."

"That is not even close to the same thing," Alexandria said. Her grip on the steering wheel grew even tighter. "Clara said your heart stopped."

As if it was responding to being mentioned, Neve's heart gave a painful judder in her chest, the bastard.

"I don't want to talk about this," Neve said, turning her gaze to look aimlessly out the window.

"You need more time," Alexandria insisted. "To let yourself heal and grieve and—"

"Grieve?" Neve snapped. "What the hell do I have to grieve?"

"Neve—"

"No one died!" Neve was shouting now. "I'm alive and so are my sisters. . . . They're just not *here*. But they're alive. I would know if they were—" Neve's throat closed on the word "dead," like her body wouldn't let her put that out into the universe. Like not saying it out loud could somehow keep it from coming true.

Neve *would* know if they were dead. She had to know. Even if the part of herself that had always been connected to her sisters, where their emotions had always bled slightly together as if they were the single entity some folklorists insisted, was cold and dark now, Neve had to believe that she would know. She couldn't fathom that she was just . . . walking around in the world while her sisters were dead and gone. Neve knew it had happened before, in previous lifetimes, but this time the reincarnation cycle wouldn't kick in and bring them back together. The spell was broken.

Then again, the Gate was still closed and, with the exception of Aodh, keeping the rest of the pantheon inside. So maybe when Neve finally kicked it in this life, she'd just wake up in the next, with her sisters and no memories of this whole shitshow. Neve flinched away from the thought, even as some part of her longed to believe that there was another life to look forward to, one where she'd never learned the truth about what she and her sisters were guarding. It would be so much simpler.

But no. Neve didn't want to forget. Forgetting was what had started her down this path in the first place; the fact that she didn't remember, when her sisters did, even if Bay and Mercy hadn't remembered everything. Besides, Neve had felt it when her sisters and Alexandria came through the Gate, even if she hadn't recognized the feeling until much later. The magic of the Gate was different. It had changed, if not broken completely.

"You need to let yourself rest," Alexandria said, as gently as ever, but her kindness grated.

Like she was in any place to judge, Neve thought sullenly. Like Alexandria wasn't the poster child for smiling through the pain and keeping herself busy to ignore the mind-bending psychological trauma of being kidnapped by her girlfriend's family who, by the way, also killed her parents.

"I can't."

"God, Neve, you—" Alexandria snapped, smacking one hand on the wheel. Neve waited, but the rest of the admonishment didn't come.

At first, way back when they'd met and Alexandria had cheerfully inserted herself into Neve's life without taking no for an answer, her constant movement had set Neve on edge. It was distracting, the way Alexandria was always in motion, tapping her fingers or chewing on a pen or ripping erasers into tiny pieces without even thinking about it. So when Alexandria cut off mid-sentence, her body suddenly going completely, utterly still behind the wheel, Neve knew that something was wrong.

"What's happening?" Neve asked, her voice going low with urgency.

It took Alexandria too long to answer, the seconds dragging by like molasses. "I don't know," she said finally. Hearing her voice would've been a relief, except she was still so scarily still. "I don't know. I feel . . . itchy. Like before."

Neve remembered that night in the rain, when Alexandria had woken her up because she couldn't sleep, because something was pulling on her. Every time something had happened with the Gate, Alexandria had known. She'd been able to sense it.

Alexandria seemed to have reached the same conclusion. "We have to go," she said, shaking off the momentary paralysis and slamming her foot down on the gas. "Here." Alexandria yanked her phone out of her pocket so fast that it spun out of her grip. Neve caught it with one hand. She didn't need any additional prompting, punching in Daughter Maeve's number.

"Neve!" Daughter Maeve's voice was high and strained. "Where are—"

"The Gate," Neve snapped before Maeve could finish asking the question. "I think something is happening. Get the barrier up."

She hung up without waiting for Maeve to respond before tapping into Alexandria's messages and opening the group chat with the rest of their friends.

Like The Library: This is Neve. Don't come near the beach. Explain later.

The barrier was already live and shimmering when Alexandria pulled the car to a stop just within the gossamer curtain of magic that kept the rest of Newgrange Harbor from seeing what was happening a few miles down the beach. Sand spat from beneath the tires and Neve lurched out the passenger door. The stone that had been cold and unyielding this morning was a smear of color as magic sparked it back to life.

Something was wrong. Something besides the obvious.

"Stay here," Neve ordered, slamming the door closed behind her. Alexandria shouldn't have been there in the first place, but there wasn't time for that argument and Neve knew she probably wouldn't win it anyway.

"Cousin!" a cheerful voice called. Aodh dropped off one of the rocks above the Gate onto the sand below, grinning. His head lolled to the side slightly, arms loose by his sides as he looked her up and down. "You're looking well."

Neve's breath caught in her chest, fear momentarily freezing her muscles. They pulled so tightly over her bones that Neve thought they might snap. The knot of scar tissue on her chest burned with the memory of his sword carving through her.

Behind him, the Gate roiled. The magic coming off it was oily and noxious, and suddenly the smell of low tide in the air was overwhelmed by the scent of rot.

Aodh's grin stretched wider, revealing teeth that were unnervingly white and just a little bit too sharp. Unconsciously, Neve ran her tongue over her own teeth, seeking out points. Did she smile like that?

"Come *on*," Aodh jeered. He spun in a little circle, throwing his arms wide. "Don't look so glum, Nemain. Don't you want to see your sisters again?"

Anger, as bright and fleeting as lightning, zipped through her nerves. Neve shook off the stillness and ripped her dagger out of her belt, holding it steady as she waited for the anger to catch. The base of her throat warmed, as if she was building to a scream, but the place inside her—at the very core of her, where her power should have been—was still dark and cold and empty. There wasn't anything there to feed the spark, and it fizzled quickly, leaving her even colder than before.

"Shut up," Neve growled. The rasp of her ruined voice sounded pathetic.

Aodh tilted his head to the side again. Neve had the sense that he was weighing her against the version he'd known a thousand years ago, the girl Neve had seen in the mirror just a few hours earlier and whose voice she was suddenly hearing in her head.

She clutched her dagger in her hand, willing it not to shake. He had to go. Right now.

Aodh's eyes dropped to the blade and then returned to her face. "Do you really think you're ready for round two, cousin?" he asked, rolling his eyes. He hadn't even gotten out his own weapon, just continued to slouch carelessly in front of the seething Gate.

Neve bared her teeth.

"Pity. Who's going to look after your human when you're gone, I wonder?" Aodh shrugged, raising one shoulder and dropping it. "Or should I say humans?" His emphasis on the plural came out like a hiss. "You've got a colorful little collection, don't you?"

The bottom dropped out of her stomach. No. How did he know about them? How could he—

Did you really think they were safe while you were moping around and being useless? snarled the voice in her mind.

"Don't talk about them," Neve growled. The words were barely audible, rumbling low inside her chest, more feeling than sound.

"Are you going to make me?" Aodh asked, sounding genuinely curious. "You can't protect them. You can't even protect yourself. You're half-baked, cousin. Vestigial. Badb and Macha were useless too, but at least they were finished."

The whole world went quiet except for the thundering of blood in Neve's ears and the scream steadily building in her head. Hearing Mercy's and Bay's names, their true names, flung at her so carelessly made Neve reel like she was in the aftermath of an explosion, everything off-kilter and not quite real.

Numb, Neve felt herself lurch into motion. Her limbs still didn't feel quite like they belonged to her, but that also meant it was easier to ignore the ache of her injuries as she pushed herself to move faster. She closed the distance between her and Aodh in a few long strides, her dagger angled to cut his weaselly, shithead heart out of his chest.

Aodh sighed, his sword appearing in his hands. He didn't even have the courtesy to look worried as he dropped into a stance that Neve had been taught when she was barely big enough to hold a training blade. "Oh well. If you insist."

Later, she would wonder if it was her and Aodh's doing, their violent intent to cut each other into little pieces, or some other unknown condition that caused the Gate to churn and bubble, the last of the unyielding stone giving way to swirling, rot-colored magic.

Even later than that, Neve would wonder why she and her family had never known *what* caused the Gate to open, only that it did. She would poke at that gap in their knowledge, in their ability to do their job and keep anything from getting out of the Gate, until it bled.

At the moment, however, Neve was a little busy trying to change her only remaining blood family into past tense, so her situational awareness wasn't at an all-time high.

A sound like a thunderclap drew her attention back to the Gate. It was still seething, still giving off the same acrid magic, but even with her vision as screwy as it was, Neve could tell that this was different from every other time she'd seen it open before.

Neve was facing the Gate, so she had the tiniest bit of lead time to throw herself out of the way of the *thing* that ripped from the stone.

Aodh was not so lucky. Neve had the impression of claws and teeth before a massive gout of blue blood sprayed into the sand. Aodh screamed in pain and shock, staggering away from the thing that had mauled him.

"No," he said, his expression open with shock as another shadow grew closer and closer to the mouth of the Gate. "No, that's not right." Blood drenched the fabric of his shirt and his arm hung limp at his side, but he didn't seem to notice.

Behind him, the Gate spluttered again, the churning, rotted magic spitting out a second dark shape that resolved into serrated teeth and sharp, unnatural angles.

What the hell is that about? Neve had time to think before the second creature was on her.

She moved, her body reacting before her mind could catch up. This was something she knew, something she had trained for. The fight was in her blood and she knew what to do.

Neve ducked under the first clumsy swipe, letting her momentum carry her into a roll that had her ribs shrieking their displeasure. Her breath was already thinning, coming in short, erratic gasps.

Instinct and training weren't going to do much good if her body quit on her, and Neve was still far from fighting form. She had to finish this, and quickly.

The creature speared the ground where Neve had been a moment before, its claws coming close enough to snag the fabric of her heavy winter jacket. It wasn't her armor, not by a long shot, but the heavy insulated padding was the only thing between her and the claws trying to stab her in the chest. Again. It wasn't an experience Neve cared to repeat.

Neve managed to skitter out of the creature's reach, jogging backward on her heels and finally getting enough room to actually look at the thing. It didn't move like anything she'd ever seen, its disjointed limbs jerking haphazardly. It was slower, too. Neve wasn't usually faster than the things she was fighting, but even in her current state she managed to outspeed it.

It looked . . . premature. It was all harsh angles and shifting bone fragments beneath a casing of loose flesh that looked moments away from sloughing off entirely. Festering, ichorous spools of magic dripped from it like drool, hissing whenever it hit the ground.

Neve knew the creatures she and her sisters had called demons. She had seen them come in a hundred different forms, a thousand shapes and sizes. All of them were dangerous, all of them were horrible, and—as Neve had learned at the cost of everything she'd ever known to be true—all of them were family.

But these creatures? They were unlike anything she'd ever seen.

A pained grunt drew Neve's attention back to Aodh, who was still busy with his own murderous shadow.

Why is it attacking him? Neve barely had time to wonder

before she slashed at the creature again. Blood and dripping flesh splashed against her wrist, and Neve bit back a scream as they ate into her skin like acid. Her fingers spasmed and she managed to keep hold of her dagger, but only barely.

The creatures that had come through before were chaotic and destructive, but they united under one goal: kill the Morrigan and get free. Aodh, while unable to get through the Gate himself—not without Alexandria's intervention, at least—had been an integral part of that. So why the hell would they attack him? They were on the same side.

Apparently, no one had told them that.

Aodh shouted a curse as his creature slipped into his guard, opening up a new wound on his arm before he could spin away.

Seizing on her lapse in attention, Neve's monster screeched, snapping its jaws at her hard enough that Neve heard a crack from the force. A dripping tongue lolled, drooling saliva and bone chips onto the sand. Neve's stomach heaved. She thought she might be sick for the second time today, dodging out of the way as the creature came at her again. It was faster this time, but Neve was still able to scramble out of range. Her heart was pounding hard now, her lungs burning. The fight had barely started and Neve knew she wasn't able to keep this up for much longer.

As the creature skated past her, overshooting and unable

to control its momentum, Neve saw an opening. She pivoted on one heel, dagger held tight in her hand, as she aimed at the creature's center of mass. Neve had no idea if the thing had a heart, or if it was just blood and viscera sloshing around in there, but the chest region was always a good guess.

What's if it's Bay?

The thought came out of nowhere, striking Neve like a blow to the back of the head, quickly followed by: *Or Mercy?*

Neve froze, her dagger only inches away from the creature's flank. The whole world felt like it had slowed down around her as she peered at the monster anew, desperately searching for anything familiar in the unpleasant wreckage of muscle and sinew of its body.

The creature snarled, taking the opportunity to right itself and fly at her again.

Get out of the way. She willed her muscles to move, but they'd locked together and wouldn't obey her.

Somewhere just beyond her periphery, Neve heard Alexandria scream. It startled her back into motion, but Neve knew even as she tried to dodge that she wasn't going to make it. She could see the trajectory of the creature's claws and where they would shred through skin and sinew. This time the feeble protection of her puffer jacket wouldn't be enough.

The lack of pain was a surprise, as was the fact that her

insides did not become outsides. But the most surprising thing of all was the lanky shape that collided with the creature a split second before it reached Neve.

Aodh and the thing rolled down the beach in a tangle of limbs. When they finally came to a stop, Aodh was on top, straddling the creature with his knees pressing down hard where its shoulder joints should be. Neve saw the flash of a blade in his hand.

"Don't!" she shouted before she could stop herself.

Aodh's head snapped to her, long enough for the creature to jostle itself free. Aodh shouted in pain as claws ripped up his already battered torso, and this time there was no hesitation before he plunged his blade into the thing's neck.

Neve swallowed a scream of horror as the creature howled, writhing and spitting foul magic like sparks before it collapsed in on itself. It had to be dead, but it wasn't like any of the so-called demon deaths Neve had seen before. There was no explosion of scorching ash; the thing just sort of melted, coagulating into sludge that mingled with the blood in the sand. Neve could see a matching puddle a few feet away, all that remained of the other demon.

The resulting silence was eerie, broken only by the crash of waves behind them and the screeching of seagulls above. The Gate had gone still again. Neve no longer felt the flare of its magic in her gut.

From where he still kneeled in the pool of monster gore and blood, Aodh tilted his head up to meet Neve's gaze. His eyes were wide and unfocused, pupils blown wide with pain and shock. He looked like a kid. He'd *saved* her. Why would he do that?

There was a pulse in the air as the barrier around the beach came down, and when Neve looked again, Aodh was running, leaving a trail of blood behind him.

Neve staggered to her feet, intent on following, on seizing the opportunity to cut him down while he was injured enough that she might actually have a chance.

"What the hell was that?" Alexandria's voice called, halting Neve in her tracks.

Neve didn't know whether she was talking about Aodh, the Gate, or the new flavor of abominations that had crawled through, but her answer to all three was the same:

"I have no idea."

CHAPTER SIX

It was about that time that the Daughters showed up. Helpful timing, as always.

"What . . ." Daughter Maeve's voice cracked as she looked at the damage to the Gate and the mess of blood and monster goop around Neve and Alexandria. "What the devil happened here?"

Neve knew it was just a figure of speech, but the reference to devils just reminded her of the lie she'd been fed her entire life.

"The Gate opened," she snapped, getting to her feet and taking Alexandria with her.

"How is that possible?"

Neve rounded on Aoife, jabbing at her with her finger. "How the hell should I know? I'm not the one with magic, am I?"

Aoife jerked back like she'd been struck. "That's not—"

"Are you . . . are you both all right?" Daughter Clara cut in before Aoife could finish.

Neve saw red. "Of course not! Jesus Christ, do we look okay?" she demanded, feeling an ugly spike of vindication when Daughter Clara flinched. "Thanks for all your help, by the way. The Gate's closed again, but good luck if it opens, because there's new shit coming out of it."

She didn't wait for a response to that, or wait to see the Daughters' reaction to the revelation that the Gate was throwing up insensate goop monsters. Instead, Neve hooked her arms around Alexandria's waist as gently as she could and guided them both back into the relative safety of the convent.

Besides aggravating old wounds and ripping open some scar tissue that should've stayed put, Neve discovered she was remarkably unscathed once she had calmed down long enough to give herself a thorough once-over. Alexandria, more importantly, didn't have a scratch, though there was a kind of faraway look in her eye that Neve knew from experience was the beginning of shock.

Once Neve was relatively certain she wasn't going to bite their heads off and that Alexandria wasn't about to have a panic attack, she and Alexandria went and found the Daughters again. Maeve, Aoife, and Clara were collected in the library, their heads bowed over a bunch of books older than all of them combined. Or maybe not. Neve had never questioned the authenticity of the books in the Daughters' collection before, and she'd read only a handful of them. The rest could be filled with manga and scribbles for all she knew.

The thought only served to remind Neve how much she didn't want to speak to any of them right now, or ever, but she'd said it herself: in this life, Neve's knowledge of magic was minimal at best, and whatever the hell was going on with the Gate was magic bullshit all the way down. So, gritting her teeth the whole time, Neve stumbled through an explanation of everything that had happened, starting with Alexandria's bad feeling.

No one said anything for a good two minutes after she was done. The Daughters all stood whey-faced and silent. Clara looked like she was trying not to cry. Aoife was glaring. Maeve just kind of looked old.

"That's . . ." Aoife started, clearing her throat loudly. "We need to look into this, obviously. If the parameters of the Gate spell have changed . . ." She trailed off, eyebrows furrowing as she glared into the middle distance. "This is serious."

Daughter Aoife, witch and master of understatement. Neve rolled her eyes.

"Is it . . ." Alexandria asked haltingly, twisting her fingers together. "Did I do this?"

"What?" Neve asked. "No."

"Well—" Daughter Aoife started, but Neve whirled on her.

"*No,*" she said again, more emphatically this time.

"You don't know that," Alexandria said, looking miserable.

Yes, I do, Neve thought. Even as she thought it, she knew it wasn't true. Neve didn't know that Alexandria wasn't responsible for whatever had happened to the Gate.

"He said I was the key," Alexandria said, still wringing her hands and looking at the floor. "Before. Um, behind the Veil. Aodh said that I could travel between the worlds, which is why they needed me to get out."

Neve felt the sour tang of Alexandria's fear and pressed herself against Alexandria's back, hugging her from behind. She dropped her chin onto the top of Alexandria's head, hoping the weight would be grounding instead of smothering.

Alexandria's voice was just a little bit steadier when she spoke again. "If that was true, shouldn't the Gate be open now? All the way?"

Daughter Aoife's glare into the middle distance only intensified. "I don't know," she admitted after a moment.

Why not? The question rose to the top of Neve's mind without prompting. Why didn't she know? Shouldn't the Daughters know how the Gate spell worked, considering they'd been around since Neve and her sisters made it?

"I don't know either," Neve said slowly, more questions fizzing and popping in her brain, Mentos dropped into Diet Coke. She felt sick, abruptly overcome with a feeling like déjà vu times a million. Only the weight of Alexandria in her arms kept the room from swaying around her. "Bay and Mercy didn't know either."

Talking about her sisters didn't help soothe the nausea currently waging war on her insides, but Neve locked her jaw and pressed on.

"When they turned eighteen, they didn't know about the Veil or the Gate or how we made either of them. They only started to remember any of it once we were there. That's not . . ." Neve struggled to come up with the words to express her sense of being completely untethered from the reality she'd known and accepted her whole life, and every lifetime that had come before. Why didn't they know? Why didn't they remember making the Veil at all?

"You really don't remember, do you?" Aodh had asked her when they'd met for the first time in this life, before she'd remembered who he was. *"Makes sense. Why bother remembering the people you betrayed and abandoned? Easier to pretend that you were right about everything when you don't remember the other side."*

Neve shook her head. "Why would we do that?" she asked, looking at the Daughters in turn. "Why would we make ourselves forget?"

Because we didn't want the chance to go back, offered Nemain's voice in her mind. Neve shook her head harder. That wasn't right. It didn't feel right; it didn't feel true—or maybe that was just easier for her to stomach.

Neve gritted her teeth and forced herself to focus and stop going in circles.

"We don't know," Daughter Maeve said after a moment that dragged on for longer than it should have.

"What *do* you know?" Neve snapped, but this time she just

felt sorry at the look of exhaustion that passed over Maeve's face.

"We know that Alexandria is connected to all this some-how," Clara offered gently, as if that made Neve feel any better. "And we know that the spell has changed." She spoke directly to Alexandria now as she said, "And we know that whatever ability you have to bring people through the Gate, it's clearly limited. That's not nothing."

It sure as hell wasn't a lot.

Pain spiked through Neve's skull again, and she thought of the white fog that seeped out from behind the door in her head. More specifically, she thought of what lay behind it, memories from a dozen lifetimes and even further back than that, to their first life. She wasn't yet eighteen, so she shouldn't have remembered anything, let alone her life before the Veil. But maybe she'd start to remember that too, like Bay and Mercy had when they all went through the Gate. Maybe the right memory would slip through at any moment and Neve would remember everything. She'd finally have answers.

Yeah, right, Neve thought with a sigh. *As if it would be that simple.*

"We'll figure this out," Daughter Aoife said, nodding her head like she could just will it into being. "And we'll get Bay and Mercy back."

Neve felt another little stab of anger at that, as if get-ting her sisters back was an afterthought. As if it wasn't the

Daughters' fault that they were gone in the first place.

"Thanks," Alexandria said woodenly. She shuffled from foot to foot before giving Neve a sidelong glance. "Would you mind if I stayed here tonight? I, uh . . . with Aodh still running around, I'm not super comfortable—I don't want to go home."

She didn't want to put her aunt and uncle in danger, Neve translated mentally.

Maeve inclined her head. "Of course. You should both get some rest."

Don't tell me what to do, Neve thought petulantly. But she couldn't deny that she was exhausted and Alexandria was dead on her feet. Besides, Neve much preferred that Alexandria stay here, where there was at least the illusion of safety, than anywhere else.

"Come on," Neve said. "You can wear something of mine."

Ordinarily, she would've expected some dumb joke about reaching the swapping-clothes dating stage, or something that would've made Neve blush, but Alexandria just nodded.

"Sorry about the mess," Neve said when they reached her attic bedroom. It wasn't in great shape. There were clothes and weapons strewn everywhere, as well as a dozen heavy books scattered on the bed. Neve had taken them from the library in a panicked haze, searching for anything that might tell her how to get Bay and Mercy back. She hadn't been successful. Obviously. But she'd kept the books.

Honestly, Neve hadn't slept in her own bed since the day of the library heist. Instead, she'd been alternating between Bay's and Mercy's rooms, stealing their pillows so she always had at least one that smelled like them.

"I've seen worse," Alexandria said with a brave attempt at a smile. She sighed, finding an unoccupied space on the bed and sitting down before grabbing one of the books and flicking through it at random.

Neve waffled in the doorway, unsure what to do. She was exhausted. It had been one hell of a long day, and despite her irritation with Daughter Maeve for saying so, Neve desperately needed to rest. But today hadn't just happened to her, and Neve had no idea if talking about it would make things better or worse, especially after the inquisition downstairs.

She hadn't yet come to a decision when Alexandria spoke, not looking up from the book in her lap, some dusty text on magical theory that Neve had gotten about ten pages into before abandoning.

"Why is magic just math?"

That was not what Neve had expected her to say, but Neve probably should have learned by now to expect the unexpected when it came to Alexandria.

"Dunno." Neve shrugged, shifting some of the other books and discarded clothes so she could sit down on the bed as well. "My understanding is baseline at best."

"What, you never wanted to wave a magic wand and cast spells?"

Neve stretched her arms over her head until her joints cracked. Alexandria made a face. "No," Neve said. "Not in this life. I was a little busy learning how to use a sword. Also, I'm dogshit at math and I'm like ninety percent sure there aren't any wands involved."

"So,"—Alexandria made a considering noise—"can anyone learn how to do this stuff? All the theorems or spells or whatever? Or are you born with it?"

Neve disliked the direction this conversation was going, but not enough to lie about it. "I think anyone can learn. It's hard, though, and dangerous. There's a lot more to it than memorizing spells and whatever."

The Daughters told them that centuries ago, when the world was newer and quieter, witches were much more common. Magic was more common, full stop. But it wasn't an infinite resource, and as history marched on, fewer and fewer people were able to access it safely. Plenty tried and even more hurt themselves or died in the attempt. Aoife had explained it once, that to use magic was to make yourself a conduit for a force of nature. Guiding and shaping it into the form you wanted was like trying to direct a flood through a plastic straw. Ninety-nine percent of the time it was safer to get out of the way.

What are the
school toda
making her
into wakefulness to find
of them had gotten muc
once it wasn't because o
Alexandria finally thoug
she had over a hundred t

For whatever reason,
hadn't set them at ease.

What followed was a l
ing as she and Alexandr
noon *again*.

It had taken until the
down from that conversa
time before they had to be
they'd gotten the explan
getting ambushed at sch
have happened if Alexand

Within the nest of pil

Then again, everything Neve knew about magic was from Aoife, so that could all be bullshit as well. Who knew? Maybe magic was as easy as snapping your fingers and wishing hard.

Neve watched Alexandria digest that, her fingers drumming absently on the book cover. Alexandria made a noise under her breath, humming like she was trying to come up with the words for something.

"Is this my fault?" she asked again, so quietly that without her freaky hearing, Neve wouldn't have been able to make out the words. "Did I do this?"

"No," Neve said immediately. "Jesus, no. None of this is your fault, literally none of it."

Alexandria took a deep breath through her nose and Neve prepared for a verbal panic attack, a mile-a-minute spiral like the first time they kissed.

"Are you sure?" Alexandria asked instead, still in a voice so small that Neve felt her heart break a little.

Neve just reached over, pulling Alexandria into a hug. She kissed both of Alexandria's cheeks, tasting salt, and only hugged her harder, taking care not to bruise. "Yes," she said. No preamble, no further explanation, just the assurance that absolutely none of this was Alexandria's fault.

She couldn't say the same for herself, or her family, but Neve hung on to Alexandria like a lifeline and just hoped beyond hope that Alexandria might eventually believe her.

Alexandria huffe
from Neve's embrac
lasers from my eyes

Neve smiled. "Th
give her an idea. Sh
ages ago, with how
Alexandria getting
learning how to figl

extra barrier between them and the world, while flimsy as hell, made them both feel a little bit safer, and also it was as cold as absolute tits in the attic—Alexandria's eyes were so dark that Neve could barely distinguish her irises from her pupils.

Damn, she was pretty.

Alexandria made a face. "Your morning breath is horrible," she said.

Neve grinned and pulled Alexandria close, pressing kisses all over her face while Alexandria shrieked and tried to squirm away.

"Oh my god." Alexandria rolled to the right, managing to yank both of them and half the blankets onto the floor. "Halitosis, thy name is Neve."

Neve laughed, letting Alexandria shove her into the bathroom, and returned five minutes later with clean teeth.

"Wait," Alexandria said when Neve went in for another kiss. "Breath check."

Rolling her eyes, Neve opened her mouth and exhaled before Alexandria finally let herself be kissed.

All told, not a bad way to wake up in the morning, even with everything going on around them.

"No," Alexandria said when they finally broke apart. Her hands were pressed against Neve's chest and her cheeks were pink. Neve probably looked the same; she could feel the heat all the way to the tips of her ears.

Neve blinked, trying to unwind whatever train of thought had led to that answer.

"No, you can't talk me out of going to school," Alexandria said, clarifying. Which was helpful and Neve appreciated it, even if it was exactly the opposite of what she wanted to hear.

"Look." Alexandria cut Neve off before she could launch into some ineffective argument or other. "Yesterday happened. And I am freaking out about it. But sitting around is only going to give me more time to think about it and honestly, I'm already, like, one tiny inconvenience away from a meltdown."

Neve sighed, all her half-formed arguments vanishing. For all that Neve hadn't wanted to go back, now that she considered the alternative, staying in the convent and not being able to do shit while the Daughters dove through historical records and spellbooks would be a good way to drive herself insane.

"The Daughters aren't going to like it," Neve said, mostly to herself. She didn't think they would understand that Neve and Alexandria needed to put space between themselves and . . . the everything.

"They're not *my* moms," Alexandria said, shrugging.

They're not mine, either, Neve meant to say. For whatever reason, the words didn't make it out of her mouth.

The Daughters were already in the kitchen when Neve and Alexandria made their way downstairs. The three of them looked worse for wear, like they hadn't slept much the night before.

Good, Neve thought, shoving away the pang of worry for her haggard guardians. They *weren't* her moms, no matter what Alexandria said.

"Good morning," Maeve said, putting down her mug of strong-smelling coffee. Normally, the Daughters favored tea, but apparently that wasn't getting the job done if they were pulling out the stronger stuff.

"Did you sleep all right?" Clara asked. Her tone was tenuous, and Neve bristled at the quiet, hopeful look on her face, like Neve might have just woken up and forgotten everything. It made her want to arch her back and hiss.

"Fine, thank you," Alexandria said before Neve could do exactly that. Then, helping herself to some of the coffee: "And thank you again for letting me stay the night."

"Of course," Maeve said. "You're welcome as long as you like."

Alexandria hesitated, fiddling with the handle of her mug until Neve started to worry that she might drop it and burn herself. Neve took that as her cue.

"So, we'll be going," she said bluntly, nodding at the door.

Maeve's eyebrows climbed toward her hairline. "Going where?"

"School."

The reaction was as dramatic and immediate as Neve had predicted, and she felt her blood pressure skyrocket. Boiled down, though, the Daughters' arguments were the same as Neve's had been yesterday: it was too dangerous, Aodh was still loose and unaccounted for, it was safest to stay close, blah blah blah.

"You done?" Neve asked when the Daughters finally stopped talking long enough for her to get a word in edge-wise. Maybe not the most tactful way to go, but Neve had never been the tactful one in her family, and Bay was gone, so the Daughters would just have to deal.

"This isn't something you can just run away from," Maeve said severely, drawing herself up. Neve immediately felt the instinctive need to apologize, to shrink away, like she was about to get grounded.

"I'm not," Neve snapped. "I'm the only one *left*."

Maeve flinched a little. "What about Aodh?" she asked after a pause that hung heavy in the air. "You're in no shape to fight him if he turns up again."

That hadn't stopped her yesterday, Neve thought sullenly, though bringing it up probably wouldn't be helpful, so she kept it to herself.

"He's hurt," Neve said slowly. Aodh might be stronger, but he'd gotten his shit rocked pretty good in that fight. "I don't think he's going to try anything."

That last bit was bullshit; Neve had no idea what was going on in her cousin's head. But she was running out of excuses for the Daughters to let them go, and she really didn't want to challenge Daughter Aoife to keep them in the convent by force.

"Besides," Alexandria jumped in, picking up Neve's train of thought instantly because she was wonderful and brilliant, "he knows I'm connected to the Gate, right? And that Neve is protecting me. Even if he wanted a rematch, he would be on his own against whatever came through. I can't exactly fight, so his odds are kind of bullshit."

Not yet, anyway, but Neve was hoping to rectify the not-being-able-to-fight thing as soon as this afternoon. She should have done so earlier, honestly. At least taught Alexandria the basics. Neve wondered if she could scavenge some armor that Alexandria could wear under her clothes, or at least under the outer layers. None of Neve's current set would fit, and Bay's and Mercy's castoffs from before they turned eighteen were way too big. Maybe there was something at the Three Crows she could make work. Neve made a mental note to swing by after school.

"Fine," Daughter Maeve said after a long, drawn-out silence that made Neve's skin itch. She slid something across the kitchen counter and Neve caught her phone before it could drop to the ground and shatter. "Keep this on you and call us if anything happens."

Neve pocketed the phone and gave Maeve a lazy two-finger salute, grabbing her backpack from its stool on the way out the door. Alexandria followed, mumbling effusive thank-yous the whole way.

"Jeez, I always forget how scary they are," Alexandria said once they were in the safety of Neve's car.

Neve rolled her eyes. The Daughters weren't scary. Maybe Aoife, sometimes, but the other two . . . nah. Liars, yes. Scary, no.

Absently, Neve rubbed at the scar on her chest, feeling the ache as new hypertrophic tissue tried to patch over the damage she'd done during the fight yesterday. It had been over in moments—Neve's training sessions had been longer than that when she was barely old enough to hold a practice blade—and she was still aching and sore as if she'd been through Samhain all over again.

It could've been worse. It would've been, in fact, if Aodh hadn't tackled the creature before it could slash at her. Neve turned that moment over again and again in her mind, polishing the memory until it shone, but it didn't provide any additional clarity.

Why would he do that? Why bother getting between her and the thing trying to kill her when he'd tried to gut her just a few weeks ago?

Neve recalled the memories that had spilled forth when Aodh had done . . . *whatever* he had done to her head behind

79

the Veil. They'd only been glimpses of the past, but Neve felt an echo of affection for the bright-eyed, smiling boy she'd remembered before she shoved it down. It wasn't hers, not in this life; it was Nemain's. Affection or no, Aodh had a thousand years' worth of resentment he'd already taken out on her vital organs.

Still. Neve and Aodh were the only gods . . . demons—*whatever the hell they were*—left. That wasn't nothing.

The thought made Neve feel like she'd been punched in the stomach. With everything that had happened yesterday, she'd almost been able to ignore the fact that Bay and Mercy were gone, that two thirds of her soul were missing. The cold in her chest began to spread out, ice crystalizing in her blood with the reminder that she was alone.

"What do I even call myself now?" Neve heard herself ask aloud. Which was not remotely the most pressing question, but she couldn't bear to think about Bay and Mercy a second longer.

Alexandria looked up from where she'd been doodling in her sketchbook. She'd been unusually silent the whole ride. Neve was willing to bet that if she looked, she'd see pencil recreations of the new monsters imprinted on the pages. Kind of upsetting, as far as meditative habits went, but Neve wasn't in any place to judge what was or was not a healthy coping mechanism.

"What?"

Neve opened her mouth, closed it again, and then started over. This was not what she'd anticipated talking about, but she'd already started, so what the hell.

"I don't know what I am anymore. We thought we were gods and they were demons, but we're all the same. Does that make us demons or them gods?" she wondered aloud. "Or both? Or neither?"

Neve had asked Bay a similar question when they'd been behind the Veil. "Very old," Bay had said, which hadn't been helpful at the time and wasn't helpful now.

"I don't know," Alexandria mused. She scratched a hand through her hair with a sudden faraway look that said she'd found a new research topic to hyperfocus on until she found a satisfying solution.

"Sidhe," Alexandria said at lunch.

Puck startled at Alexandria's sudden arrival as she plonked her tray down on the table next to them.

"She?" Puck repeated.

"Yeah," Alexandria agreed. "S-I-D-H-E."

"That is . . . not what that spells."

"It's Irish," Alexandria informed them, grinning and pleased with herself. Puck still looked baffled.

Neve looked at Alexandria sidelong, raising an eyebrow. "Fairies? Really?"

"That's not a direct translation," Alexandria said, as if Neve didn't know that. "And it's just a suggestion."

Neve shrugged her shoulders, trying not to think about how Mercy and Bay would react to being called fairies. In a different language, but still. Mercy would probably say it was homophobic and then laugh at her own joke. Neve's stomach hurt again.

She would see their reactions when Bay and Mercy were home, Neve told herself firmly. In the meantime, it was as good a name as any. Though Neve still felt a prickle at rearranging a centuries-old taxonomy that had been a cornerstone of her identity. She sighed, scrubbing her hands across her face. She knew that she was the one who'd brought it up, but what did it matter what they were, or what they were called? Neve was still mostly human, for another few months at least. The rest of it could fall off a cliff for all she was concerned.

"What are we talking about?" Michael asked, sitting down next to Puck with Ilma right behind. From the look on his face, he'd overheard a bit of the conversation and was just as confused as Puck.

"Neve's, uh, mythology project," Alexandria said, giving him a significant look that was about as subtle as a train crash. "About sidhe."

"What, like fairies or something?" Tameka asked, joining them. Simon was with her, and Neve felt herself settle a little with all of them there together. "Isn't that what that means?"

Neve started to wonder when she had collected so many folklore enthusiasts who knew the meaning of "sidhe" off the top of their heads before realizing that she was probably the reason her friends knew this stuff in the first place.

She was also the reason her friends were in danger, her brain helpfully supplied. Aodh knew about them, at least in passing, which was already way too close for Neve's comfort.

Neve pulled her phone out of her pocket and opened up her chat with Alexandria.

Neve: How would you feel about making it a group lesson?

She and Alexandria hadn't revisited Neve's suggestion of learning self-defense, but it stood to reason that the rest of their friends might benefit from knowing how to throw a punch. If anything, it would give Neve a reason to have them all in the convent, where she could see them and where she knew it was safe.

"Well, since everyone knows that Neve's dickhead cousin is running around, anyone want to learn to fight?" Alexandria asked the group, which was an easy enough way to answer Neve's question.

Puck and Ilma looked a little less than enthusiastic, the only two outliers among the rousing chorus of support for the idea.

"Not today or anything," Neve said, suddenly a little bit

overwhelmed with the logistics, even though it had been her idea in the first place. Just because *she* knew how to fight didn't mean she'd be any good at teaching other people to defend themselves. Neve didn't really know the reasonable limits of human strength and speed, and her martial education had been pretty weapons-centric.

Neve had watched Simon trip over empty air before, and Alexandria's fidgeting caused her to launch her pencils across classrooms about once a week. Giving any of them live steel would be a good way to lose a finger.

Maybe Neve hadn't thought this through. Actually, scratch that: she definitely hadn't thought this through. But the offer was already made and it *was* a good idea, even if Neve didn't have the faintest clue where to start.

"Give me a couple of days to get shit squared away," she said, trying to balance the need to give herself time to fig-ure out how to do this—and most importantly, how to do it safely—and the warring desire that her friends know how to defend themselves as soon as possible.

Puck and Ilma still didn't look totally convinced.

No pressure, Neve texted them quickly while the others were distracted. It's just an idea

Ilma: Can I think about it?

Neve: Of course

Puck just texted a series of emojis that Neve assumed was

their way of saying they agreed with Ilma and would think about it as well.

Neve had to think about it too, and she spent the rest of the lunch period and most of the following classes making a list of things she might need. Most she'd be able to scavenge from the convent, but Clara's human-safe painkillers and bruise ointments were only stocked at the Three Crows. Neve and her sisters had never needed them, but they were great for business, and Neve would rather be safe than sorry.

The ancient wood door of the shop creaked loudly when she opened it that afternoon. Later, Neve would imagine it was a warning. Her arm snapped out, catching Alexandria in the chest before she could take another step into the shop. They both agreed that with Aodh still running around, even if he was injured, if was best for them to stick together.

They might have been wrong about that.

"Ow," Alexandria complained. "What the hell, Neve?" She pushed at Neve's arm and then shifted as if to move past.

Neve was faster. "Don't," she said. Something in her face, her tone, the sudden rigidity of her body, must have translated, because Alexandria didn't try again.

"Something's wrong," Neve said, trying to locate the source of whatever was putting her so violently ill at ease.

The shop looked normal, or as normal as it ever did for

an occult shop run by three not-gods-but-not-humans-either, two of whom were MIA, and occasionally their lying guardians, one of whom was an entire witch. Decorative geodes of varying size and magic potency lined the shelves, glittering in the yellow light from the lamps hanging above. The candles and bundles of herbs were all in their rightful places. None of the books had been torn from the bookshelves. Everything was where it was supposed to be.

Except Bay and Mercy, obviously. Neve didn't know why she felt disappointed; she knew they weren't just going to magically show up the second she walked through the door, like nothing had happened. She hadn't realized that was something she was even hoping for until the crush of disappointment made her legs feel leaden.

Neve waited for her unease to lessen, but something was still wrong, and it was sending her nervous system into high gear.

Blood. Neve didn't know why it took her so long to recognize the metallic tang in the air, but all of a sudden it dawned on her. She could smell blood, a lot of it.

"Stay behind me," Neve said in a low voice. She began to creep forward, feeling Alexandria hanging close at her elbow.

The smell, overpowering now that she'd recognized what it was, only got stronger as they made their way deeper inside the shop. With every step, Neve felt dread sink its cold fingers into her, turning her icy and numb from the inside out.

"Neve, what—?" Alexandria started, but Neve barely heard her over the high-pitched ringing that erupted in her ears as she finally saw a splash of blood. It glittered against the dark wood of the doorframe that led into the back of the shop. And it was blue.

Neve surged forward, ripping her dagger from her belt and holding it steady, wishing for her sword.

There wasn't much farther to go. Not much farther some- one *could* go. The storeroom wasn't that big, and as Neve stepped through the last row of tall shelves, she could hear high, panicked breathing through the ringing in her ears. Bloody handprints smeared the shelves where Neve and her sisters stored merchandise, and footprints slid across the pol- ished floor in a frantic, scrambling pattern as they made their way to the very back of the store.

This deep in the storeroom, the copper smell was over- whelming. Neve felt bile rise in her throat, sour and painful where it hit the abused flesh behind her tongue. She hissed at the sting and the labored breathing hitched.

Bracing herself for what she was about to see, Neve turned the final corner. She expected a mess of primary colors, red hair and blue blood as one of her sisters slowly bled out in the back of the shop that had been a second home to them.

She was almost right. There was blood everywhere, pooling

below a pale, long-limbed body that was slumped in the corner, one arm wrapped around a torso that was so stained with glittering blue that Neve couldn't tell the original colors of the clothes beneath the carnage.

Aodh's pain-glazed eyes slid between Neve and Alexandria. He sighed. There was blood on his teeth. "Oh, now this is just embarrassing."

CHAPTER EIGHT

To everyone's surprise and maybe even her own, Alexandria moved first. Before Neve could even think about stopping her—before Neve could process what she was seeing, let alone react to it—Alexandria was across the storeroom. A new splatter of blue-gold blood added to the grim tableau on the walls as Alexandria's fist connected with Aodh's cheek, snapping his head to the side.

The sound of the impact finally spurred Neve to move instead of staying frozen like an idiot. She looped her arm around Alexandria's waist, hauling her back before she could hit Aodh again. More specifically, before Aodh could react and do something horrible.

Alexandria fought Neve's grip, twisting like an angry cat, her eyes blazing like she was trying to light Aodh on fire with her mind.

"I'll kill you," Alexandria was saying, over and over. "I'll fucking kill you, you asshole—"

"Ow." Aodh pressed the pad of his thumb against the place where Alexandria struck him. It had been a solid punch. Neve couldn't tell from this distance, not with the gore spattered across Aodh's skin like a grisly Jackson Pollock painting, but she suspected that it had already begun to bruise. Neve made a mental note that Alexandria might not be starting from square one if she knew enough to keep her thumb outside her fist when she threw a punch.

That's my girl, Neve thought with a fierce, vindictive swell of pride.

Her girl was still very much trying to wriggle out of Neve's arms, clearly intent on taking out a decade's worth of anger and fear on Aodh while she had the opportunity.

"Let me go," Alexandria shouted, loud enough to make Neve wince.

"Don't," Neve said lowly, arranging them so that Alexandria was in front of her, with Neve's back to Aodh. He could definitely still hear her, but she was doing her best under the circumstances.

"Why not?" Alexandria snarled. Her whole face was twisted up with fury that Neve recognized, the pain and rage lighting her up from the inside. "He's hurt, he's—" Her voice choked off raggedly and Alexandria growled in frustration, casting her eyes downward and blinking back sudden tears.

"It was a good punch," Neve said. She didn't mention that it was a lucky shot, and the only reason it had connected was because she'd caught Aodh by surprise. Neve didn't need to tell Alexandria the kind of damage he could do, even like this.

"I hate him."

"I know. Me too," Neve said, ignoring the flash of remembered, fleeting affection she'd felt earlier.

Alexandria's shoulders sagged and Neve let her go, only a little worried that she might try to go for Aodh again. But Alexandria was smart—a hell of a lot smarter than Neve and not nearly as reckless.

"I'm right here," Aodh whined, calling their attention back to him.

Neve turned to face him. He looked way too smug for someone who was bleeding out on the floor and had just been punched in the face.

She wasn't looking in a mirror, wasn't anywhere near her own reflection, but all of a sudden Neve could see—sense, feel, maybe—the other version of herself sneering. Her upper lip curled in a snarl.

He's right here. He's hurt. Why haven't you killed him yet?

Why hadn't she? She hadn't even thought to do it. Hell, her first impulse was to keep Alexandria from hitting him again. What was wrong with her? Aodh was injured, he was . . .

He was injured. Neve's eyes snapped back to Aodh. He was very, very injured. Neve had known as much when he'd fled the beach yesterday, but she hadn't realized it had been *this* bad.

She wouldn't have survived it, Neve thought abruptly. The

worst of his injuries had been meant for her, before Aodh had gotten in the way. He might have saved her life.

"You saved me," Neve barked, her skin suddenly feeling itchy and too tight. "Why?"

Aodh heaved a deeply put-upon sigh, propping himself up on his elbow despite how obviously it hurt him. Blood gushed afresh out of some wound in his side, and Neve felt a small, potent part of herself hiss and spit. It was too similar to how she felt every time Bay or Mercy was injured in battle, and Neve crumpled up the feeling and stomped on it before it could take hold. "Is that how you say 'thank you'?" he asked.

"And *what*, exactly, is she thanking you for?" Alexandria snarled, uncharacteristic venom in her voice.

Aodh turned his head, glancing lazily at Alexandria. It was an unnerving expression to see on a face that so resembled Neve's own.

Alexandria met his gaze without blinking. "You tried to kill her," she said, like Neve was the only one he'd hurt here.

"But I didn't," Aodh pointed out. His grin was beginning to look forced. There was still blood on his teeth. "Doesn't that count for something?"

"No. It doesn't." Alexandria crossed her arms over her chest.

Aodh sighed like Alexandria was the one being unreasonable here, rolling his eyes toward the ceiling. It was a good show. He looked almost perfectly at ease, like he'd staggered into the Three Crows and bled everywhere for fun and there was nowhere else he'd rather be. Only the slight strain in his neck and clench of his jaw gave him away.

"Well, you're welcome for the voice, at least," he said, gesturing at Neve. He didn't look away from Alexandria. "The rasp is much more attractive, don't you think?"

This time, Neve saw Alexandria's lunge coming and stepped between them. Alexandria gave a frustrated yell.

Aodh's laugh echoed off the ceiling, high and unkind, before it dissolved into a wet hacking cough.

Good. Served him right, Neve thought, tamping down the surge of secondhand anxiety on his behalf. It was involuntary, she told herself firmly, a reaction to seeing so much blood that, until recently, had only ever belonged to Neve and her sisters. It didn't mean she cared.

"What do you want?" Neve demanded, trying to change tack before he provoked Alexandria into trying to hit him again.

"Same thing you do," Aodh said. The strain had made its way into his voice now, belying the cavalier attitude.

"Doubtful," Alexandria muttered, still partially obscured by Neve's body.

Aodh's smile grew pointed. "Hate to break it to you, but Nemain and I are on the same side."

"You are not—" Alexandria started.

"Don't call me that," Neve snapped at the exact same time. Their words overlapped, the sentences running into each other. Aodh shot her a knowing look. Neve wanted to stab him.

"My name is Neve," she said again, as calm as she could manage. There was a part of her that kept waiting for heat to rise in her throat, for the anger that had always been as natural as breathing, but it didn't come.

Aodh made a face. "It's not, though, is it?"

"And we're not on the same side."

"You don't want your sisters back, then?" Aodh asked innocently. "That's unexpected. You three were always so completely codependent. But if you're content to let them rot behind the Veil for the rest of eternity, fine."

Neve's knees turned to water and her legs suddenly seemed to object to holding her weight. Ice stabbed at the very heart of her, at a place deeper and more important than Aodh had ever reached with his own blade. She clenched her hands into fists to keep them from shaking.

"That's what I thought," Aodh said with a knowing look, despite Neve's efforts to mask the wave of dread that threatened to pull her under. "Where was this worry for the rest of us, I wonder? Did you care so much when it was me you left behind?"

A spike of pain drove through her skull, and Neve's breath hissed through her teeth. She tried to blink away the white fog that appeared in her periphery, but it had come on too quickly for her to fight. Neve sucked in another breath, her lungs burning with the effort, and then the storeroom winked away and she was somewhere else.

"You can't just leave me behind!"

Aodh's face was a mask of shock and pain. He flung the words at her in a voice that straddled the line between hopelessness and rage.

Neve—no, Nemain, she was Nemain here. She wasn't Neve yet and wouldn't be for a long, long time. Nemain looked at the weapon held ready in Aodh's grip. The pang of guilt she'd been feeling was easily overshadowed by contemptuous self-assurance. This was the only way, and she knew it.

"Put that away," she said in a voice that was so unlike how she would sound in the future, several dozen lifetimes from now. "Are you really going to fight me? After everything? You had your chance, and now this is the only way to keep us safe."

Aodh's mouth twisted. "What are my options, Nemain, when you're trying to leave me behind?"

He stepped to the side, dropping into a defensive stance that Nemain knew well. They'd learned it together. The movements were practiced, easy, almost thoughtless. They'd done this a hundred times, a thousand, practicing and sparring before either of them was big enough to hold a proper sword and they had to use the terrible blunted ones instead.

"You weren't supposed to find out like this," Nemain heard herself

say. You weren't supposed to find out at all, *she thought. Another stab of guilt there, but it was distant and expertly suppressed.*

"I won't let you," Aodh said. His voice cracked but his footwork never stumbled. He adjusted his grip on his sword.

Nemain's eyes tracked the movement. "You won't kill me," she said, utterly certain. Then, haughtily: "You couldn't if you wanted to."

Aodh was fast. He was strong and angry and excellent, *but she was better. He knew it too, and Nemain felt only resignation as he charged at her.*

Neve's chest throbbed painfully as reality reasserted itself, her breath coming in stuttering little gasps that had nothing to do with the injury to her lungs.

What the hell was that? Neve thought, even though she knew the answer. It was her. Past her. Neve Prime, the original from before the Veil, the Gate, and any of the rest of it. The girl Neve had seen in the mirror.

Neve shuddered, unable to shake the creeping feeling of wrongness that accompanied the memory. She felt sick, like the floor was rocking beneath her feet. She shouldn't have seen that. It was too early; she was too young. She gritted her teeth as her heart panged in her chest again. It was as if her body was trying to make up for lost time, taking all the guilt she should have felt and force-feeding it to her now.

And she did feel guilty. She didn't want to, and maybe if she was the same person she had been before all this, before the Veil, before the reincarnation cycle, before Alexandria and their friends, she wouldn't feel guilty now. But Neve was different. She was so fundamentally different, and her heart ached for the boy she and her sisters had left behind. The memory of his face, the betrayal and heartbreak she saw there, was seared behind her eyelids, and for a moment Neve wished that she was back in the memory because it hadn't hurt so badly in the past.

It wasn't enough, though. The memory, the guilt, it wasn't enough to make Neve forget everything he'd done.

"That," Aodh said, nodding at Neve and killing any hope she might have had that her trip down memory lane had gone unnoticed. It was a stupid thing to hope for, all things considered, but still. "That's what I want."

Alexandria exhaled harshly through her nose. From her position behind Neve, she hadn't seen the play of emotions as Neve had come back to herself. "What are you talking about?" she demanded.

"Nem—*Neve*—made the Veil," Aodh said, making a show of correcting himself. Neve growled at him. "She knows how to unmake it, since apparently whatever *you* did was temporary," he said, waving a careless hand at Alexandria.

"Give me one reason," Neve said, still shaking off the memory. She had the sense of wandering through the dark, knowing that there was a cliff somewhere ahead of her but not where it was. Like one wrong step would send her into free fall. "One reason why I don't just kill you now and be done with it."

She should. It was the right thing to do. Neve should have done it already, instead of hedging and hesitating like this. Mercy wouldn't have hesitated. Bay wouldn't have either, though Bay might have been upset after the fact. But they both would have acted. They wouldn't have just stood here and chatted with the person who had ruined Alexandria's life, killed her parents, and very nearly killed Neve.

"You can't," Aodh said archly. Maybe it was residual bleed-through from the memory or maybe he was too hurt to hide it anymore, but she could hear the slight tremor in his voice beneath all the bullshit and bravado. "You need me, because you sure as hell won't be able to handle what comes out of the Gate on your own." Then, after a pause, as if he could sense her next question: "And I can't kill you, because you know how to open the Gate, even though you *conveniently* let yourself forget. Our interests are aligned, cousin."

Neve glared. Like hell was she going to help him open the Gate and set loose an army, but she needed a way to get to Bay and Mercy. And he was right: Neve wasn't strong enough to take care of this new flavor of monster. Not as she was and not on her own.

Neve wanted him to be wrong. But he wasn't. Son of a bitch.

Alexandria gave a spiteful snort. "Yeah right, like we'd ever help—"

"Fine," Neve said at the same time. Alexandria's mouth dropped open, her eyes going wide with outrage.

Aodh smiled, flashing his blood-stained teeth again. Neve already regretted this.

"This is going to be just like old times."

CHAPTER NINE

"Hey, so, quick question," Alexandria said after hauling Neve back into the main room of the store. Her face was a study in indignation, from the tight seam of her mouth to the spots of color on her cheeks. "Have you completely lost your mind?"

"No," Neve said, pitching her voice down and hoping Alexandria would do the same because Aodh could definitely still hear them. "No, I haven't, but I'm on my own and—"

"You're not on your own!" Alexandria hissed. "Stop saying that! You have me. And you have the Daughters."

Neve scowled. Right, the Daughters, who had been lying to her for a thousand years about who and what she was, and had cheerfully let her and her sisters kill and be killed for a lie.

"They can't help me with this," she insisted, because none of that would be persuasive to Alexandria. "And neither can you." She didn't mean it as an insult or a criticism, but that didn't stop Alexandria from looking like she'd been slapped.

"He's a monster," Alexandria said, recovering quickly.

So am I.

"I know," Neve said. "But right now, that monster is all we've got." She pressed her keys into Alexandria's hand. "Take my car and go home."

Neve needed to get Aodh back to the convent, and despite whatever little truce they'd sketched between themselves, she didn't trust him in an enclosed space with Alexandria. Not to mention that Alexandria might be pissed enough to attempt vehicular manslaughter. This was the best option of a bad bunch.

If the look on her face was anything to go by, Alexandria disagreed. But she took the keys.

"This is wrong," she said before turning and walking away, leaving Neve alone in the store. Neve stayed there for a long moment, watching the door, still trying to come up with some explanation that would make any of this okay.

"She'll get over it," Aodh said, abruptly behind her.

Neve turned with a scowl to see him leaning in the door-way that led to the storeroom. He was still bleeding; Neve was going to have to clean it up. She was only slightly mollified by the fact that he truly looked like hell. Beneath the blood, his skin was waxy and gray, and it looked like the walk from the back had taken what little remained of his strength.

Unfortunately, it couldn't keep him from talking. "Who knows, maybe this will bring us all closer together as friends."

"Shut up."

. . .

Neve hadn't given much of an explanation when she called the Daughters and told them to meet her at the Three Crows, but they showed up in record time. Neve had shoved Aodh back in the storeroom to keep him out of sight, hoping to have a chance to explain before the Daughters inevitably lost their shit.

"Neve?" The bell over the door chimed, and Neve steeled herself for what she knew was going to be an extremely unpleasant conversation.

Before she got a word out, Aoife's eyes flashed, and the air in the shop went thin and brittle. Magic gathered in Aoife's palms and dripped off her fingertips. The smell of ozone mingled with the lingering stench of blood did not help settle Neve's unruly stomach.

Neve sighed. So much for that plan.

For their parts, Clara and Maeve didn't have as colorful an outward reaction, but both of their faces went taut and grim when Aodh poked his head out from the back.

"Hello, Maeve," Aodh said, inclining his head almost cordially at the Daughters, who looked like a trio of crows in their black dresses and veils. "Aoife. Clara." He squinted at the two of them before flashing his teeth in a smile. "And still together, I see. Good for you."

Aoife made a noise of outrage, but Maeve stepped forward before she could do anything more.

"Neve," Maeve said, her voice tightly controlled.

Neve explained with as few words as possible, watching the Daughters' expressions.

To Neve's surprise, Aodh didn't take the chance to jump in when the Daughters stood in stony silence, digesting Neve's objectively insane proposal. He just watched the four of them with an amused gleam in his eye. He had one of his fingers in his mouth, digging out the blood under his nails with his teeth. Neve grimaced and looked away.

She fought the urge to fidget as the silence began to drag. She knew that she'd put the Daughters in a corner, springing Aodh on them like this. Which had kind of been the point.

If he's here, that means he's not out there, Neve thought pointedly, in case Aoife was listening.

Aoife's thunderous expression only darkened; she was definitely listening.

Finally, after the silence had dragged on for so long that Neve's eye had begun to twitch, Maeve regarded Aodh.

"You will not harm anyone else."

Aodh made an *X* over his heart. "Promise." He opened his mouth again, and Neve felt the hum of air vibrating as he started to speak, but Aoife was faster. She crossed from the door in three long strides and pressed one crackling fingertip against Aodh's forehead. It reminded Neve a little too much of what Aodh had done to her, back behind the Veil when he'd broken the door in her head.

"None of that, either," Aoife said darkly. Neve felt the pulse of Aoife's magic taking hold.

For the first time, Aodh's smile dropped. He glared, the promise of violence written all over his face, and Neve bent her knees slightly, prepared to leap at him. But Aodh remained perfectly still as spellwork crawled over his skin, branching out from Aoife's fingertip. It flashed over his mouth and circled twice around his throat before disappearing again.

"That feels a bit targeted," Aodh said stiffly when Aoife stepped away. He rubbed at the spots where the magic had been visible a moment before. "Ugh. I suppose the Daughters of *Danu* would have a spell custom-made for me." He flung the words like an accusation, but Neve didn't know what he meant. "That's a lot of power. Sure you can spare it?"

Aoife's eyes narrowed, but she didn't dignify his question with a response.

A lot of power? What did he . . . ? Neve thought of the route the magic had taken over his mouth and around his neck. Keeping him from speaking.

Keeping him from speaking because he could mess with people's heads. Neve went cold. She hadn't thought of that and wanted to kick herself. That was one hell of an oversight.

Aodh rolled his eyes, looking more annoyed than murderous now. "Oh, fine. If it makes you feel better." He paused. "I thought after a thousand years you wouldn't still be so *boring*."

Neve was regretting this already.

"Neve," Maeve said once they had returned to the convent. Despite their clear reservations, the Daughters were going along with the plan. For now. And Aodh was injured enough that the bare-bones supplies at the Three Crows wouldn't be enough.

It had been a *very* tense ride home.

Neve winced at the severity in Maeve's tone. Clara and Aoife were escorting Aodh to the infirmary, both of them looking stiff enough to snap.

"Before you ask what I was thinking—" Neve started, waiting until Aodh was well out of earshot to speak.

Maeve didn't let her finish. "You weren't thinking," she said, bearing down on Neve like a natural disaster. "You can't have been, or else you wouldn't have done this."

"What else was I supposed to do?" Neve asked, her hands spread wide in front of her.

"What you were trained to do!" Daughter Maeve snapped.

Neve reared back, her mouth dropping open. "What I was trained to do?" she repeated.

"That's not—"

"No, fine, let's talk about it," Neve shouted, squaring her shoulders. "What was I trained to do, Maeve? What were any of us trained to do? Because from where I'm standing, you three let us kill our family over and over and over again for no reason."

"There was a reason," Maeve replied hotly. "He's dangerous. Too many of your family agreed with him and wouldn't listen. It was going to be war."

The words had the smoothness of repetition, of being carried through the centuries.

"That's not good enough!" Neve shouted, and Maeve's eyes widened with surprise, as if she'd thought the argument was over. "You can't tell me that between the three of us, this was the best we could come up with?" Neve waved her arm to encompass the convent, the Gate, the whole thousand-year shitshow. "You really expect me to believe that locking our family away and forgetting they existed was the best solution? That's insane. You hear how insane that is, right? And what about everyone who didn't agree? They got shoved into limbo too? Forever?"

"It was the only way," Daughter Maeve said, but there was a quaver in her voice that hadn't been there before. "It was the only way we knew to keep everyone safe."

Neve snorted. "Safe? Yeah, right." She yanked down the

collar of her shirt to reveal the ugly snarl of scar tissue. "This felt really safe, Maeve."

"You don't know," Maeve said, shaking her head minutely. "You don't remember."

"Why not?" Neve shot back. "Why don't we remember? Why would we let ourselves forget?"

She waited, but Maeve said nothing.

"That's what I thought," Neve growled. "You don't know either. And I don't know what's worse: that we forgot, or that you never asked why."

Maeve made a strangled sort of sound, but Neve had decided that she was done. It had been a long-ass day, and she couldn't stand the look on Maeve's face a moment longer.

CHAPTER TEN

O h, good, you're still alive," Alexandria said when
Neve answered her call the next morning. Her
acidic tone failed to disguise the relief in her voice.

"I'm still alive," Neve said, trying not to sound irritated.
She really didn't need a repeat of yesterday's argument.
Besides, Alexandria was well aware that Neve was alive. Neve
had texted her more than once to tell her so, remembering
how poorly Alexandria had reacted the few times Neve had
gone radio silent in the past.

"Well, I'm glad he didn't kill you in your sleep," Alexandria
said tartly when Neve didn't take the bait.

"Aoife upped the wards," Neve said, still straining for calm.
"And I don't even think he stayed here last night."

"Didn't—" Alexandria spluttered. "Why would you bother
letting him in at all if you're just going to let him waltz out
the front door?"

It was way too early in the morning for Neve to have a
headache, but she could already feel one forming behind her
eyes. For the moment, it didn't feel supernatural, but she knew
how quickly that could change.

"Aoife again," Neve said tersely, explaining the dart of magic Aoife had injected under Aodh's skin. Neve was still thinking about what he'd said, about the Daughters having a spell ready-made to neutralize his ability in particular. It itched at her brain, but Neve couldn't figure out why. She didn't think she'd get a straight answer from Aodh even if she did ask, and she didn't want to even start with the Daughters at the moment.

"So, what, you just tag him like a migratory bird and call it done?"

"What do you want me to do?" Neve asked, even though she knew the answer. Alexandria wanted the same thing as Maeve, though Neve doubted Alexandria would phrase it the same way. They both wanted Aodh dead, and neither seemed to realize that Neve did too. But so long as Bay and Mercy were gone and the knowledge of the Gate spell was locked in her head, this truce was the best they'd get.

What happens when you do remember? Neve's past self asked. *Are you really going to let him have an army? Are you really going to let him live, after everything he's done?*

Neve wished her past self would shut up.

Neve wished Bay and Mercy were here. She wished a lot of things. Right now, she mostly wished not to be having this fight. Again.

After a pause, Neve heard the sound of a car honking outside.

"I have your car, remember?" Alexandria said, still on the line.

The tension didn't lessen once they were at school. Alexandria had told their friends everything that had happened, which saved Neve the trouble of having to do it herself. Small mercies.

"I can't believe you're helping him," Tameka said under her breath when they all congregated during one of the periods when everyone's study hall overlapped. Newgrange Harbor High School's class schedule was a work of arcana so dense that even Aoife would have trouble sorting through it. Neve mostly went with the flow or skipped altogether if she couldn't remember which class was next.

She sort of wished she'd skipped now, because then she wouldn't be having the same conversation for a third—no, fourth—time.

"I'm not helping him," Neve said without looking up from the worksheet she was pretending to be working on. So far, she'd filled out her name at the top and nothing else.

"I prefer to think that we're helping each other," said a voice suddenly at Neve's elbow.

Neve nearly hit the goddamn ceiling, slamming her hand down in surprise hard enough that the table rattled and she could hear the old wood creak loudly.

"Also, you're spelling your fake name wrong," Aodh added, propping his chin in his hand as he scanned the worksheet.

Neve's jaw ached from clenching it, and there was so much adrenaline thrumming through her limbs that she thought she might vibrate out of her skin. Around them, the humans had gone completely still, as if Neve and Aodh were the kind of predators that couldn't see something until it moved.

"What are you doing here?" Neve gritted out.

Aodh looked confused, his eyebrows meeting in the middle of his forehead. Despite the mess he'd been just the night before, he looked almost completely healed now. Neve's chest throbbed. She hated him.

"You're the one with self-induced amnesia, cousin," Aodh said. "Am I just supposed to trust that you'll be kind enough to share when you remember how you locked us all up for a thousand years?" The look on Neve's face must have been enough of an answer, because he continued. "I thought so. Hopefully some quality bonding time will help trigger something in that thick skull of yours."

He reached out as if to poke her in the forehead. Fear lit her up like a Christmas tree and Neve reacted before she could think, yanking the knife she had at her waist and plunging it into the closest bit of him she could reach.

Aodh looked at the dagger pinning his sleeve to the table. "Really?"

"Everything okay back there?"

Neve's head snapped to the front of the classroom.

Somehow, she'd forgotten that she was still at school, surrounded by humans who didn't know what she was and who would probably not react well to her stabbing someone in the middle of class. Also, there was definitely a rule against having knives at school.

"Yes," Alexandria said without missing a beat. She gave the study hall teacher—a substitute whose name Neve didn't know—a smile. "Sorry. I saw a bug."

The sub looked a little dubious, but Neve shifted her body and quickly stowed the knife.

"All right," the sub said after a pause. "Please go back to work and keep the volume down."

Alexandria nodded, the smile dropping off her face as soon as the sub turned away.

"That," Aodh said, his eyes shining with laughter, "was an overreaction."

"Go away," Neve snarled.

Aodh leaned back in his chair, limbs loose and at ease. "Are you going to stab me again?"

"Only if you deserve it."

"That's rude."

"Go away."

Aodh cocked his head to the side, gray eyes sweeping over her before lazily surveying the rest of the classroom. Neve's stomach dropped. It was nearly the same feeling of being overcome by a memory, except Neve didn't need to look into the past to know where she'd seen that expression before. She'd seen it in her own mirror, felt it on her own face when she was being a cocky asshole.

The sudden similarity did not make her feel better.

"Are you going to make me?"

Neve's teeth clacked together as a dozen impotent threats stacked up on her tongue, each more pathetic and less actionable than the last. Aodh's considering look morphed into a delighted smile. Neve had a very vivid mental image of ripping off his arms and beating him with them.

"*Anyway*," Aodh said, cheerfully looking away from Neve as she tried her best to fry him with her mind. He regarded the humans at the table, who, besides Alexandria, hadn't moved or spoken, and all looked like they were in various stages of shock. "Hello, humans. I'm Aodh. I'm sure we'll be seeing a lot of each other."

When the bell rang to signal the end of what felt like the longest study hall in existence, Neve was not subtle about hanging back, putting herself between Aodh and her friends as they all but ran out the door. Alexandria looked like she might try to linger, but Neve gave a minute shake of her head. Alexandria filed out with the others, though not before giving Aodh a look that could have stripped paint.

"Come on. Let's have it, then," Aodh said when the classroom was empty save for the two of them. He wasn't looking at her, instead making a show of reading the many multicolored posters on the walls. Neve knew better than to think she might have an advantage because he was distracted.

She also knew that the next class would be coming soon, which meant that her window of opportunity was closing fast.

"What are you *doing* here?" Neve demanded. She didn't let herself think, aiming a punch at Aodh's kidney. Despite how he might look, there was no way he was totally healed in less than twenty-four hours, and Neve had seen enough of the damage to know where to aim.

She didn't have time to brace before Aodh grabbed her forearm in an iron grip, and then her back hit the wall hard enough to expel all the breath from her lungs.

Neve wheezed, her body trying to curl in on itself, but Aodh was in the way. He pressed his forearm against her throat, choking any sound before it could escape.

"Don't get cocky, cousin," Aodh said. His face was a blank mask, completely devoid of expression. "You already had your chance to kill me and you didn't take it."

Neve bared her teeth at him. Her whole chest seized up, caught on an exhale like her useless lungs had forgotten how to inflate.

"So we," Aodh said calmly, ignoring Neve's increasingly frantic pulse, "are going to play nice. And once the whole family is together again, we can go back to trying to kill each other. How does that sound?"

"Have you always been this desperate for attention?" Neve wheezed. "Or did you just get too used to calling yourself a king?"

"Maybe I was wrong," Aodh said in a cold, dead voice that chilled Neve down to her bones. "I thought you actually cared about each other, but clearly you don't mind your sisters being stuck with all the rest of them."

Neve flinched.

"I'm not the only one who's angry," Aodh said, low and menacing. "The three of you did a lot of damage and we had a long time to consider what would happen if we ever got free." He shrugged, a gesture that would have been utterly blasé if not for the hate that blazed across his face. "You'll only have yourself to blame if there's nothing left to save."

Neve couldn't move, couldn't speak. She could barely hear anything beyond her heart hammering a panicked rhythm in her ears. Even worse, Neve felt her eyes well over with tears before she could blink them away.

The voice in her head, the memory of Nemain, screeched at the show of weakness.

You shouldn't have made me like this, then, Neve thought, trying to shove her away. She felt as if she were splintering, the sliver of herself that was left without her sisters beginning

115

to break down even further from the strain of being hurt and scared and so alone. *You shouldn't have made us human, or made us forget.*

"Good talk," Aodh said, and released her.

Neve staggered, only just able to keep her shaking legs from collapsing. By the time she managed to catch her breath, students were already making their way in for their next class and Aodh was gone.

CHAPTER ELEVEN

He didn't stay gone. Neve wished it was just a threat, a shitty power play to remind her that he'd kicked her ass before and could do it again whenever he wanted.

But no. Aodh stuck around. She didn't see him as often around the convent—maybe it was the presence of the Daughters that he was avoiding, she didn't know—but he became a frequent and upsetting fixture at school.

Neve couldn't wrap her head around the *why* of it, nor could she pin down when he'd pop up next. None of the teachers seemed to notice him. Their eyes just kind of moved over him like he wasn't even there.

Aodh had caught her eye and grinned the first time it happened, when Neve wasn't able to mask her expression in time. "She's under a lot of stress, poor Aoife," was all he'd said.

Neve had immediately thought the worst and spent the rest of the day obsessing, worrying that Aoife's spell had failed and that Aodh was going to plant himself in the minds of the Newgrange Harbor population like a persistent weed. She'd very nearly gone back to the convent to check, to find another solution if Aoife couldn't keep up with the spell. But

Neve didn't feel anything shift in the passive weave of magic, nothing that told her Aodh was messing with people's heads. Which didn't mean that it wasn't happening, but it was enough for Neve not to fly off the handle and assume the worst.

More proof that his powers had, at the very least, been severely limited came soon after. Whatever he was doing to the teachers and admin didn't extend to the rest of the student body. Neve felt the eyes on her and Aodh whenever he was around, chatting about nothing or just lurking and making everyone deeply uncomfortable. As far as Newgrange Harbor knew, there were only three Morgan siblings, but Aodh looked so like Neve that there was no way someone wouldn't put it together. Their hair was a slightly different color and his had more of a curl to it, but they had the same eyes and the same rangy build. He wasn't taller than her, thankfully—Neve didn't think she would be able to cope with that on top of everything else, though they both easily cleared six feet. Seizing on a petty impulse, Neve resolved to wear her lifted boots for the foreseeable future.

Her human friends, naturally, were not handling any of this well. For the first few days they had all been jumpy as hell, constantly looking over their shoulders and flinching at sudden noises. It made Neve's stomach hurt to watch, but she couldn't exactly tell them that everything was going to be okay, could she?

I know you're scared, she didn't say. *And I don't blame you. Please let me make it up to you. Please let me try, for once in all my useless lifetimes, to actually help.*

Puck: I want to learn how to fight

The text pinged in the group chat a week or so after Aodh had decided to enroll part-time at Newgrange Harbor High School.

Ilma: Me too

Neve's phone buzzed with a chorus of assents. In the haze of the last week, between the Gate opening and all Aodh's everything, Neve had nearly forgotten about that proposal.

Neve: Are you sure?

They knew that Aodh might be at the convent. But he was also at school and wherever the hell he wanted to be, waiting for the door in Neve's head to leak a relevant memory—which had yet to happen. Neve hadn't remembered anything else, in fact. She still didn't have any idea what she was going to do if—*when*—she finally did remember, and she had no way of knowing when Aodh's sudden patience would run out. When it did, it would probably be best for everyone that her friends know the very basics of how to defend themselves.

Neve: Okay. After school

Having a distraction was good; it helped keep her calm. It was even better to have a distraction that might mean the difference between the squishy and horrifically important humans in her life living or dying. Not that any of them would ever be able to take Aodh, or any other monster that came out of the Gate, even if they'd been training for their entire lives. But surprise was one hell of a tool. They didn't have to be warriors. They just needed to hit hard and run like hell. Neve didn't know when the Gate would open next or what fun new nightmare would come out of it when it did, but she would feel a tiny bit better knowing that her friends might have a shot at getting away.

That didn't solve the original problem with this plan, which was that Neve had no idea what she was doing.

Bay would be good at this. Mercy . . . probably not as good. She'd heckle and crack mean jokes, but it wouldn't matter, because at least she would be there. With Neve. Both sisters would be, instead of trapped somewhere she couldn't reach.

A lump formed at the base of Neve's throat. She missed her sisters so suddenly and so fiercely that it hurt like a wound. In her mind's eye, the empty place inside her yawned ever wider. Neve felt the tips of her fingers going numb, icing over.

She didn't give the Daughters much notice, but by the time the small caravan of cars pulled up to the convent, there was enough food in the kitchen to feed a small army, and the training yard was inexplicably bigger than Neve could ever remember it being. It was warm, too, warmer than it had any right to be. Neve didn't really mind the cold—despite the numbness spreading through her like an infection, she ran warm (thank you, supernatural metabolism)—but she doubted her friends would be as comfortable, considering it was nearly February. When she squinted, Neve could see purplish starbursts reflecting in the dim light. Aoife.

Neve's lip curled. The Daughters had another thing coming if they thought that any of this would make up for what they'd done.

"Need a little help?" Daughter Maeve asked, hovering just inside the door as Neve finished showing her friends around and, with dubious confidence, had them start warming up. Michael had shot her a skeptical look before shrugging his shoulders and beginning a lap around the ring. Tameka, Simon, Puck, and Ilma had followed suit, though none of them looked fully convinced that Neve knew what she was doing. Alexandria had given her an encouraging smile at least.

"He keeps showing up," she said shortly. Neve didn't need to specify who she was talking about.

Maeve inhaled sharply through her nose but otherwise stayed aggravatingly calm. "You're all right."

It wasn't a question but an observation. Neve still snorted. "Physically? Yeah." Neve meant that Aodh hadn't hurt anyone, though she knew good and well that his continued presence wasn't doing favors for anyone's mental health.

"If it comes down to a fight—" Maeve started gravely, no doubt about to warn Neve about the pointlessness of this whole endeavor; kill it dead before she could manage to fail at it herself.

"I know," Neve snapped. Then softer: "I know. But I don't know what else to do."

Some part of her, the recently reawakened Nemain in her head, hissed and spat at the admission, and Neve cringed away almost as soon as she'd said it, hating her own honesty and vulnerability. But Maeve was here and Neve was alone, without her sisters, and she didn't know how to do this.

Neve growled out a sigh, deflecting, and ran her hands through her hair. She should have worn it in a braid today, but she wasn't as good at braiding as Bay. Her stomach hurt.

"All right, then," Maeve said briskly, nodding. She surveyed the six humans in their yard, and Neve realized that this was probably more humans than had ever been in the convent at one time.

"What are you doing?" Neve asked when Maeve turned to go inside.

"Getting Clara," Maeve replied. "Or did you forget who taught you girls to fight in the first place?"

Neve was left to goggle at the space Maeve had left behind for only a minute or so before she reappeared with Clara. Both of them were wearing matching determined expressions that Neve chose not to examine too deeply.

"So," Clara said in the same businesslike way she had when she was organizing her workshop or wringing small magic out of otherwise ordinary plants. "Basics?"

"Yeah," Neve said, still a little nonplussed. This was too easy. She'd sprung this on them without warning and barely let on that she needed help. Why were they jumping in like this? What had she done to deserve whatever weird, unspoken kindness was going on here? She'd been nothing but horrible to them—all three of them—for weeks. With extremely good and justified reason, but still.

Because they loved her. Obviously. Even though she was angry with them, even though she'd been prickly and awful. But knowing that didn't make anything easier.

"I'm assuming no weapons?" Clara asked, oblivious to Neve's conflict or choosing not to comment on it. More kindness Neve didn't deserve.

"Just self-defense," Neve said. Her shoulders were somewhere around her ears, and she kept waiting for one of the Daughters to break the charade and shove it in her face. There was another shoe somewhere, waiting for the opportunity to drop, but Neve couldn't see it.

"Let's get started, then," Clara said, rolling up her sleeves. She took a step out into the yard before stopping and glancing back at Neve. "Shouldn't you get your sword?" she asked.

Neve started. She hadn't trained in weeks, hadn't been in any shape to train without injuring herself further. "Now?" she asked, eyes darting to the humans who had stopped their warm-up and were glancing at the three of them with various levels of unease and suspicion. They knew what she was and what she could do by now, obviously, but there was a difference between knowing and seeing firsthand. Besides the brief scuffle outside the Gate, her friends—again, besides Alexandria—had never really seen what Neve was capable of. Neve wasn't sure she wanted that to change.

But right now it didn't seem like she had a choice. "I think you've had enough bed rest, dear," Maeve said, not unkindly. "Go get your gear. We'll get started."

Still thoroughly dazed at the turn this afternoon had taken, Neve did as she was told and retrieved her short-sword from the armory. The moment she felt the familiar weight of her blade in her hand, some of the restless energy that Neve hadn't even noticed was humming beneath her skin began to dissipate.

Even though she knew better than to let her focus wander with a blade in her hand, Neve kept one eye on her humans as Maeve and Clara had them run some drills. Easy ones, just to get an idea of what they were working with. Neve felt herself wince a little, remembering how the Daughters had put her and her sisters through their paces when they were little, before they graduated to live steel and started training on their own. Honestly, Neve was feeling a little stupid for not suggesting this earlier.

Watching out of the corner of her eye while she did some of her own drills to warm up, Neve was grateful she'd thought to suggest that everyone come in their gym clothes. Maeve and Clara were tough as hell, even if they were accommodating for humans, and if Neve's friends weren't sweating already, they would be soon.

Neve waited until Maeve and Clara had explained the next drill and the group began the exercise before she started on her own in earnest. She was out of practice and had over-exerted herself yesterday, so she had no choice but to take it slow.

Basics. That's what she'd requested for her friends. Maybe Neve should take her own advice. Ignoring the part of her that wanted to launch into complicated drills and formations, Neve tightened her ponytail and went all the way back to the start. It felt weird, doing this on her own. There was a reason Neve had been avoiding the training ring, besides the obvious. It was just another reminder that Bay and Mercy were gone.

Neve pressed her lips together, swallowing a sob. She needed to keep it together. She was going to get them back, and she would have to be able to fight when she did. Bay and Mercy needed her to be strong.

She closed her eyes, focusing on the unbalanced weight of her short-sword in one hand and her dagger in the other, and allowed that to inform her stance as she rearranged her body into position. With her eyes closed, it was much easier to pay attention to her breathing, hearing it hitch and feeling herself wheeze even when she wasn't doing anything too strenuous.

Her lungs *should* heal, according to Clara, who had done her best and looked desperately unhappy when she told Neve that the rest was just up to time.

Neve squeezed her eyes tighter, trying not to dwell on that. Her lungs would heal or they wouldn't. Clara had done everything she could, and Neve wasn't doing herself any favors by obsessing.

She also wouldn't do herself any favors if she overextended herself now. With her focus still on her breathing, Neve moved from one stance to the next, paying attention to how her body shifted and reacted to each one. Which ones hurt more, which ones hurt less. There weren't any that didn't hurt, but Neve was slowly starting to accept that the low-grade pain in her chest was her new baseline.

Neve had spent her whole life pushing her body to its limits and past them, again and again and again. She knew herself, her strength and speed and the way her body moved. When she'd woken up after returning from the Veil, it wasn't just her connection to Bay and Mercy that was gone: Neve's connection to her own physical self was gone too, and she'd had to learn all over again.

Even though it hurt a little, it felt good, too. Gentle, almost. Like Neve was being reintroduced to herself.

Neve knew she was going to be sore by the time she finally finished the last of her slow, methodical drills, and she opened her eyes just in time to see Alexandria throw a pretty good punch before overbalancing and nearly falling on her ass. She and the rest of the group were sweaty and breathing hard by the time Maeve and Clara decided to call it quits.

"Jesus Christ, no wonder you're so cranky if you spend all your time doing this shit," Michael complained. The words materialized in puffs of vapor that floated upward from where he'd bent nearly in half, hands on his knees. Puck made an equally exhausted noise of agreement.

No one else verbalized their critiques of Neve's attitude or the training session, though every one of them looked like they'd been exercising for hours under the hot sun. Neve was just the teeny-tiniest bit impressed with the Daughters.

"Same time tomorrow?" Maeve offered, raising a steely gray eyebrow to a chorus of groans.

Neve laughed, pressing her fist against her mouth to stifle the sound.

They did come back. Every other afternoon for the rest of the week, in fact. Daughters Maeve and Clara seemed happy enough to put together a human-safe training plan, and it got everyone out of the way while Aoife spent her time trying to diagnose what the hell was going on with the Gate and how they were going to get Bay and Mercy out without setting Aodh's army loose.

It was going better than Neve had thought it would. Tameka, Simon, Puck, Michael, and Ilma were making good progress, especially considering their lack of baseline fighting skills. They still went jumpy and silent whenever Aodh showed up, but some of the abject fear had dissipated. Neve wasn't sure if that was a good thing or not.

She still wasn't sure why he was bothering her, despite his insistence that he was waiting for Neve to remember, and one night, while thumbing through yet another magic textbook in the library, she said so out loud.

"Maybe he's lonely," Aoife replied after a long moment.

Neve rolled her eyes so hard that she could actually watch her brain cells reject that little theory outright.

"Yeah, okay," she said dismissively, returning to the book. *Lonely.* Right.

CHAPTER TWELVE

You leave your left side open."

Neve had barely taken a step back inside the convent, tying her sweaty hair into a bun to get it off her neck. She flinched hard, one hand going for the sword on her back before her brain caught up to her.

"Don't jump out at people who are armed," she snapped. Her heart thudded painfully in her chest, and Neve had to pull thin breaths in through her nose until it calmed again.

Aodh grinned at her from the spot where he'd been lurking near the doorway. He gave the impression of movement despite standing still, Neve noticed. Like gravity didn't have the same hold on him as it did other people. There was a weird slouchiness in the way he stood, a stark contrast to Neve's own rigid posture. He was always just a little bit tilted, as if his connective tissue was more elastic than it should be.

"What are you doing here?" Neve growled.

"I can't pop in to visit?" Aodh asked.

"No."

"Call it a surprise inspection, then."

Neve snorted. "Yeah, well, if you've got an issue with

how I fight, you should take it up with the dickhead who stabbed me."

Now it was Aodh's turn to huff, as if Neve were being over-dramatic and he hadn't *literally* stabbed her. "You do like to complain about that, don't you?"

Neve didn't dignify that with a response, shouldering past him.

"You know, you used to be a lot more fun!" Aodh called after her.

Unlike every other time a memory had slipped through the door in her head, this time there was no warning. No head-ache, no fog, no nothing. Neve was in the convent one minute, and the next, she was gone.

There was a weight in her hand, a blade that was lighter than it should have been. That was the first thing she noticed. The second was that it was made of wood, a crudely carved training weapon.

The third thing, which she really should have noticed first and foremost, was that the hand holding the wooden dagger—her hand—was way too small.

Neve blinked, adjusting to a vantage point that was much shorter than what she was used to. Her vision was warped and strange for a few dizzying moments before it reconciled with itself and solidified, but it still wasn't quite right. She wasn't entirely sure how, but Neve was in two places at once. She was both participant and spectator, watching the scene that unfolded beneath her and a part of it at the same time. Maybe that meant she wasn't actually anywhere, because this was a memory. Could she be in two places and also nowhere all at the same time? Probably not. But also . . . maybe?

Her head hurt.

Before she had the chance to adapt to suddenly being several years younger and significantly smaller, a high-pitched cry came from just outside her vision. She didn't react in time to block the smarting blow that knocked her into the dust.

"Not fair!" Little Neve's voice came out high and reedy. She glared at the boy who towered over her, his head blocking out the light of the sun.

"It's not my fault you're too slow," said the boy. The blade in his hands was also wooden, though much larger, clearly meant to train him to hold a longsword. Backlit by the sun, the only feature she could make out clearly was his halo of copper-red hair.

"Aodh," little Neve whined as she jumped to her feet, confirming Neve's suspicions about the boy's identity.

The two of them whirled around with their makeshift weapons, all eagerness and energy with barely any technique behind their movements as they hacked and slashed at each other. Their forms were sloppy, growing limbs held loosely like they weren't exactly sure what to do with them yet. Which, if their utter lack of coordination was any indication, they clearly did not.

Neve felt the burn in her untrained lungs, the familiar strain of exertion instead of the pain she'd been living with for months. The *ache in her muscles was welcome. It was exciting. There was no creak from bones that hadn't healed right, no tightness from tissue still knitting itself back together. Just boundless energy that Neve barely recognized as her own. She couldn't remember ever being so small. She could remember the joy that lit her up from the inside, the thrill of violence, of pushing her body to the limit without any knowledge or care of the consequences. Those she had felt not too long ago, though the memories felt like they belonged to a different person. A person Neve was struggling to recognize with every day that passed. A person she wasn't even sure she liked.*

As quickly as the memory had come, it was gone again. It spat Neve back out in the same place it had taken her, only this time when she forced the spots out of her eyes, she found several concerned faces looking back at her.

"Shit," Neve mumbled. The dizziness that had been missing earlier hit her all at once. The floor tilted beneath her, and Neve stumbled back a step.

"Nemain?"

The voice behind her was older than it had been in her memory. Once again, Neve felt like her consciousness was bisected between the past and the present. Instincts from this life told her that she wasn't safe, that she needed to run or fight or do *something*. But the echo of her much younger self was calm, regarding Aodh with the kind of comfortable familiarity that Neve had only ever felt with her sisters.

Now solidly back in her own body, in her own time, Neve felt the ragged edges of the void in her chest, the one she hadn't really known was there until she'd met Alexandria, until she'd been dragged by her hair into friendship with her humans. The grating, empty feeling that something was missing. Something had been carved out and away, and she hadn't noticed.

It was him, Neve realized with a start. She'd been missing him. Which *sucked.*

The thought, absurdly, nearly brought tears to her eyes. Neve blinked them away furiously. It wasn't her, she told herself. It was . . . the other her. The not-her from before the Veil. The one she'd been just a few minutes ago, young and excited and happy.

Neve thought her head was going to split in two as she tried desperately to reconcile the dissonance. It felt like she was at war with herself and whichever side won, Neve still lost. It was too much, too confusing.

"Don't call me that," Neve snapped. She didn't turn back, didn't look at him. There was too great a chance that if she did, she'd see the little boy from her memory, who had been nearly as dear to her as her sisters. Neve didn't think she could handle that.

It took her longer than she would've liked to feel settled again. But after she'd showered and changed into sweats, Neve was going to look for Alexandria. She'd been staying over-night more often than not, which her aunt and uncle didn't love but hadn't tried to stop yet.

Neve was about to go and ask if she would be staying again tonight when Alexandria burst into the bedroom like she'd been shot from a cannon.

"I'm sorry," she said, all in a rush.

Neve blinked, because that was usually her line. Alexandria's face crumpled, and she looked away, gnawing at her lip like she was about to burst into tears.

"No, nononono," Neve said quickly, reaching for her. She took Alexandria's face in her hands, cupping her chin. "You're okay. You're fine. I'm just confused."

Alexandria's eyes were still pointed stubbornly to the side, unblinking, like if she dried them out completely, they wouldn't be able to betray her by welling up. "I just feel so stupid," she admitted after a moment that felt like an inhala-tion before a storm. "You and the Daughters are taking all this time to teach us how to fight and I'm . . . I'm terrible at it. And it's not like there aren't a million other things you could be doing to keep everyone safe, and instead you're wasting time with me. I'm a liability."

Because she was an idiot with no filter, Neve said, "Of course you are."

Alexandria's eyes snapped to her, out of outrage or shock,

Neve wasn't sure, but she was already backpedaling. "That came out wrong," she said sheepishly. "I just mean . . . you've been at this for what, ten seconds? My sisters and I train for years, and we keep training, because this shit is hard."

"I just thought . . ." Alexandria trailed off, managing to bury her face in her hands without moving out of Neve's grip. Then, muffled by her palms pressed into her cheeks: "I don't know why I thought any of this would be easy. Like I'd put my mind to it and come out a superhero." She huffed out a harsh sigh without revealing her face. "It's stupid."

Neve carefully rearranged their bodies, pulling Alexandria into a hug. Alexandria's arms were still tight against her body, the backs of her hands pressed against Neve's shoulder.

"It's not stupid to want to help, or keep yourself safe," Neve promised. Alexandria made a muffled, wet sound but did not come up for air. "It's not," Neve insisted.

"I just . . ." Alexandria said eventually, finally lifting her head to reveal dark, shining eyes. "I thought I might be *special.*" She spat the word. "This whole thing is because of me—don't argue with me. I am not in the mood," Alexandria said, cutting Neve off before she could so much as open her mouth to protest. "And because I'm an idiot, I thought that would mean I would just get this stuff and it would be easy, and I could save the day. But I'm not . . . anything. I still don't know what I did on the beach, but I know it has to do with the

Gate and—" She sighed, resting the top of her head against Neve's collarbone. "It was dumb."

"It's not easy for me, either," Neve said after an awkward pause, scrambling for something comforting to say and just coming up with the truth. Alexandria shot her a skeptical look, one dark eyebrow rising toward her hairline. "I mean, I don't know what you did either and if it was magic or something else, but just this? Just fighting? It's hard as hell. Bay, Mercy, and I are literally built for this and it still takes years and years to be any good."

Alexandria didn't look convinced.

"I'm serious," Neve insisted, nudging her shoulder. She stretched her arm out, running her fingertips over the scars on her forearms. "Half of these are self-inflicted because I wasn't paying attention or was going too fast or got unlucky once or twice. No one expects you to suddenly be a superhero—it would be crazy unfair if we did."

Not to mention, Neve thought but didn't say because it was more upsetting than helpful, despite training all their lives, despite their abilities and their strength, she and her sisters still died. Every new lifetime, every new link in the chain that went back a thousand years, was because they hadn't been good enough, strong enough, fast enough. In the end, the three of them had died, over and over.

Neve sucked in a breath through her teeth, imagining

for a moment she could see her own entrails spilling out of her stomach like writhing wet ropes. She squeezed her eyes tightly closed, and the hazy gore was gone when she opened them again. Her heart still hammered so hard, she thought Alexandria would be able to feel it.

Something else to look forward to in the steady drip of memories. Neve didn't want to think about that. She had enough trouble sleeping without remembering each and every one of her—extraordinarily violent—deaths.

Alexandria shrugged her shoulders. She looked disappointed for another few moments before she forced a smile. "I guess I've been watching too much anime, huh?"

Neve chuckled and let the subject drop, choosing instead to let them sit in companionable silence. This wasn't easy—none of this was easy. It never had been.

Alexandria would figure it out, but it might take a little time. Neve just hoped that they had it.

CHAPTER THIRTEEN

Neve had no memory of falling asleep. One second she was in her bed with Alexandria sprawled halfway on top of her like an affectionate octopus, and the next Neve snapped back into consciousness. Alexandria's face was inches from her own, and it took Neve a moment to realize that she'd been shaken awake.

"Something's wrong," Alexandria said. In the thin moonlight that came in through the window, she was deathly pale.

Neve sat up, any remaining sleepiness vanishing at the sour tang of Alexandria's fear in the air.

"Like before?" Neve asked, already reaching for her sword under her bed.

"I don't know. I don't think so."

That wasn't encouraging.

Neve crossed to her closet and began piecing her armor on over her clothes. If the Gate was opening again, she wasn't walking into another fight without it.

Unsurprisingly, the Daughters were already awake when Neve and Alexandria made it downstairs.

"We'll have the barrier ready, just in case," Aoife said. Neve nodded. That meant she didn't know exactly what was going on either. Also not a great sign.

Neve nearly asked where Aodh was but stopped herself. She didn't think he stayed at the convent overnight, and in any case, there was no need to invoke trouble before they knew what they were dealing with.

"I'm coming with you," Alexandria said before Neve could even attempt to convince her otherwise. Neve sighed.

"What are you—?" Alexandria asked when Neve made a quick detour into the armory, returning with a modified chest plate. She hadn't managed to retrofit a full set yet because she was neither a leatherworker nor a metalworker and sizing down already existing pieces was a *giant pain in the ass.*

Neve thrust the chest piece into Alexandria's hands. "Put that on. Over your shirt. And if things go sideways, be ready to run."

Alexandria caught the armor, managing not to drop it before slipping it on over the shirt she'd worn to bed the night before. Neve frowned; she'd have to take the chest piece in some more for it to fit right, but it was something. It would do for now, at least.

The cliff beneath the convent didn't look like it was about to implode into a portal, but Neve knew from experience how quickly that could change.

As she got closer, Neve finally understood what Alexandria

had meant about it being something different. She could feel the twinge of magic in her gut that was undoubtedly from the Gate, but it wasn't nearly as strong as before. The air was clear of rot-colored magic, so far at least.

"I am just now remembering," Alexandria said, pressing close to Neve's side as they approached, "what happened last time we came down here in the middle of the night."

Neve remembered that night in the rain and the huge monster that had gotten halfway out of the Gate before the cliff had solidified around it.

Who were they? Neve wondered, then steeled herself against the maelstrom of guilt that followed. Her one consolation was that whoever they were, whoever they'd been, death hadn't been permanent.

It really wasn't much of a consolation. Again, Neve racked her brain for why she and her sisters would set the spell up like this. Why they would force themselves to forget and turn their lives—all their lives—into an endless cycle of death and violence. It just didn't make any sense. None of it. Neve had only experienced a few flashes of her first life, but she couldn't believe any version of herself would think this was the way to keep people safe.

"I want to touch it," Alexandria said, dragging Neve out of the spiral of her thoughts. "That's probably a bad sign, right?"

"Probably."

Neither of them spoke, and the Gate didn't appear. The tiny pulse of magic that Neve could feel remained steady.

"You should touch it," Neve said, twitchy and impatient.

"I thought you said it was a bad idea!"

It definitely was, but if something was going to happen, Neve would rather be waiting for it than be taken by surprise.

"I don't want to go back there," Alexandria said quietly.

Neve shifted, stowing her knife in order to reach down and grab Alexandria's hand. "You won't."

She couldn't promise that and they both knew it, but at least this time, if Alexandria went through, Neve would go with her.

Like she should have gone with her sisters. Neve's stomach hurt.

Alexandria exhaled, steadying herself. She squeezed Neve's hand tighter. "Okay."

The flicker of magic didn't react as Alexandria reached out toward the cliff, but when her fingers made contact, there was a popping in Neve's ears, like the barometric pressure had plummeted. They both held their breath, but nothing else happened for a long moment when Neve barely trusted herself to breathe in case she set something off.

Alexandria made a small noise at the same time that Neve felt something shift. Nothing violent, and for a second, Neve thought that she'd imagined it.

"Holy shit," Alexandria breathed, tugging on Neve's hand. "Look."

Instead of the swirl of magic that usually accompanied the Gate's opening, there was only a slight distortion. At first it looked like a trick of the light, before gradually more and more of the cliff faded away and the rough-hewn stone appeared almost translucent.

A flash of movement caught her attention. It was so small that it should have been next to nothing, but considering the endless gray behind the stone, it was like someone had lit a flare.

"Hello?" Neve called, keeping hold of Alexandria's hand.

There was a staticky flicker in the gloom, as if she'd flipped to the wrong channel on a shitty old box TV, before two hazy outlines materialized. Neve couldn't make out the details; there wasn't enough definition in any of the shapes for that, but her heart nearly beat out of her chest as the part of her that was her connection to Bay and Mercy, which had been cold and empty since they'd vanished, sparked back to feeble life.

Neve plunged forward, pressing her free hand against the cliff. But despite whatever was allowing her to see into it, the Gate was still firmly closed.

"Mercy?" Neve shouted. The harmonics of her voice were already shifting, building toward a half-desperate scream. "Bay? Is that you? Can you hear me?"

"We're . . . can't—Neve!"

The spot started to dim again, taking the shapes of her sisters with it. Neve did scream this time, a wail of useless, impotent anguish.

"No," she cried. "Please don't, please don't leave!"

But they were already fading away, their silhouettes obscured by the churning gray behind the cliff. The flare in her chest was already gone, drowned out by emptiness that seemed even colder than before.

"Was that . . . ?" Alexandria ventured after the Gate had solidified beneath her hand.

"Bay and Mercy," Neve whispered. "They're alive."

They were alive. Neve hadn't let herself think otherwise. She'd insisted that she would know if Bay and Mercy were truly gone, but there had been a part of her that had feared the worst. But they were alive. More than that, they were able to communicate through the Gate somehow. Neve didn't let herself get bogged down in the logistics of that, not right this minute.

Bay and Mercy were alive, which meant they were in danger. Panic surged anew. She needed to get to them and she needed to do it *now*, which meant she needed to remember how they'd made the stupid thing in the first place.

The door in her head was already cracked. Aodh had done that. Maybe it was time to break the damn thing down.

CHAPTER FOURTEEN

N o," Daughter Maeve said when Neve said as much. Returning to the convent had been a bit of a blur. It was still hours before sunrise, but none of them were going back to sleep tonight.

"Absolutely not," Clara said at the same time, all the color draining out of her face.

Neve had expected this, known there would be opposition the second the idea popped into her head, but that didn't make it any easier to swallow.

"Naturally," she snarled. "Gods—I mean god, I mean . . ." Neve broke off, anger tying her tongue in knots. Her fists balled at her sides and it took several deep breaths to get her temper back under control again. "It's like you want them to stay gone," Neve said as soon as she was able, flinging Aodh's accusation back in their faces. "Makes it easier, right? Two fewer people who know that you've spent the last thousand years lying to us."

"Neve," Maeve said, aghast.

She should stop. She should swallow the acid on her tongue and beat her anger into a training dummy, maybe scream a little and rip open her stitches again. But now that Neve had started, she couldn't make herself stop.

Clara's face was bloodlessly pale, her mouth pressed into an unhappy line. "That's not—"

"You were supposed to take care of us!" Neve cried, and maybe she was screaming, because the Daughters froze. "What was the point?" she demanded, throwing her arms wide enough to encompass the convent and everyone in it, everyone who had lived in it for all those pointless, bloody lifetimes. "We have died over and over and over, and for what? What was so bad that we had to lock our family away and then forget they ever existed? Convince ourselves that they're monsters so that we get to be heroes for killing them?"

"We tried to keep you safe," Maeve said in a tremulous voice.

"Well, you didn't! You failed, like, a dozen times over. And now Bay and Mercy are *stuck* there. I saw them! They're in danger and I need to get them out, so I need to remember!" Neve's chest ached as she breathed raggedly. "I mean, did you even love us at all, or was that bullshit too?"

"That's enough!" Aoife shouted at the same time that Clara let out a sob and covered her mouth with her hand. The air in the hallway suddenly stank like ozone. Neve felt the hair on the back of her neck stand up.

"How can you even ask that?" Aoife demanded. Lightning

crackled, sparking in the depths of her eyes, which suddenly looked very, very dark. "Of course we do. Everything we do—everything we have done—is to protect you girls."

Neve snorted, overcome with the sheer absurdity of it all. Because Aoife meant it. Neve could tell. They all did. But that wasn't good enough, not even close.

"Yeah," she spat. "Well done with that."

She would do it on her own. She would figure it out and find a way to remember without their help.

Neve found herself in the library, wrenching books off the shelves more out of a desire to do something than because she thought there would be anything even remotely useful.

She shouldn't have brought it up with the Daughters in the first place. She should know better by now, and it wasn't as if she even technically needed them anyway, in theory. Maybe it was the stress of thinking the Gate was opening, or sleep deprivation, that had caused her to open her big stupid mouth. Maybe it was the utterly naive hope that they might actually do something helpful.

Maybe Neve was already too exhausted and unmoored from having two thirds of her soul ripped out of her chest and she was looking for comfort. It didn't matter either way. The Daughters weren't going to help her, which meant that, yet again, Neve was on her own.

She snapped a book closed hard enough that a cloud of dust leaped from the pages. She sneezed, wiping at her eyes with the back of her hand.

Neve didn't even want her memories. She hadn't for weeks now, and the irony was not lost on her, how quickly her attitude had changed about the whole thing. It felt like all she had ever wanted was to remember, but now Neve couldn't think of anything she wanted less. It was so stupid. She was stupid.

Neve swiped at her eyes again, which were still watering from the dust and definitely not from anything else. What a joke.

The Nemain in her head, the one who kept sneering at Neve in her reflection, made a noise of disgust. *Weak.*

Yeah, maybe, but at least Neve was still here, not some asshole who had set all this in motion and then died, leaving Neve to deal with the consequences.

She probably shouldn't keep thinking about her old self, her original self, as a completely separate person. That *had* been her, no matter if Neve didn't remember living that life. Even if it had been purposefully sealed away for some unknown and deeply aggravating reason. She was Nemain, even if she didn't have her memories. These were her mistakes, no matter how much she wished she could foist them on someone else.

It was a good thing she wasn't in therapy, because Neve was

sure her doctor would have a field day with this line of thinking. Once they got past the reincarnated-not-a-god-kind-of-a-monster-with-family-issues-you-wouldn't-believe thing.

Neve braced herself as she heard the familiar sound of Alexandria's footsteps.

"I'm good at math," Alexandria said quietly.

"I don't know why I bother," Neve said, slumping back against the bookshelves she was sitting against with a huff.

Alexandria made a face before sitting down beside her. "What?"

"You." Neve waved a hand at all of her. "I keep thinking I know what you'll say next but I'm always wrong."

"That's part of my charm," Alexandria said, nudging her shoulder against Neve's.

"You're good at math," Neve said, returning them to the first and still utterly baffling track of this conversation.

"I am good at math," Alexandria agreed. "Which no one ever expects because I also like art, because people are reductive."

"Also because you're gay."

"There's that," Alexandria said without a moment's hesitation, nodding sincerely at Neve's nonsense. "But magic is, like, ninety percent math, right? It's all metaphysics and spell theorems. So if you tell me what you're trying to do, maybe I can help?"

Neve loved her. There wasn't any dust to blame this time for the tears that welled in her eyes.

"Or not," Alexandria said, backpedaling frantically as soon as she saw the tears. "Or I can just keep my mouth shut because I don't know jack shit about any of this and am clearly making it worse."

"You're not," Neve promised her, sniffling just a little. "You're not, I promise."

"Yeah, clearly I'm doing a bang-up job, making you cry," Alexandria said. She slouched forward with her shoulders around her ears, leaning against her knees. "Great girlfriend moment."

"No, I mean it," Neve said. "Thank you."

Alexandria shot her a look. "Right, I'm the one with weird reactions to stuff." She sighed. "Is there something I can do? To help?"

"Probably not."

"Well, shit."

Alexandria fidgeted with the tied strings on her sweatshirt, alternating between chewing on the end of one and trying to unravel the other.

"It's bad, then, right?" she asked after a bit "Whatever you want to do that will help you remember?"

That was the thing; Neve didn't even know if it was bad. She didn't even know if it was possible, except of course it was, because Aodh had done it to her, at least partially.

"There's a ritual, when we turn eighteen," Neve explained. "All the memories and the rest of it come back on their own, but it helps us sort through everything. It's . . . overwhelming, otherwise."

Alexandria whistled. "I can imagine. A thousand years' worth of memories all at once sounds like a lot."

It was. Even with the ritual to help them process it all, Bay and Mercy hadn't been themselves for months after their eighteenth birthdays. It had been terrifying, seeing strangers looking out at her through her sisters' eyes as Neve glimpsed versions of them she hadn't met and didn't remember yet.

"I don't even think it would work," Neve admitted. "Even after they turned eighteen, neither of my sisters remembered anything about the Veil or why we made the stupid thing in the first place."

"Like matryoshka dolls," Alexandria said inexplicably, continuing when she saw the look on Neve's face. "The Russian nesting dolls . . . you know what I'm talking about. You open them up and there's a smaller version of the same doll inside."

Neve frowned, struggling to see the connection. "We're not Russian."

"Oh my *god*, you are the most literal person in the entire world," Alexandria complained, poking Neve in the chest, which didn't seem fair. "No, listen. It's like . . . you guys talk about your lifetimes like they're links in a chain, right? And when you turn eighteen, you can access all of them. You can see all the dolls and all the patterns, but until then, all you've got is the one on the outside."

"Okay . . ."

"But for whatever reason"—Alexandria was speaking more quickly, warming up to her own theory while Neve struggled to keep up—"you made it so that when you got all those memories back, the first life was missing."

"The little doll in the middle?" Neve ventured.

"That's right, yeah. You're trying to get to those pre-Veil memories without getting bogged down by a thousand years' worth of experiences in your head at the same time."

"And how do I do that?" Neve asked when Alexandria trailed off.

Alexandria's eyebrows scrunched together and she frowned. "I have no idea."

Neve turned that over in her mind, because it wasn't as if she had anything better to do or any other solutions at the moment. There was no guarantee that the original version of herself, Nemain, Neve Prime, would even know how she and her sisters made the Veil in the first place, or why.

She recalled the very first memory that had slipped through when Aodh had taken an ax to the door in her head. She had been so certain that he was a danger—that they all were, their whole family. That creating the Veil was the only way to keep everyone safe.

Neve had no idea when those memories existed in context of each other. Hell, she wasn't even sure if she could trust them. For all she knew, it was all fake, some trick of neuro-chemistry as her traumatized brain tried to make sense of everything that had happened to her. The dissonance felt like nails scratching at the chalkboard of her mind, a dizzy-sick feeling like vertigo times a million.

But why would we forget? That was what she kept tripping over, the bit of this whole thing that nagged her. Why would they have done that to themselves? To assuage their own guilt, like Aodh had accused? Maybe.

Neve knocked her head back against the bookshelves with a hard thunk. This wasn't helping. She could theorize all she wanted, but the fact of the matter was, Neve—*this* Neve, the one from this lifetime and no other—hadn't been there. She didn't know. The only other person who was there had tried to kill her, and even if he was lonely like Aoife had suggested, even if he'd once been that excited kid Neve had sparred with so happily, Aodh didn't know any more than she did.

She didn't remember. It was the most frustrating thing in the world, this erratic drip of memories that came with no warning and even less context. Neve could glimpse flashes of the past, see the tiniest bit of the innermost matryoshka doll, if she insisted on using Alexandria's metaphor, through the hole Aodh had made.

Neve sat up like she'd been stabbed in the ass, the movement scaring the shit out of Alexandria, who yelped and clutched at her chest, eyes massive.

"What the hell, Neve?"

Neve didn't answer, because she knew how to get to the smallest doll. And Alexandria was not going to like it.

CHAPTER FIFTEEN

Neve was aware, in the way she sometimes was that something was about to be a complete and utter shitshow, that this was a bad idea. Even if it wasn't, not telling Alexandria was definitely a bad idea. Once, not telling the Daughters *also* would've been a bad idea, but at this point Neve just presumed they were going to do the least helpful thing and moved on from there, even if her stomach twinged a little bit at the thought of keeping things from them.

Ask for forgiveness, not permission; wasn't that how the saying went?

Though Neve wasn't sure the phrase really held water when she was asking her stab-happy cousin to break her brain. Again.

Bay and Mercy would hate it too, no doubt. They would lose their collective shit, and Bay would cry, and Mercy would try to convince Neve to reconsider, and maybe stop her by force. But they weren't here. That was the whole issue: they weren't here and Neve had no idea how to get to them. She couldn't keep waiting around for the Gate to open on its own.

Even if it did, what did that get her? A fight with creepy shadow monsters that may or may not have her sisters inside them before the Gate closed again, leaving her back at square one with nothing to show for it.

Aoife was trying, Neve knew that, but she also knew that it was taking too long. Reverse engineering magic like this was next to impossible, and since none of them thought to have a handy note titled "This Is How We Made the Gate; You're Welcome, Future Us," they had nothing to go on. And even if Neve was willing to wait until she was eighteen—and she categorically was not—those memories wouldn't even help. Bay and Mercy hadn't known either.

They didn't know and they weren't here, and Neve couldn't keep doing nothing. Not when she finally thought she could do something about it. Even if that something meant asking Aodh for help, and even if that help might scramble her brain like an egg.

The only problem now—besides all of it—was that Neve had no idea how to find her pain-in-the-ass cousin without asking Aoife to track him, which would probably give up the game.

It was Saturday, so her friends were all in their respective homes and weren't scheduled to come over to train until Monday or Tuesday, depending on how they felt after the weekend. Normally, Neve would spend her days off with her sisters, but without them to fill the silence, the convent felt even bigger and emptier than normal.

Neve was still working out how to get out of the convent without arousing suspicion when Alexandria poked her in the side.

"We're going on a field trip," she said.

Neve blinked, waiting for further explanation.

Alexandria sighed, scrubbing the back of her hand over her eyes. Neither of them had gotten very much sleep the night before, but Alexandria looked like she'd been up for days, not hours.

"Are you—?"

"I think we need some air," Alexandria said before Neve could finish the question. "Okay?"

Neve nodded and didn't push further. Mostly because of the look on Alexandria's face, but also because this was the excuse Neve needed to get out of the convent and find Aodh.

Which she specifically didn't mention to Alexandria because Neve really didn't want to fight about it.

The Daughters looked slightly dubious but didn't try to stop them when Neve said that she and Alexandria were leaving.

"Keep your phone on you," was all Daughter Maeve said. Clara wouldn't even look at her, and Neve thought that maybe their willingness to let her go had more to do with her shouting at them the night before than anything else.

The thought made guilt trip heavily in her chest before Neve tried to suppress it. What did she have to feel guilty about? Everything she said was the truth.

Neve knew what Bay would say if she were here. That the Daughters were doing the best they could. Mercy probably would've been just as pissed as Neve, but even she'd probably admit that it was an impossible situation.

Neve wished they were both here so she could tell them to shut up to their faces. But more than that, she just wished they were here.

"Where are we going?" Neve asked after Alexandria had driven into Newgrange Harbor proper. They weren't on the road to the school or the Three Crows or the Abbotts' house. It wasn't a big town; there weren't a whole lot of places to go.

"I just . . ." Alexandria said after a minute, turning onto a road that Neve finally recognized. "I need to be somewhere else."

The overhang looked pretty much like Neve remembered it. The road stopped abruptly before a plot of tall grass that had yellowed but still stood upright despite the cold winter air off the ocean. The shale still made her nervous, and Neve found herself listening hard to the stone as they walked over it, preparing to move in case something crumbled.

Everything looked reasonably stable as Alexandria sat against the large stones that formed a semicircle looking out at the ocean. Today, the slate-gray sky nearly matched the ocean below, making the horizon impossible to see against the ocean. It was a little like being inside a storm cloud before it broke.

Which reminded her.

Neve took off her coat and dumped it over Alexandria's head. If they were going to be out here, she might as well be warm.

"Thanks," Alexandria said with a small smile, sliding her arms into the coat. It was laughably too big on her, and Neve was reminded how much she liked it when Alexandria wore her clothes.

"Company, yes or no?" Neve asked. She thought she knew the answer, but she didn't want to assume.

After a second, Alexandria nodded. Neve sent the text. With any luck, the rest of their friends would be here soon.

"What's happening to me?" Alexandria asked. She was still looking out at the water and wrapped Neve's coat closer around herself.

Neve hummed, buying herself time to answer. "I don't know," she said eventually.

"Am I even human?" Alexandria gazed out at the endless gray expanse of sea and sky, gnawing on her lip and determinedly not looking at Neve.

"What?"

"Never mind," Alexandria huffed. She crossed her arms over her chest, shoulders creeping up toward her ears.

"No, I mean it," Neve insisted. "You don't . . . you don't think you're human?"

"Well, how can I be?" Alexandria burst out. "Could a normal person have broken the Gate like I did? Could a normal human do what I did last night? No."

"That's not—"

"It doesn't matter."

"Yes, it does."

The silence that followed left too much space for Neve to think. How long had Alexandria thought that? Neve knew that Alexandria blamed herself, knew how guilty she felt, but she didn't think that meant Alexandria thought she wasn't *human*.

"I don't want to talk about this," Alexandria said before Neve could manage to put her thoughts into some semblance of order.

"You are human."

"Says who?" Alexandria shot back.

"Says me."

"Well, what the hell would you know about it?" Alexandria snapped. Then her mouth shut with a nearly audible click, lips pressing into a thin line.

Neve looked at the ground, her eyes tracing the lines of shale underfoot. She'd never wanted to be human before, not really. There was no reason Alexandria's comment should hurt like it did.

She doesn't mean it, Neve told herself.

Who cares if she does? growled Nemain in the back of her head. *You're* not *human.*

It was true, but that didn't stop it from feeling like an insult. What would Neve know about being human anyway, apart from the fact that she wasn't? What did she care, when she hadn't wanted anything to do with them until a few months ago?

Maybe because she was supposed to have more time to *be* human, as much as she was capable. Another few weeks, at the very least. She hadn't appreciated it until it was too late, and now Neve had to puncture the little bubble of time she had left in order to access memories she couldn't fathom hiding in the first place.

"I—" Alexandria started.

"Everything okay?"

Tameka's voice sailed over the tall grass before Alexandria could finish. The rest of the group had shown up much sooner than Neve had expected, but then again, it was a small town.

"You guys all right?" Michael asked, his eyes flicking between Neve and Alexandria.

Neve left it up to Alexandria whether or not to explain, her focus suddenly drawn to a spot just around the bend of the overhang. It was beyond where you could walk safely without worrying about tumbling into the ocean below, nearly out of eyesight from the little stone semicircle, and Neve was abruptly positive that Aodh was there.

She almost called out to him to let him know he wasn't as subtle as he thought he was, but Neve didn't want to give him any more attention, and she didn't think her friends would appreciate his presence. He wasn't *doing* anything, so if he wanted to lurk, that was fine.

Besides, she still needed to talk to him.

"Neve?" Simon was saying when Neve started paying attention to the conversation again. She had the impression that it wasn't the first time he'd said her name.

"Sorry, what?"

Simon made a face. "Just seeing if you were good. You kind of went away for a second."

Neve tried for a smile. "Yeah, I'm fine. Didn't get a lot of sleep last night." *Also my cousin is being creepy again and I didn't want to bring attention to it.*

No one really looked convinced. Neve couldn't help but think of the last time they were all here. Everything had felt so much easier. She remembered listening to the others swap stories and laugh, a stark contrast to the strained silence that fell over them now.

What was there to laugh about, really? And what else would they—any of them—talk about other than the supernatural disaster that Neve had dropped into their laps?

Just something else she'd ruined.

Simon and Ilma were making a valiant effort, but after a little while even they gave it up.

Neve's stomach twisted. Alexandria had wanted to get away, and Neve had thought company would help, but it looked to her like she'd just brought everyone together to be scared and miserable.

"I—" she started, rubbing the back of her neck uncomfortably.

Before she could finish, something shifted beneath her feet, followed by a cracking sound so loud that even the humans heard it.

"Move," Neve said, standing in an instant. It took the others a second longer to react. "Move!"

It felt a little ironic, Neve would think later, that she'd worried about this exact thing the first time they'd come here. Someone—Michael, she thought—had given her a hard time about it, snickering at the idea that Neve was afraid of heights.

It wasn't the height she was afraid of; it was what lay at the bottom.

Neve felt the world slow around her as her focus sharpened on a single objective: get the humans to solid ground.

Easier said than done. She was so much faster than they were, but Neve couldn't outrun a rockslide.

Simon and Tameka were the closest to the grass, and they managed to stagger to safety on their own. Two safe, and four left in danger.

Neve reached for the closest bodies to her, catching Alexandria and Michael by the waists and hauling them away as the shale continued to fall apart beneath their feet.

Someone screamed.

"Stay here!" Neve ordered, already turning back for Puck and Ilma.

Ilma was closer, one hand already outstretched as Neve lunged for her. The stone underfoot gave way with a sickening crunch that Neve felt in her bones, and then her stomach leaped into her mouth as she began to fall.

There wasn't time to move—there wasn't time to think. Blood and wind rushed in her ears. Neve wasn't sure how she managed it, but somehow she reeled Ilma in close, twisted, and hurled her bodily across the crumbling outcrop. She barely had time to hope that Ilma had landed safely before the edge of the cliff dropped out of view and Neve plunged toward the sea.

CHAPTER SIXTEEN

Neve braced, trying to control the tension in her body so it didn't crack into pieces when she hit the surf below.

When the impact came, it was so unexpected that Neve's eyes flew open. Her shoulder screamed in pain as something stopped her descent, grabbing her arm to pull her out of free fall and damn near dislocating something in the process. Her mind still hadn't quite caught up to the fact that she was no longer falling when she hit solid ground again.

"Neve!" someone shouted.

Neve's head swiveled back and forth. Tameka and Simon had been okay, and she'd gotten Alexandria and Michael to safety. A quick glance revealed a very shaken but alive Ilma, so that left—

"Puck," Neve rasped. She turned too quickly and her stomach lurched as her inner ear unbalanced and she felt like she was falling all over again.

"They're okay."

Neve didn't know who said it, not really able to pick out voices through the blood still rushing in her ears. She whirled again, ignoring the burn of bile in her throat as her stomach rebelled, and finally saw Puck. Their face was drained of color and there was a thin coat of shale dust in their hair, turning it prematurely gray, but they were okay. Everyone was okay.

Including her. *How*—?

Neve saw the flash of red hair out of the corner of her eye at the same second she recalled that Aodh had been lurking at the overhang. Which didn't explain why he'd bothered to save Neve—again—or Puck. Or why he wasn't hanging around to gloat about it.

"Is everyone all right?" Neve asked, her voice coming out tight and breathless. "Ilma, are you—?"

"I'm fine," Ilma promised.

"I think," Alexandria said, looking wide-eyed at the group of them, "I think we're all okay."

Neve nodded once. No one was hurt. Thank whatever god was still listening.

No, thank Aodh, which was infinitely worse.

"I'll be right back," Neve promised. She only caught a glimpse of the six confused faces before she sprinted off in the direction she'd seen Aodh last.

Unfortunately, there was no way she could catch him if he didn't want to be caught. Neve didn't get a mile down the road before her lungs started to burn.

"Wait!" Neve shouted at the empty street as she staggered

to a halt. She ground her fist into the scar on her chest, trying to force the fire out. "Jesus Christ," she swore.

"No, I'm Aodh."

The voice came from directly behind her and Neve jumped, already throwing a punch before Aodh caught her fist.

"Don't *do* that," Neve gasped, wrenching her hand out of his grip.

Aodh cocked his head to the side, smiling. It looked forced. "It's funny."

"Why did you do that?" Neve demanded.

"Because I like scaring you."

Neve could strangle him. "No, not *that*. You saved me." Again. "You saved *Puck*. Why?"

Aodh shifted, hunching his shoulders slightly before he straightened up again. It was a strangely vulnerable gesture. It made him look young, like he regretted coming back to talk to her when he might have gotten a clean getaway.

"Never a bad thing to have you owe me even more, cousin," he said archly, making a show of inspecting his fingernails. Which, incidentally, were still covered in gray shale dust.

"Bullshit."

The smile dropped off his face, not into blank nothingness but into a scowl. "What you believe is up to you," Aodh said, turning to go.

"What, and you're just going to leave?" Neve shouted,

grabbing his shoulder and spinning him back to face her.

Aodh recoiled, his mouth opening in a wordless snarl that made Neve think of an irate cat. "You sound like Danu," he spat.

Neve's brows knit together. "What the hell does that mean?"

The day was already overcast, so Neve didn't notice the white fog drifting into her field of view before the headache split through her skull. She winced, blinked, but before she could hear Aodh's response, she was someplace else.

"It's not fair."

Neve was in two places at once. She observed the version of herself from the mirror, from the newest of the memories, though that was so deeply relative as to be nearly meaningless at this point. At the same time, she was there, in that moment, looking at an Aodh who was identical to the boy-king nightmare shithead plaguing her.

Neve's chest panged with emotion that both was and was not her own. Hatred, fear, and deep, abiding love all swirled together in a miasma she couldn't sift apart.

"What's not fair, cousin?" Neve asked in a haughty, indulgent tone that felt completely natural and also set her teeth on edge. She (some version of herself—it was getting more and more difficult to differentiate now) had a headache.

"The three of you get to leave," complained Aodh. "So do Brigid and the Dagda and everyone else. I'm the only one who has to stay home."

"Well, we're a little bit older than you are," Neve said, reaching

out and ruffling his hair. It wasn't quite the same shade as hers. It was brighter, more vibrant. Closer to Macha's.

"Not that much older," Aodh complained, crossing his arms over his chest. Nemain smiled. "I'm stuck here with Danu while you all get to see the world."

"You'll get to see it too," Nemain promised.

"When?"

"When it's safe," Badb intoned gently, joining them where they lay sprawled on the grass, gazing up at a sky that was young and so blue.

Aodh pushed himself onto his elbows, glaring at her. "Why wouldn't it be safe? They're just humans."

"And there are a lot more of them than there are of us," Badb said, sitting down beside them. "The world isn't going anywhere."

"There's so much out there," Aodh grumbled. "I want to see all of it."

"And we want to see it with you," Nemain said. "Just be a little patient."

Aodh rolled his eyes, huffing in a way that Nemain knew was mostly for show. "Fine. I suppose."

The memory began to fade as Neve watched herself—watched Nemain—lunge faster than she had ever been able to move in this lifetime, tackling Aodh around the waist. She heard them laughing long after the white fog dissipated and let the present back in.

Aodh was waiting, looking at her carefully. "Welcome back."

Neve ignored him, rubbing at her eyes with the back of her hand. The Aodh who glared at her was so strikingly different from the one she'd just seen that it was making Neve dizzy. She couldn't stop tallying up the differences, comparing Aodh to Aodh, apples to apples. She couldn't stop comparing everything he'd done from behind the Veil—orchestrating attack after attack, driving Alexandria out of her home, killing her *parents*, damn near carving Neve's heart out of her chest—with his actions since he'd come through. Saving Neve from the new monsters in the Gate, and now again. His lingering, irritating but not malevolent presence around school. And now rescuing Puck when it would've been the easiest thing in the world to just let them fall. No one would've been able to blame him—hell, Neve might not have even remembered that he had been there at all, in the aftermath.

"What?" Aodh demanded, eyes narrowing at her scrutiny. He stood stock still, clearly making an effort not to cross his arms over his chest. His usual loose, careless posture had been replaced by a stiffness that made him look like an improperly assembled scarecrow. Like his joints had been fastened at the wrong angles.

"I don't get you," Neve said, too honest.

Aodh's eyes were gray slits set deep into his face. "Clearly."

Neve saw him make the decision to leave. She wasn't sure what brought on *this* particular bout of insanity—maybe she was still raw from the memory, or maybe missing Bay and Mercy had finally driven her over the edge. Maybe she was hoping that he would finally finish what he started, kill her and be done with it.

Whatever the extremely inadvisable reason, Neve threw herself at him like she'd done in her memory. It wasn't a graceful attack by any stretch of the imagination. It was barely even an attack at all, and Neve chalked it up to surprise when Aodh didn't manage to get out of the way before she crashed into him and took them both down to the ground.

"What are you—" Aodh demanded, his face alight with outrage. For a single moment Neve managed to pin him, sitting her whole weight on his chest. The Nemain in her head scoffed. *Wrestling like children. Really.*

"Get off!" Aodh shouted, seeming to forget that he could stop her anytime he wanted. Maybe Neve wasn't the only one reliving old memories.

"Why am I still alive?" Neve demanded, the question wrenching from her throat.

"You're the one who knows how to open the Gate, stupid," Aodh growled. "Or have you forgotten that, too?"

Neve bared her teeth in a humorless smile. "You hate me. You would've found another way." She shoved his shoulders hard against the pavement.

"So eager to die, cousin?"

"No, I—"

It was at that moment Aodh seemed to remember who had the upper hand in this situation. He shoved her away, and Neve hit the ground with an impact that shuddered through her abdomen.

"If that's what you want, it could be arranged," Aodh said, standing over her. In the haze of the overcast sky, his silhouette reminded her too much of the little boy from another memory. Neve gritted her teeth hard enough that her jaw twinged in protest. At this rate, she was going to grind them into nothing. A problem for a future Neve, if such a person existed.

"Tell me why," Neve said, clinging to her question like a dog with a bone.

Aodh's eyes flashed. "Don't you have more important things to worry about?"

"Tell me!"

"Because you're the only one left!" Aodh shouted. "And you three are the only ones who might actually be worse than I am."

Neve swallowed hard. Aoife's theory that he was lonely had begun to make a grudging sort of sense, but Neve hadn't ever expected to hear him admit it out loud.

He felt *guilty*. Neve didn't know why she was so surprised, but it still knocked the wind out of her as if she'd been struck. Aodh twitched and fidgeted, any attempts to keep himself under control abandoned. It did make a kind of sense, now that she actually stopped to think about it. Aodh had a thousand years' worth of anger simmering just below the surface, and he'd spent that thousand years doing everything he could to get back at the people who'd locked him up. With good reason—his idea of fun was along the lines of arson and homicide—but still.

Aodh had hurt their family, too. He'd wrenched control from the other sidhe by force and killed anyone who'd gotten in his way. He'd said as much when Neve had met him behind the Veil for the first time.

Exile or battle. Those were his words. Even if he got what he wanted, even if the Gate opened and the rest of the sidhe came through, there would be plenty who still blamed him for what he'd done.

"Stop it," Aodh snapped. "Stop looking at me like that. You don't get to look at me like that. You don't know what it was like. The three of you left me and Danu was gone and no one would *listen*, and it was your f—"

"I'm sorry."

Aodh blinked, his eyes suddenly very wide. "What?"

"I'm sorry. For all of it. I know it doesn't matter and it doesn't fix anything or make anything better, but I still am. I don't remember, but . . . but I don't think we were right. We shouldn't have made the Veil. We shouldn't have left you."

The words hung in the freezing air, floating there like the

steam from her breath. Somehow, she'd talked herself back into the wellspring of sadness that occupied the space where her scream used to be.

"You're so different from what I remember," he said. "I don't think you—she—Nemain, the one I knew, ever apologized to me a day in her life. Not even at the end."

Neve thought of the girl she'd glimpsed in her reflection, the one who wore her face but was still utterly unrecognizable. The haughty look in her eye, the defiant jut of her jaw.

Yeah, it tracked. That girl probably didn't know how to spell the word "sorry," let alone say it with any sincerity.

"She sounds like a real bitch."

Aodh laughed bitterly. "She was."

Neve paused, something else occurring to her. "Wait, what do you mean, Danu was gone?"

Aodh's expression shuttered so completely, it was as if someone had drawn a curtain behind his eyes. "She disappeared. Before the Veil and everything that came after." His eyes cut sharply to Neve. "We thought you three killed her."

CHAPTER SEVENTEEN

Neve ignored Clara asking her where she'd been when she stormed back into the convent with Aodh, blood still thundering in her ears.

Clara followed as Neve furiously searched out Maeve and Aoife, and Neve could hear Alexandria muttering, "No, I don't know what's going on," before she pushed open the doors of Aoife's workshop. Maeve and Aoife were inside, their heads bent over one of the paper-strewn tables, and both of them looked up in alarm at Neve's abrupt arrival.

"Neve, what are you—?" Aoife's eyes landed on Aodh and narrowed. The air crackled all of a sudden as Aoife gathered magic around herself. Neve ignored that, as well as the glare Alexandria had been boring into her since Neve reappeared with Aodh beside her at the cliff. Neve wasn't even sure what excuses Alexandria had made to their friends. Her mind had turned into a haze of TV static as anger, the likes of which she hadn't felt since her sisters vanished, lit inside her. She knew instinctively that it wasn't going to last, but she clung to it as tightly as she could.

"Aoife, dear, be polite," Aodh purred. Any vulnerability, imagined or otherwise, had vanished as if it had never existed at all.

"Did we kill Danu?" Neve demanded before either of them could speak again.

Aoife's eyes grew massive. "What?"

"Did we . . ." Neve repeated with exaggerated patience. She clenched her fists, feeling like she was about to fly apart at any second. ". . . kill Danu?"

"Why would you ask that?" Clara had gone painfully white.

So it was true, then. It had to be, for them to react like this.

Neve wanted to scream. She wanted to break something. She wanted to burn every single book in this room and take the whole convent with it, then walk away from this place and never look back.

The rest of the pantheon was family in the loose definition of the term. They didn't have the technology back then, and even if they did, Neve doubted anyone would be interested in doing blood tests to see exactly how related they were. They called themselves family, and that was enough for everyone.

Out of all of them, Danu was by far the most important and probably the least written about. The rest of their family— Neve and her sisters, poor Brigid, the Dagda, even Aodh—had all made their marks on the culture in some way or another.

In books, songs, old folklore that had been written down after being oral for hundreds of years, there had been mentions of most if not all of them. But records of Danu were sparse, even for a pantheon that had mostly survived through stories. Some folklorists thought her name was actually Anu, or Dana, but besides a patchy and confusing history, there wasn't that much about her.

For Neve and her sisters—and the Daughters, too, since Danu was their namesake and the one who'd created their order—Danu was a consistent presence, if in name only. Neve had only one memory of her, but she could feel others churning in the back of her head. Danu was the closest thing their family had to a matriarch. She protected them; she might have actually birthed some of them, though Neve didn't know. And the stories that did include her always mentioned that the pantheon itself was literally named after her. Tuatha de Danann, the People of the Goddess Danu.

So it was a little bit upsetting, the thought that Neve and her sisters had killed her.

"Don't lie to me," Neve rasped. Her throat hurt and her heart felt liable to beat out of her chest. Tears burned in the corners of her eyes and she blinked them away.

Aoife spluttered, turning to Maeve for help, and whatever tenuous grip was left on Neve's self-control snapped.

"We did, didn't we?" Neve paced, winding her fingers

through her hair and pulling hard like she could somehow make things make sense by force.

She was spinning out and she knew it, her breaths coming in tight little gasps that had nothing to do with exertion and everything to do with the way her thoughts were careening out of control, scattering any last feeble semblance of sense to the wind.

"We did," Neve gasped out. "We killed her." She pulled at her hair again, which hurt and didn't make anything better. "Why would we do that—*why would we do that?*"

All the questions that had gone unanswered since Bay and Mercy disappeared—since before, since Neve had met Alexandria and the cracks in her life had begun to show—felt as if they were pressing down on her. There was this terrible pressure in her head behind her eyes.

"Neve—" someone said, trying to break through her panic spiral, but Neve was too lost in her own head, her thoughts a seething mess of white and fog and blood and pain.

"What is the point?" Neve demanded to everyone and no one. "What is the point of any of this?"

A thousand years of fighting and killing and dying over and over and over again. Of forgetting everything every time and starting from scratch but never remembering why or how they'd started all this. It didn't make sense—it had never made any damn sense, but at least before, Neve had her sisters and they could pretend that they were actually helping people. What had they spent so long fighting against? Aodh? Neve remembered the fire, the attack on the human settlement, but how was *this* the solution? All she had was that patchy, dizzy-sick certainty that creating the Gate had been the only way forward, but she couldn't remember why and it was making her head feel like it was going to split open.

Neve flinched and spun at a gentle pressure against her shoulder.

"You didn't," Daughter Maeve said. She pressed a hand to Neve's cheek gently, so gently, as if worried that Neve was going to shatter. It didn't do any good. Neve went to pieces anyway. Daughter Maeve didn't say anything, just held her close as Neve cried herself out.

"Really?" she asked when she could finally speak again. Her eyes were still stinging a little and her mouth felt dry, like she'd been sleeping with it open.

"Yes," Maeve said. Neve wanted to believe her. She wanted to believe her so badly, to close her eyes and let that be the truth and for a second pretend like any of this was okay. Just one single second where she and her sisters weren't monsters.

"What happened to her, then?" Neve asked, because she couldn't let it be that easy. She couldn't just take it on faith. She had to know.

"I would also like to know," Aodh chimed in, drawing

everyone's attention to the fact that he was still in the room with them. Neve had enough presence of mind to be embarrassed that he'd seen her cry, which was so much worse than seeing her nearly bleed out, for some reason.

Daughter Maeve looked between him and Neve. "I think we'd better have this conversation another time."

"And why would that be?" Aodh asked sweetly, arching an eyebrow. He took a book off Aoife's desk and began leafing through it.

"Because you're dangerous," Maeve replied calmly. Aodh rolled his eyes.

Neve pressed her fist against the healing wound on her sternum. She didn't need to be told that Aodh was dangerous; she knew firsthand. She'd seen it for herself, when Aodh had cracked the door in her head the first time. She saw the destruction he'd caused—an entire town burned to nothing, every living person dead—and for what? Because he was bored? She felt another stab of that dizzy-sick feeling, trying to reconcile her memories. Why would he *do* that? He'd wanted to leave—he'd wanted to see the world. What would he gain by destroying it?

"I just—" Neve said. Her head pounded. "I don't understand. This doesn't make *sense.*"

"The world was changing," Daughter Maeve said, her voice going cold. "*He* didn't want to change with it. You and

179

your family, you had always lived alongside humanity, but that wasn't good enough for him after a while."

"Is *that* what she told you?" Aodh asked, derision dripping from every syllable. "Your patron did always think the worst of me."

"It's the truth," Maeve said severely.

"Is it?"

I'm stuck here with Danu while you all get to see the world.

You'll get to see it too.

Neve squeezed her eyes shut until the dizzy spell passed. She didn't know why she was trying to argue the point anyway. Aodh had already done so much harm to every person in this room. But wouldn't she have done the same in his position? How would Neve have reacted to being left behind if it had been her?

"Danu didn't die," Aoife said slowly, interrupting Aodh and Maeve's glaring. "But she was gone even before the Gate spell was completed. We—the three of us—we never knew exactly where she went, but she'd tasked us with taking care of you, and that was our new focus."

"You never thought to ask?" Alexandria spoke up for the first time. She crossed her arms. "Your *patron* vanishes after giving you vague instructions to look after three soon-to-be-sort-of-human war gods, and you didn't ask any follow-up questions?"

"We didn't have the option," Aoife said a little coldly. Her eyes cut to Alexandria, who, to her credit, didn't look fazed. "Things were already in motion and we had to adapt quickly."

Aodh sneered. "Already in motion," he repeated.

"But we needed Danu for the spell," Neve said, pulling them back on track. That was something she knew for certain, that Neve and her sisters hadn't been able to do it on their own. "I don't . . . We must have asked for her help. But if she agreed, why wasn't she in the Veil? Where would she have gone?"

Silence fell as Aoife chewed on that. Literally, too, gnawing on the inside of her cheek like Neve did sometimes.

"Wait." It was Clara who spoke up. She ran around a corner composed of precariously stacked books and papers, nearly toppling it over in the process, and returned a moment later with a massive sheet of paper. She cleared off the main worktable quickly before unfurling it, revealing a giant spell diagram. Neve could see the lines of cause and effect and the basic shape of it, but the way they intersected and spun off was completely foreign to her. Even Neve, with her rudimentary knowledge of spell theory and C- in algebra, could see that there was something missing in the diagram. A hole where something clearly should be. There were faint marks where a pencil had tried to fill in the gap a dozen or more times before erasing its tracks, and if the crinkling wear of the paper was any indication, someone had shoved the whole thing onto a shelf somewhere when they couldn't figure it out.

"Do you remember this?" Clara said, pointing excitedly at the diagram.

Aoife's eyebrows drew together and her mouth pulled into a frown. "Yes, but I don't see how this is relevant."

"What even is it?" Alexandria asked, peering closer and very determinedly not making eye contact with Neve, which only made her feel worse.

"The barrier that comes up when there's an attack," Aoife explained, one finger running along the drawn lines on the page in front of her. "I noticed once, during, ahem, the time in between cycles—"

She meant when Neve and her sisters were dead and the Daughters were waiting for them to come back. Neve fought the urge to look at Aodh.

"—that there was an awful lot of power in the barrier. There has to be, of course, to keep everything hidden. And we have magically charged items that help it on particularly hard nights, like Samhain, but even adding those to the equation, I couldn't figure out why the spell was drawing so much power."

Aoife tapped her chin, leaving a smudge of graphite where her thumb had touched the paper. She was on a roll now, her eyes moving up and down like she was seeing the diagram for the first time. Neve thought it would probably be very exciting, if she had any idea what was going on.

"There's only a finite amount of magic in the world. We all know that," Aoife said broadly to the rest of them, who did all know that. "And this spell was tied to the Gate—again, obviously, because it's keeping everything that comes through the Gate out of sight while within the confines of the beach. Though I could never work out that connection. . . ." She gasped, one hand rising to her mouth, before she turned and kissed Clara hard on the lips. "Darling, you are brilliant."

Neve looked away, her cheeks going bright red at the sight of two of her guardians kissing, which was stupid because Neve had been in their wedding, but still.

"Thank you," Clara said a little breathlessly, blushing nearly as hard as Neve, if not harder.

"Can someone explain for those of us who don't understand magic-science?" Alexandria asked.

And for those of us who should but would appreciate the explanation anyway? Neve thought but didn't say because she didn't need a lecture about paying attention and "the importance of understanding the metaphysical world around us" on top of everything else. Bay would be all over this, Neve knew. Mercy less so, but they both paid more attention to this kind of stuff than Neve ever had.

"Even if you add our relics to the equation," Aoife explained, sketching several symbols that Neve vaguely recognized onto the diagram, "there's still a whole lot of energy being generated for something that shouldn't be all that magically complex." She added several new lines that meant literally nothing to Neve but did give the diagram a well-rounded, completed look, so that was something. Aoife tapped the new symbol with her finger. "That could be her."

Aoife paused, as if waiting for applause. Neve and Alexandria exchanged baffled looks. Whatever mic-drop moment Aoife had been expecting, it hadn't landed.

"What do you mean, that's her?" Alexandria asked. Her mouth pulled into a frown, eyebrows drawing close enough to place a little divot on her forehead between them as she scanned the lines on the paper, as if she could somehow divine their meaning by force of will.

"How do you know Danu agreed to help? How do we even know she actually went missing behind the Veil?" she asked, shooting Aodh a poisonous look.

"Well, if she was going on about a *war*," said Aodh, who'd put the book down and was peering at the diagrams with barely concealed interest, "no doubt she volunteered to martyr herself. It was her style."

"You can't generate that kind of magic out of nothing," Neve explained quickly, feeling the Daughters begin to puff up with indignation. "If she *did* agree to help, she still wouldn't be able to generate enough magic to kick-start the spell out of nowhere. Not without . . ."

The solution came to her as she spoke, the sheer obviousness of it feeling like a kick in the throat.

Aodh said that they thought Danu had died, that the Morrigan had killed her even before the Veil dropped over them and cut them off from the world. Neve had wanted him to be wrong, unable to stomach the thought that she and her sisters were responsible for any more harm, but this wasn't much better.

"She's powering it," Neve said slowly, the pieces slotting themselves together in her mind. "Danu is powering the Gate, isn't she?" It wasn't a spell. Or, it wasn't *just* a spell. Casting wasn't the only way to access magic; it was in everything. Like, for example, the matriarch of the sidhe. Danu hadn't cast the Gate spell, because she *was* the Gate spell. Or at least, she was its conduit.

Aoife nodded, some of the excited light leaving her face. "I think so."

Aodh whistled. "Shit."

The brief surge of excitement at finding an answer, any answer, was gone as quickly as it came. Neve's whole body felt heavy as she stood in the silence that followed the revelation. Danu had gone missing not because she was dead, but because she'd used herself to generate power for the Gate. She *couldn't* be dead, or else the spell would have failed ages ago.

Neve felt queasy. But this was something; it was progress. If Danu was what was holding the Gate together, even in whatever weird, warped state it was in now, then she should be able to open it back up again. Actually, if they managed to wake her up—Neve was choosing to think that Danu had been sleeping this whole time, rather than watching her family tear themselves into bloody pieces over and over again for a thousand years—the Veil might just dissolve altogether. Which would give Neve her sisters back, and also let out a whole host of very angry sidhe who'd had a thousand years' worth of axes to grind.

Neve shook her head. One thing at a time.

"Well, damn," Alexandria said, beating Neve to the conclusion. "Now we've just got to wake up Mom."

CHAPTER EIGHTEEN

That, like literally everything else—Neve didn't know why she even bothered expecting anything different, because why would *anything* be simple—was easier said than done. Apparently, along with not telling the Daughters that she was leaving to be a living battery for a spell, Danu had failed to leave any "Break Glass in Case of Emergency" instructions on how to find her again. Which was probably why everyone behind the Veil thought she'd been dead this whole time.

Aodh, predictably, was no help at all, and he had swanned off soon after their conversation. Apparently, that had been enough family bonding for him for one day, and he didn't look pleased that Danu was the solution to their problems. Well. One potential solution to one problem and the catalyst for a whole host of new ones.

But one thing at a time. Aodh might have been gone, but the fallout of his presence was not. Case in point: Alexandria was avoiding Neve.

She was perched on one of the catwalks that crisscrossed the air above the spine of the convent, doodling in her sketchbook, when Neve found her. Neve hauled herself up into a semicomfortable place on the iron lattice that she'd used to get between the attic and Bay's and Mercy's rooms a thousand times, trying to think about anything other than the fact that those rooms were currently empty.

"What do you want?" Alexandria asked without looking up from her drawing.

"You're angry with me."

Alexandria rolled her eyes, making a particularly sharp mark against the page with her pencil. "What gave it away?"

"I am naturally perceptive," Neve said, trying for a joke, which had worked before when she had done something stupid and reckless that Alexandria was angry about. Not this time: Alexandria's mouth didn't so much as twitch.

"I'm sorry," she tried again.

This time Alexandria did look up at her. "Do you even know what you're apologizing for?"

"I went after Aodh without telling you," Neve recited dutifully. "Which was dangerous, I know. I shouldn't have done it."

"Was it?" Alexandria asked. "Was it dangerous? Do you even think that?"

Neve blinked. "I don't—"

"Because from here," Alexandria continued, cutting her off, "it seems like you don't think so anymore."

"What are you talking about?" Neve demanded, thoroughly

baffled at the turn this conversation had taken. "Of course I know he's dangerous. He almost killed me."

"Oh good," Alexandria spat. "You remember. I was worried that you'd hit your head and forgotten that, since you seem determined not to treat him like he's the bad guy here."

But—

The thought rose up in her mind before Neve could stop it, a thousand excuses and dull, stinging defensiveness that she couldn't push away.

"See!" Alexandria said, reacting to whatever was showing on Neve's face before she could manage to work it out herself. "You're making excuses for him. I can see you doing it."

"I wasn't," Neve lied, wincing because lying was bad enough, but this was almost offensively obvious.

"You were!" Alexandria said, shoving her sketchbook off her lap. If they weren't both precariously perched three stories off the ground, she would probably be pacing. "God, I know you miss Bay and Mercy, but he's not—you can't just slot him in like everything he's done never happened."

Neve jerked back. "I'm not slotting him in," she repeated, balking at the implication that Bay and Mercy could be replaced, and that Neve had found the first candidate that was the correct species and was trying to force him into their spot.

"He killed my parents and ruined my life," Alexandria said. Her hand clenched into a fist around her pencil. Neve could hear the wood straining not to snap. "You can't just expect me to forget about that."

"I don't," Neve said quickly, horrified all over again. "Of course I don't. Why would you even say that?"

"Because you're acting like it never happened!"

"Because it was our fault!" Neve shouted.

Alexandria blew out a breath, looking more frustrated than ever. "That's not what I'm talking about and you know it. I don't blame you for not being able to predict that there were other ways through the Gate."

"That's not what I mean." Neve shook her head, closing her eyes and pressing her knuckles hard against her temple. "I can't remember why we did it. I have these memories that feel real, but they're all so insubstantial. I can't . . . I keep trying, but I can't remember why we were so certain that this was the only way. And that makes me think that we were wrong."

A thousand years. A thousand years of being locked away from the world. Neve could barely conceptualize that amount of time. That was why they had the cycle; that was why they had a whole ritual to help them sort through everything when the levy broke at eighteen. Neve had only been throwing herself against the Gate for a few weeks, trying to get her sisters back, but it was already turning her inside out. She couldn't fathom centuries upon centuries of doing the same thing.

"That doesn't make it okay," Alexandria said.

It didn't; of course it didn't. But if Neve blamed Aodh for everything he'd done, how could she get away with not shouldering some of the blame herself? For whatever reason, *this* was the solution they'd chosen. The Veil, the Gate, all of it. Neve had to carry the consequences of that decision, even if she didn't remember it.

But Alexandria didn't want to hear that, and she didn't want to accept Neve's apologies. Neve watched her climb down one of the ladders back to the second floor and didn't follow, just stared up at the peaked ceiling and wondered how the hell any of this was going to get better. And what the hell Neve was supposed to do if it didn't.

Aoife, now that she had a better grasp of the problem and wasn't scrabbling about in the dark anymore trying to reverse engineer a solution out of nothing, had an answer within a day.

"I think we might be able to pull her out," Aoife said, gesturing at a brand-new mess of scrawled spellwork.

"Won't that just . . . end the spell?" Alexandria asked hesitantly. "What if Aodh's army is still waiting?"

Neve had been thinking the same, though her mouth felt dry when she thought about saying so out loud. Wasn't this what they deserved? Wouldn't she have been just as angry? How could Neve justify working this hard to get Bay and Mercy, only to leave the rest of their family in there?

"No," Aoife said, looking triumphant. "All that magic won't just dissipate. The spell didn't simply end when you came through, remember? It changed. If we can bring Danu out, bring her *here*, she might be able to help us get Bay and Mercy back."

But *only* Bay and Mercy. That went unsaid.

"How do we do that?" Neve asked.

Aoife winced a little, looking pale, which was how Neve knew she was not going to like the answer. "There was a way that we—members of the Order, that is—used to be able to contact her. If we modified it a little bit, I think it might still work."

"But?" Neve prompted, because there was no way it could be that easy.

"But I think that the Gate would have to be open."

Neve filled in the rest for herself: If the Gate was open, then the new monsters would have a chance to get through, and Neve wouldn't be enough to stop them on her own. Which meant, as if the universe and magic and any gods living or dead were conspiring against her, Neve needed Aodh for what came next.

Alexandria glowered, clearly having come to the same conclusion. Their argument from earlier was fresh in both of their minds and Neve grimaced.

"More cousin bonding time. Awesome."

"He's not going to agree if he knows you're only going for

Bay and Mercy," Daughter Aoife said. Neve fought the urge to snap at her.

"Yeah, so we lie," she said instead, ignoring the way it made her feel a little ill even to suggest it.

Once again, Neve felt like she was split between the past and the present. Like she was trying to make up for a thousand years' worth of mistakes and hurt as few people in the process as possible. Whatever peace she'd made with Aodh, whatever limbo they'd found themselves in, it didn't extend to the rest of the family she and her sisters had left behind as well. There were too many things that could go wrong.

Neve shook herself. No. She needed to focus on fixing what she could, while she could. If they could get to Danu, then Danu might be able to get to Bay and Mercy. It was a big *if*, but it was the closest thing they had to a coherent plan.

Even if the thought of lying to Aodh, the thought of leaving the rest of the sidhe made Neve sick to her stomach.

Maybe Danu would know what to do. Maybe she could fix everything. Take it off Neve's hands. Or, at the very least, give her a place to start, because right now Neve felt like she was being torn in a hundred different directions. She didn't know how much more of this she could take.

CHAPTER NINETEEN

A few nights later, Neve startled awake, finding her body moving before she was even fully awake. She pulled on a sweatshirt and pauldrons, and swung her knife belt over her hips with deft, mechanical movements.

She was going to the Gate. Where else? Her body seemed to know this before the rest of her caught up, but then all of her was in agreement.

Instinctive urgency still hummed beneath her skin as Neve arrived, drawing her weapons and standing off against the Gate as if it was an enemy itself. Which it was. Of course it was. How could it not be, when it had caused so much harm?

Always blaming others, hissed Nemain's voice in the back of her mind.

"Shut up," Neve snarled, not bothering to keep the words inside for once.

"I didn't say anything."

Neve whirled, both surprised and not to find Aodh standing a few feet away, despite the fact that it was barely past midnight and freezing, to boot. He hadn't been around the last few days, since the realization about Danu. Not that Neve had been looking.

Aodh smirked, looking like he was going to say something snippy and annoying, but his smile faded as he took a second look at the expression on Neve's face.

"Little late for sparring," Aodh said neutrally. His head cocked to the side, assessing. "But if you wanted a partner, all you had to do was ask."

Neve snorted. "Right, because the last time worked out so well for me."

A look almost like hurt flashed across his face before Aodh rolled his eyes. "Probably for the best. I keep forgetting this is it for you. Last life. No more chances if we're going to open the Gate."

Last life, and as far as Neve knew, she would be spending the rest of it completely and totally alone while her sisters spent their last lives stuck behind the Veil. The thought made her feel sick. A spike of pain drove through her skull right behind her left eye.

Neve didn't want to think about this right now. Especially because his words had the ring of truth to them. She hadn't thought about it much—hadn't let herself think about the fact that this was her last life. For as long as she could remember, Neve had taken her continued existence for granted.

Sure, there was the danger of dying before she manifested and breaking the chain, but so long as she made it to eighteen, she and her sisters would just keep coming back lifetime after lifetime. It had been comforting once. Then it had been a little horrifying. More than a little. The thought of coming back again and again, dying violently over and over, had kind of turned into a nightmare.

She knew, obviously, that once the spell was broken—really broken, not the current sort-of-cracked bullshit—this was her last life. The only reason they reincarnated over and over was to protect the Gate, and once the spell was gone, the reincarnation chain would follow. This was it. Neve would just . . . keep on going and when she died, that would be the end. Maybe she would get lucky and die of old age.

Could she even die of old age?

The thought made Neve's blood pound in her ears, her stomach swooping like she'd tripped and fallen from the top of the cliff, and she instinctively braced herself for an impact that didn't come.

She didn't want to think about that. Neve's relationship with her own mortality was tenuous, to say the very least, but whether it was a comfort or a burden, the idea that she would inevitably die had always been consistent. Now all of eternity stretched before her, and Neve realized she'd never considered whether or not she and her sisters could die of old age. Or would they just . . . keep going until something killed them?

Would she just keep going without Bay and Mercy? Neve thought of her conversation with Mercy in the garden. It felt like forever ago now, even though it had only been a month or so. Mercy had said that the only thing that had kept them going when one of them died before the others was knowing they would see her in the next life. Neve's legs suddenly felt weak as she contemplated eternity without her sisters.

Neve shuddered. That sounded like a whole new genre of nightmare. She'd pass on immortality, thanks.

For all its sudden distress, it was a useless thought exercise anyway. Whether or not she would live forever wasn't really worth considering, because the odds of Neve surviving the year, let alone centuries, were slim to none. She shuddered, very aware of Aodh's eyes on her, watching her reaction.

She needed to stop thinking about this.

She needed to stop thinking, period.

"What *did* bring you out here, cousin?" Aodh asked a bit later. Neve had put her sword away and sat down with her back against the Gate, though there wasn't anything to sense anyway. The portal was utterly inactive, silent and still. It made her feel better, like she might have a split-second head start in case anything did happen.

Aodh squinted with overdone suspicion. "Unless this was all a ploy to lure me out and get my guard down."

"You caught me. This was all a setup. Well done." Neve sighed, the exhaustion from the early hour catching up to her at the same time. Her shoulders sagged and her head suddenly felt very heavy on her neck.

She didn't want to bring up Bay and Mercy. Partly because it hurt too much, drew too much attention to the great empty space behind Neve's heart, and partly because Neve wasn't sure if whatever little cease-fire she and Aodh had stumbled into applied to them. She didn't want to chance it, not tonight.

"What's your problem with Danu?" Neve asked. She didn't really expect him to answer. Mostly, she expected him to get a little bit snarly and defensive.

"I was the last one," Aodh said after a minute. "Before, I mean. I'm the youngest. The world was moving on without us, and everyone had gone to see it. Left the nest, as it were. I was the only one left, so she clung to me a little harder." His mouth twisted. "I didn't care for it."

Something was resolving in Neve's mind, some picture that she hadn't been able to put together before.

Neve felt the moment the Gate began to shift behind her. Aodh sprang to his feet, sensing it as well. Less than thirty seconds later, Neve's phone rang.

"I know," Neve said, answering Alexandria on the first ring. "I'm already here."

"I'm coming," was all Alexandria said before she hung up.

Neve wished she wouldn't, but there was nothing to do about it now. Mostly out of habit, she texted 911 into her chat with the Daughters, though they'd likely sensed the Gate spluttering to life as surely as Neve had.

There was probably a lecture in her future about sneaking out to the Gate without telling them. Or yet another tedious conversation about Aodh being dangerous. Neve just had to hope they'd be too distracted by the return of their patron to get on her ass too badly.

Or maybe Neve would die in the attempt. Hard to get lectured about running around with your homicidal cousin when you were dead.

Bad joke. She shouldn't think like that. At the very least, it was probably tempting fate, considering the monsters the Gate was about to barf up.

"It's not them," Aodh said under his breath. His sword was already in his hand, his grip abruptly reminding Neve of Mercy's, even though his blade was smaller. She'd never taken the time to appreciate his style, not really. She'd been a little too busy trying not to die to really pick it apart, but she could see from his stance that, even though he held his weapon like Mercy did, he favored speed over Mercy's brute strength. He was better built for it too, slimmer than Mercy, closer in build to Neve and Bay, though they were all bulky for their age—and in the Morgans' case, gender—compared to humans.

"What?" Neve asked, eyes darting to him, but Aodh's focus was fixed on the seething Gate.

"What comes through. They're not your sisters. So don't hesitate." He gave a smile that was so obviously meant to be comforting that Neve had to look away.

Neve felt her hackles rise, instinct wanting her to snap at him before she swallowed it back down. She had hesitated the last time the Gate opened, and it had almost cost her.

Instead, Neve nodded before turning back to see the Daughters begin their part. The plan was simple: Neve and Aodh would take care of whatever came through the Gate in order to give the Daughters enough time to contact Danu and bring her through.

Simple, however, did not mean easy.

"How much time do you need?" Neve called, shouting to be heard as the wind kicked up. The world didn't like having holes blown into it. Neve was sympathetic.

"Eight minutes!" Clara yelled back.

Eight minutes. Not that long in the grand scheme of things, but Neve knew better. With the exception of Samhain, their battles at the Gate were usually quick and brutal affairs. Even with their strength and stamina, even with their train-ing, Neve and her sisters couldn't fight forever. And now Neve didn't even have her sisters, and she was in rougher shape than ever.

Eight minutes. Neve's eyes cut to Aodh. He was all healed up from the last time, and they knew what to expect, but Neve still found herself running the odds. Could they last eight minutes? Give the Daughters long enough to call to Danu like a magical, interdimensional alarm clock?

Could she trust him for that long? The thought was quiet, wriggling in the back of Neve's mind.

The Gate heaved and spat, the stink of rot suddenly curdling in the air. Purple-black magic swirled and sparked, revealing shadows already moving within.

Neve didn't have a choice. Trust or no, the Gate was opening and Neve had to focus.

Eight minutes.

Neve and Aodh were both moving before the first shadow even tore itself out of the cliffside. It was just as lumpy and misshapen as the last batch, weird ichorous flesh oozing across its frame like something horrible and not yet finished.

Neve's sword bit into it a split second after Aodh's, dousing them both with black-gray goop that sizzled and burned where it touched her skin.

It's not them, Neve repeated, refusing to look for the shapes of Bay and Mercy in the shadows that tore into the world. She hoped Aodh was right. *It's not them.*

It could be, though, even if they weren't themselves. Mercy and Bay could be any one of these creatures, warped and fleshy and awful simulacra of themselves, just like the rest of their family that had managed to come through the Gate.

Why did we do this? Despair was a weight on her limbs, slowing her to a crawl. Her sword and dagger were unimaginably heavy, and Neve found herself trembling. *Why did we think this was the right thing to do? How did we get it so wrong?*

"Move!"

Aodh's voice cut through the fog of guilt, and Neve jerked out of the way to avoid the yellow teeth that nearly sank into her neck. She hit the ground hard and rolled with the momentum, breath coming in harsh pants. Her chest hurt already and they'd barely started.

Aodh's face was flecked with black goop that left red burn marks behind. His gray eyes were bright, reflecting the pale moonlight overhead. "Get your shit together, cousin," he snarled.

Neve hauled herself back to her feet, this time not allowing herself to think as she moved. She was not a person; she was a body, a pair of blades, and she had one goal: survive.

But it felt as though no time had passed before Neve's limbs grew heavy from exertion. Her chest burned. She could feel the exact shape of the injury as if it were a brand instead of a stab wound from the same sword she saw flashing in her peripheral vision, hacking at the monsters that crawled through the Gate.

Neve hoped that whatever the Daughters were doing was working. Even with Aodh's help, she wasn't nearly fast enough to avoid the teeth and claws and burning flesh intent on tearing her apart. Her clothing stuck to her skin, blue-gold blood weeping from several long, deep cuts along her back and arms.

Heat built in her throat as if her body recognized that she was fighting and was preparing to scream. It felt like Neve had swallowed a coal, or was holding back tears, but she didn't scream. Couldn't scream. The rage, the spark that had transformed the burning inside her into a sound so powerful that it could freeze her enemies in their tracks or even kill them outright, was nowhere to be found.

Swallowing hard and shaking her head to keep the blood out of her eyes, Neve tried to summon it up again and again, but there was nothing. She was an unlit pilot light, a bomb without a fuse. Her power had gone cold and dormant because Neve wasn't angry. Not the kind of angry that warscreamed.

Neve bared her teeth in a snarl, hating herself, hating her sisters, hating the monster that bore down on her even though it was her fault it was like this. But it wasn't the same as before; it didn't create the same spark, not even close.

The creatures were uncoordinated, their movements jerky, but they were fast. Unpredictable, too, and Neve kept finding herself on the back foot as she stabbed at anything that got too close.

Her ears were ringing and blood dripped in her eyes. Neve cried out as a claw tangled in her ponytail and yanked, snapping her head back. The world tilted and she hit the sand hard.

Somewhere behind her, someone screamed, but Neve couldn't really hear anything other than the snarling monster inches away from her face. Sharp claws stabbed high on her arm, teeth closing on her shoulder with a wet ripping sound like it was trying to tear the damn thing off.

Neve was screaming now too, but it wasn't the warscream she needed. Her vision was going white as her nerves overloaded with pain, cortisol pumping into her system to keep her from going into shock.

Neve swung her free arm, stabbing her dagger into the fleshy bit right above the mouth where the rest of the face should be. The monster howled, releasing her, and Neve scrambled away. Her sword arm hung uselessly at her side, still connected to the rest of her, barely. Bits of her shoulder dangled in ragged, meaty strips, and blood poured down her front.

"Neve!" Alexandria shrieked from somewhere behind the fighting.

"Don't let her through!" Neve yelled without looking back, unwilling to take her focus off the remaining shadows. The Gate wasn't spitting out any new monsters now, but there were still two staggering drunkenly around the beach. They weren't working in tandem, not anything so organized, but their frantic speed and unpredictable movements made them difficult to kill either way. Aodh wasn't in nearly as bad shape as she was, but Neve could still see blood where they'd managed to wound him.

"What are you—Neve!" Alexandria shouted again. Her voice sounded like it was coming from the same distance away, which Neve counted as a good sign. "I can help, I can—"

A roar cut her off and Neve lurched backward as the monster she'd stabbed lunged for her, evidently not as dead as she'd hoped. Half-baked or not, these bastards were hard to kill. Neve blamed the goop and distinct lack of visible anatomy.

Moving only caused more blood to flow out of the wound on her shoulder, but Neve didn't have a choice as the monster tried to finish the job. She slashed at it, making purchase with her dagger and scalding the skin of her wrist. It was a miracle she managed to keep hold of the blade long enough to stab the creature again, then again, until it stopped moving and finally melted away, skin sloughing off and seeping into the sand. Bile rose in Neve's throat, and she didn't know whether it was from the monster or the pain. Didn't really matter.

Then, finally, the slow build of the magic the Daughters had been calling hit its zenith. Neve held her breath, waiting for something, anything, to indicate that the spell had worked.

But all she saw was the Gate, still spitting rotten magic, and one of the two remaining monsters lunging at Aodh.

"Duck!" She didn't think, didn't wait for him to reply or act, just threw her dagger with all the strength she had left. The force of the throw drove the blade deep into its oozing flesh and the monster screamed. It wasn't enough to kill it, but it bought Aodh enough time to finish it off.

There was heavy, expectant silence, and then, like the cliff had been split apart by an earthquake, an almighty crack appeared. It bisected the Gate, sending even more foul magical sparks flying into the air, and Neve had to hold up her good arm to keep the cloud of dust and sand from getting in her eyes. When she blinked through the grit, the crack in the Gate was still there, yawning even farther open, and deep within, the silhouette of a woman approached.

Neve felt her focus pull toward the Gate, toward the newcomer, forgetting that there was still one monster left.

"*Neve.*" Alexandria's voice was high and terrified. Neve hadn't realized she'd gotten so close.

Idiot, Neve heard the voice of her former self snarl. *You should have made sure the other one was dead.*

Neve dropped her shoulder, angling her body between the remaining creature and Alexandria. Then Alexandria did something batshit insane. Instead of running, or ducking behind Neve's bulk, or doing anything else even remotely reasonable, Alexandria threw her weight forward as Neve hunched down. The result was Alexandria landing halfway on top of Neve's back like they were doing a shitty ice-skating trick.

Neve didn't have time to adjust to the unexpected weight before she saw Alexandria's arm in her peripheral vision, reaching for the creature. There was a horrible sizzle as her hand made contact, seizing whatever bit of the thing's oozing flesh she could grab, and Alexandria pulled.

Then the whole world exploded.

CHAPTER TWENTY

Neve's ears popped and her stomach roiled at the sudden drop in barometric pressure. The air around her seemed to compress and then expand, sending her flying backward. Bits of jagged rock ripped up what remained of her jacket and tore into her exposed skin, but Neve wasn't focused on that at the moment.

She fought to her feet, blinking away the cartoon stars that danced in front of her eyes as she sought out Alexandria.

The Gate was still again and scored with white pressure wounds where the stone had buckled under the force.

Alexandria stood in the epicenter of the detonation, her face pale beneath the monster gore splattered on her cheeks. She hadn't moved an inch despite the visible evidence of violence all around her. Her arm was still outstretched, elbow locked in place.

Unlike Alexandria, the rotted monster that had come through the Gate hadn't been spared the brunt of the explosion, and it hadn't been flung away like Neve. Alexandria's hand still gripped its arm, but the gooey, sizzling flesh of the creature had stripped away. Neve had thought that beneath the casing of skin might have just been a slop of blood and organs, but the shape of the creature—no, the person—in Alexandria's grip was undeniably familiar.

If not for the instinctual hum that buzzed beneath Neve's skin—if not for the fact that she'd seen the creature come out of the Gate—Neve might have thought they were human. Then, for a terrifying second, she thought they might be *Danu*.

She didn't have enough time to get a good look, to say something or move closer. Neve barely had time to confirm that the sidhe wasn't Bay or Mercy before Alexandria jerked her hand away.

As soon as she removed her hand, there was a scream and a flash like lightning. Neve swore, throwing up her good arm to keep her retinas from burning out of her head, and when she looked again, Alexandria was alone. The only sign that someone else had been there at all was a collection of black dust already disappearing into the sand.

Behind them, still coated with blood and rotting bits of monster flesh, Aodh swore loudly. His eyes were enormous, his mouth slightly agape in the most unguarded expression Neve had ever seen him wear.

"Nemain, look out!" shouted a voice that Neve knew intimately and had never heard in this lifetime. Dizzy-sick nausea ripped through her before a figure pulled Neve behind her, putting herself between Neve and Alexandria.

Neve's first thought was that Danu looked a whole lot like Neve and her sisters. Or maybe it would be more accurate to say that they looked like her, considering she'd come first.

Neve's second thought was that, in her gray dress, Danu looked soft.

The steely look on her face as she regarded Alexandria, however, was anything but.

"No, wait," Neve said, staggering forward, her good arm outstretched while the other hung limply by her side. "It's okay."

Danu looked between Neve and Alexandria, and then her eyes flicked to the gouge in the earth where Alexandria had . . . detonated. Neve didn't know. Alexandria still hadn't made a sound, her mouth slightly open as she tried to understand what the hell had just happened. Neve didn't blame her.

"What's going on?" Danu asked. "What's happened? It's too—" Something appeared to click in her mind. "Where are your sisters?"

"The Veil," Neve grit out. Talking took more energy than usual all of a sudden. Her tongue felt heavy and unwieldy in her mouth. She'd lost a lot of blood. "We were wrong," she said, swaying a little on her feet. Behind Danu, the crack had sealed back up, and the beach was relatively still. Everything had sort of dissolved into swirls of color, but Neve could still sense the Gate behind the unassuming façade of stone.

Neve kept trying to explain, to tell Danu what had happened

and why they'd taken so long to come and get her, and to apologize for putting her in that position in the first place. But the words wouldn't come out right and her arm hurt and so did her head, with the kind of pain that made it feel like it was going to split right down the middle. There was also Alexandria to consider. Neve was aware that Alexandria was still with them, which was good, and that Daughter Clara was taking care of her, which was better.

Then they were moving and had lost Aodh somewhere along the way. Probably at the boundary to the convent, though Neve couldn't be sure. But she heard Alexandria yelling and then Aodh wasn't with them anymore.

That was probably for the best.

All thought spun out of her head as firm hands gripped her arm and snapped it back into place. The scream that tore out of her throat was the closest to a warscream she'd managed in months.

"Nemain, you're going to be all right," someone whispered. Normally, Neve would tell them not to use that name, that her name was Neve, not Nemain, but from this voice, it was okay. "You're going to be all right, sweet girl. I promise. Everything is going to be all right."

Neve wanted to believe her. More than anything, Neve wanted to believe that everything was going to be okay. But she didn't. She just hurt.

. . .

Alexandria wasn't there when Neve finally came to. Time had gotten kind of squishy on her for a while there, and Neve wasn't sure how long she'd been out. She tried to sit up and found her sword arm bound in a sling, which reminded her of the first time she and Alexandria had met, way back in the fall. When sidhe were still demons, Neve was still a god, and Bay and Mercy were still on this plane of existence. It had been less than six months, and Neve's whole life was different. Mostly for the worse.

Neve reached for her phone with her free hand, but the bedside table was empty.

Slowly, because she knew the drill by now and didn't want to earn herself more bed rest by overdoing it, Neve levered herself out of the bed, careful to make sure her legs would hold her weight before continuing to the door. She half expected one of the Daughters to burst in the moment she put her hand on the doorknob, but she couldn't hear anything in the hallway outside. No hushed voices or footsteps.

It was . . . weird. There wasn't anyone as Neve plodded out of the infirmary room and through the spine of the convent. The echo of her solitary steps seemed even louder when Neve began to wonder if she were alone in the convent. The thought made her whole body go cold.

Don't be stupid, she tried to tell herself. She wasn't alone here; the Daughters wouldn't have left her. Neve was being paranoid after waking up alone and without her phone. It was fine. She was being dumb.

Dumb or not, Neve moved a little quicker as she traced her way through the most traveled areas of the convent. Her breath released in relief when she finally heard voices coming from the direction of the library.

"This is not—" a hushed, tense voice was saying as Neve rounded the corner. She stopped quickly, instinct urging her to slink back a step, press against the wall, and make herself small so they didn't know she was here. "I do not blame you, but this is not how I meant this to happen."

"We're sorry, my lady," Daughter Clara said, her voice careful and measured. "But we didn't have many other options."

"No, no, I understand," the hushed voice—it had to be Danu's—said, sounding aggrieved and put-upon. It made Neve's stomach turn. "I just . . . this is not how I intended our reunion to go. I'm worried. The human—"

"Alexandria," Daughter Clara corrected, sounding a little sharp.

"Yes," Danu acquiesced.

Neve's heart twisted. Where *was* Alexandria? Was she still here? Was she okay? And what the hell had she done back there?

Dimly, Neve thought that if Alexandria didn't think she was human before . . .

"Alexandria is important to Neve—Nemain," Daughter Aoife said. "And she's suffered greatly because of what we put in motion."

Put in motion. Like they'd simply set up the dominos and the way they'd fallen, everything that had come after, was separate somehow.

Neve waited for the quicksilver flash of anger to rise up at that, at the Daughters trying to remove themselves from the responsibility, but she found that she didn't have the energy. She couldn't blame the Daughters without heaping even more blame at her own feet, and Neve was already suffocating under the weight of all the wrong she'd done. That they all had done.

She was so tired.

Part of her, the part she recognized from her first life, Nemain, wanted Danu to make this all better. Neve was so used to that part of her always urging for action and violence, sneering and scowling when Neve shied away from it. But now she felt the girl she was, the girl she had been, want nothing more than for Danu to fix it for her. For all of them.

Neve took a step back from the door. It couldn't be that easy. She didn't deserve for it to be that easy, even if she wanted it to be. Even if the Neve she was now, in this life, wanted the comfort of someone telling her that she was going to be all right.

Besides, Nemain didn't have Alexandria.

She wasn't hard to find once Neve started looking. Neve found the door to her bedroom closed and knocked gently, even though it felt strange to be knocking on her own door.

"Can I come in?" Neve called softly. She waited a moment before letting herself in anyway.

Alexandria was curled up under a mountain of blankets, clutching the stuffed raven she'd given Neve like her life depended on it. Her face was wet with tears.

"I'm sorry," Alexandria said before Neve could get a word in. Her already pale face blanched further as her dark eyes landed on Neve's sling. "I'm sorry, I should've been down there with you. Are you—"

It was cumbersome with only one arm to maneuver, but Neve managed, pulling Alexandria into a hug so tight that it nearly squeezed the breath out of them both. Alexandria sniffled, tears wetting the fabric of Neve's shirt, but Neve didn't care. She just held on tighter.

They stayed like that for a long while, the two of them clinging to each other.

"I—" Alexandria mumbled against Neve's chest.

"You saved me," Neve cut her off before she could apologize again. "You saved my life."

It wasn't the first time, but Neve didn't think Alexandria would like to be reminded of how she and Bay and Mercy had dragged Neve out of the Gate.

"What am I?" Alexandria asked, the question muffled and soft, like she was afraid of the answer.

"You're Alexandria," Neve answered after a long minute. "And I'm Neve."

"She looked at me like I was a monster."

Neve didn't have to ask who Alexandria was talking about. The look on Danu's face was seared into Neve's brain.

"I don't even know what I *did*," Alexandria said, picking up steam now. "I was just scared and I didn't think and I *pulled* and . . ." She broke off, sniffling again. "Why is this happening to me?"

"I don't know," Neve said. It felt like that was all she ever had to say anymore. There was so much she didn't know, so much she couldn't remember.

"I'm scared."

"I know," Neve conceded after she'd let the silence drag on for a little bit too long. "I'm scared too." She huffed out a humorless laugh. "I don't think I've ever been this scared in my life. I've never been alone before. I don't really know how." As if that wasn't completely obvious.

Neve tilted her head back and scrubbed her fingers through her greasy hair. She needed a shower. "This is my last life, I think." Alexandria started, but she didn't interrupt. "I think what we did, I think what we're trying to do . . . either way, I'm pretty sure this is it. And I want to get my sisters back more than anything, but even if—*when*—I do, I only have a little bit more time to be human."

She smiled, but it was hollow and aching. "It's dumb. It's so dumb, but I never wanted to be human before we met, and now I only have a few more months left, and I'd really like to be human with you. For as long as I can."

There was nothing but dead air when Neve finished speaking. Alexandria was looking at her, wide-eyed and thunderstruck, and Neve almost apologized, almost asked what that look was for, before Alexandria closed the distance between them and kissed Neve like she would die if she didn't.

Neve had a single flash of coherence before she was overwhelmed by a lapful of Alexandria, who seemed determined to kiss every single last thought out of Neve's head. With only the briefest moment of hesitation, Neve kissed her back, holding Alexandria close as she began to suck bruises down the length of Alexandria's jaw, her neck, and with only a slight delay as the T-shirt between them disappeared, her chest.

The whole thing really was extraordinarily human.

CHAPTER TWENTY-ONE

D anu and the Daughters were still in the library when Neve and Alexandria finally felt brave enough to face them.

"Why do I feel like I'm about to meet your parents for the first time?" Alexandria asked, making an attempt at humor. She was wrapped in one of Neve's sweatshirts, the hood pulled over her hair, and she'd yanked the sleeves up so that she could hold Neve's hand without the fabric getting in the way.

"They're not—" Neve started, before seeing the small smile on Alexandria's face. She huffed. "Fine."

They didn't really have a plan, but the second Neve saw Danu and the Daughters clustered around the big table in the center of the library, she was seized by some latent youngest-child instinct, some guilt that bypassed the rest of her brain and communicated directly with her mouth.

"It's my fault," Neve said, the words coming out jumbled and fast. "Ours. Mine. I . . . we got it so wrong and we convinced you to power the Gate and we shouldn't have and now everyone is trapped and Bay and Mercy are trapped." She was starting to sound like Alexandria now, everything coming out in a haphazard run-on sentence, punctuation and breathing be damned. "And the rest of the family . . . even if we let them out they're going to be so angry and they should be angry but it's our fault, no one else's—I'm sorry. I'm so sorry and I want to make it right and I don't know how and I'm scared and—"

Neve made a muffled sound as long, gentle arms looped around her and Danu pulled her into a hug. Irritation sparked at being cut off so abruptly, but it was smothered a moment later as Neve just melted. She squeezed Danu back, not bothering to be gentle because she didn't have to.

"I'm sorry," Neve said again, mumbling into the fabric of Danu's dress. It was soft and the smell made Neve think of gentle rain and cool air and *home*. In her mind, she heard the clarion call of safety and protection the likes of which she hadn't felt since before Mercy and Bay disappeared into the Gate. Neve couldn't remember the last time she'd felt wholly, truly safe.

"Don't be," Danu said, thumbing away tears that Neve hadn't even noticed spilling onto her cheeks. "You have nothing to be sorry for."

That wasn't true, but Neve didn't contradict her, sagging like her guilt-stricken ramble had left her without any internal scaffolding, like a balloon with a slow leak, collapsing under its own weight.

"I just want them back."

Gentle fingers wound through her hair, like Bay used to do

when Neve had a nightmare. "I know. We'll get them all back. I promise."

"We were so wrong," Neve murmured. "We ruined everything."

Danu hummed. "You did no such thing. We're a family. Everything will work out."

Neve wanted to believe her. She wanted to trust that everything was going to be okay now. She was so tired and still hurting and everything was her fault. All she wanted was for someone to swoop in and take care of it for her, give her a soft place to land for the first time in her seventeen exhausting years of life.

She felt so old all of a sudden, like all her lifetimes were catching up to her at once, even though she wasn't yet eighteen and still couldn't remember them. The weight of a thousand years of bloodshed and violence hung off her bones, and even as strong as she was, Neve felt herself bending beneath the burden.

I'm only seventeen, she thought, which was a very seventeen-year-old thing to think. She was only seventeen and it shouldn't hurt this much.

A shuffle from behind her reminded Neve that she and Danu were not alone. Neve extricated herself from the warm circle of Danu's arms, watching Danu's face as she reached for Alexandria.

"This is Alexandria," Neve said, hesitating for a second as she tried to think of the best way to explain. They hadn't talked about it beforehand, and Neve wasn't sure what was okay to tell.

Alexandria gave her hand a squeeze, nodding once. All of it. Okay. Neve had a sense of déjà vu as she launched into a hurried explanation of everything that had happened since she'd first met Alexandria in the fall. Like the last time she'd done this, Alexandria picked up the story in some parts when Neve started to falter.

"I know the rest," Danu said gently when they got to the part about Neve getting stabbed and Alexandria and her sisters dragging her through the Gate. Neve gave a wan smile, grateful that she didn't have to retell that part. It was bad enough just thinking about it, and from the ill expression on her face, Alexandria felt the same.

Danu regarded them with pale blue eyes that felt as though they were staring through muscle and bone straight into their hearts. Neve wondered if Danu could see the great yawning emptiness inside her where her connection to her sisters should have been. She wondered if Danu was comparing her to the Nemain that Danu had known so long ago. Neve knew in her gut that she did not measure up.

"I'm sorry," Danu said after a long moment that left both Neve and Alexandria fidgeting and uncomfortable, like they'd been caught sneaking out and were about to get grounded. Danu looked at Alexandria and inclined her head slightly. "When we set the parameters for the spell, a human who would walk between worlds did not exist. You were hypothetical. And I'm sorry for everything you have suffered at the hands of my family."

Neve rankled a little bit at calling Alexandria "hypothetical," like when they'd designed the spell they hadn't thought about how it might affect the unlucky human who fit the bill. Which they almost certainly hadn't, now that she thought about it. Neve sighed. Her past self was such an asshole.

"It's . . ." Alexandria swallowed hard, clearly fighting the impulse to say that it was okay. It was not even close to okay. "Bay and Mercy," she said, refocusing herself with a little shake. "How do we get them back?"

"That is a little bit tricky," Daughter Maeve said, speaking up for the first time since Neve and Alexandria had joined them. "We've been discussing it."

"But before any of that," Clara cut in, "you two need to eat."

"But—"

But nothing. Clara would not be dissuaded, insisting that Neve and Alexandria both needed to take care of themselves after everything that had happened. Neve thought she saw Danu's eyes go a little cold at that, but the look was gone before she could be sure.

As much as she hated to admit it, Neve was starving. Healing took a shit-ton of energy, and Neve's arm had been hanging on by some sinew and a prayer by the time they had gotten her back to the convent. It still hurt like a son of a bitch and would be useless for the next week or so, but it had been set and the worst of the wounds had already begun to knit themselves back together. She was lucky, all things considered. Neve was pretty sure her body's ability to heal itself ended at "regrowing limbs like a gecko."

Neve and Alexandria sat at the table after their offers to help had been waved off, watching Danu and the Daughters in the kitchen. It was weird how easily Danu fit into the space. For Neve's whole life, it had only been herself, her sisters, and the Daughters in the convent. Even having Alexandria visit had sent Neve into a tailspin the first time, as her worlds collided in a way that made the edges between them feel blurry.

There was none of that now with Danu. None of the panicky sense of wrongness, like Neve was looking at one of those dumb spot-the-difference puzzles, trying to figure out what was missing. Danu just slid into place without making a ripple, like she had always been there. Or was always meant to be there.

Neve wondered what her life—what her lives—might have been like if she and her sisters had done things differently. If they hadn't insisted on making the Gate and Danu hadn't sealed herself away in order to power it. Was there any other universe where they would have ended up here? Probably not.

Maybe that would've been for the better. Neve gnawed on the inside of her lip, trying to force herself from being so damn maudlin.

"So," Danu said once Neve and Alexandria had eaten enough to satisfy Clara, who had been watching the two of them like a hawk. Mostly Alexandria, who tended toward not eating when she was stressed. Neve made up for it, ravenous from the effort of healing as she put down as many calories as possible to encourage her arm not to fall off.

"What do we do?" Neve asked in a rush, the question bursting out of her. She felt anxiety humming through her body like electrical static and half expected the hair on her arms to start standing on end. "The Gate . . . it's not going to last now, right? With you gone?"

Danu nodded. "We have a little time. I think our first priority is your sisters."

"What about everyone else?" Alexandria asked.

Danu's eyes cut to her and there was that little flash again. "Our family is . . . large. And complicated. And unfortunately, it seems that even after all this time, your cousin still *insists* on causing problems." Danu sighed, rubbing her temples. She looked just like Bay when she had a headache.

For the first time, Neve registered Aodh's absence.

"What . . ." Neve started, but the question faded, still half-formed in her mouth. "Why did he . . . ?" she tried again, with no more success. There was so much she wanted to know, so much she didn't understand, that Neve had no idea where to start.

Thankfully, Danu put together the pieces.

"Your cousin had some notions about the world," Danu said with distaste. "And about humanity. I tried to dissuade him, but he wouldn't listen to me. He wouldn't listen to you three, either. There would've been bloodshed."

Neve's stomach twisted. Aodh had said that he and Danu hadn't seen eye-to-eye. Neve remembered how eager he had been to see the world. When had that changed to fear-mongering and hate? And why hadn't it carried into his actions since coming through the Gate? Neve couldn't square it in her head; the edges of the puzzle kept shifting the moment she thought she might have a grasp on them.

"But why make the Veil?" Alexandria asked abruptly. "Why make Neve and Bay and Mercy forget? Why set them up so they would be stuck fighting, maybe forever? Why—"

"That is complicated," Danu said, leveling a look at Alexandria. "I don't expect you to understand."

"But—"

"The most important thing now is retrieving your sisters," Danu said firmly. "I worry about what could have happened to them, being behind the Veil for so long on their own. Your cousin is persuasive, and I don't doubt that they're in danger."

Ice crawled through Neve's veins until it felt as if she were frozen solid. She'd thought the same, but it was different hearing it said aloud, and by Danu, of all people.

Neve thought of the mob that had swarmed her and her sisters when they'd been behind the Veil themselves. Not all of them; most of the sidhe were just trying to live, from the looks of things, but enough that it would be a problem if they decided to take a thousand years' worth of rage out on Newgrange Harbor.

Not that they didn't have a right to be angry. Not that Bay and Mercy being gone for even the smallest fraction of the time hadn't driven Neve nearly out of her mind.

"As for the rest . . ." Danu said, reaching across the table and taking Neve's hand. Neve squeezed it gratefully. "I think I can get through to them."

The sense of relief was nearly as dizzying as the feeling before a memory dragged her under.

"You can?"

"Yes. I think it will take time, but we have some of that left. First, we retrieve Badb and Macha, and then we can bring our family home."

Neve still had a couple thousand questions and Alexandria

had even more. Chief among them was how Bay and Mercy were supposed to get out of the Gate without turning into mindless goop monsters. Aodh had only managed because Alexandria had pulled him out when the spell was still in flux. Neve had no idea if that would work a second time. She didn't understand why it worked the first time either.

"We're hoping," Aoife chimed in, "that Danu will be able to pull the spell apart enough to let them come through."

"When?" Neve demanded, nearly standing up in her chair.

"In a day or so," Danu admitted after a moment, looking chagrined that it wouldn't be sooner. "Unfortunately, I am a little bit depleted as I am. I'm sorry."

Neve felt herself flush hot with shame and looked away. Of course Danu was drained. She'd been a living, breathing power source for a thousand years. It was amazing that she was alive and talking after all that.

"But don't worry," Danu assured her. "I'll handle it. Everything that comes after, too."

It nagged at Neve a little, the smooth nonanswers and promises that Danu could just wave her hands and make a thousand years of mistakes and violence disappear. Who the hell knew, though? Maybe she could. Danu was their matriarch for a reason, and if anyone could make the rest of the sidhe listen, it was her. She'd gone along with Neve and her sisters' plan in the first place; it only made sense that she would help make things better now.

Siphoning off the rest of the magic would only take a few more days. Neve had waited this long.

Hang on, she thought, willing her sisters to be able to hear her wherever they were. *Just a little bit longer.*

CHAPTER TWENTY-TWO

There was a plan. And for once, Neve didn't have to worry about every eventuality, every way it could go wrong. She knew her part. She had her marching orders, she had someone to tell her what to do, and Neve couldn't believe how settled it made her feel. She felt calm and centered in a way she hadn't for months.

Her sense of calm only solidified the longer Danu was with them. To Neve, it was as if she had always been there, slotting easily into the ebb and flow of life in the convent without any resistance whatsoever. She worked with Clara in the garden and helped Aoife design the spell that would starve the Gate until she was able to poke a hole big enough for Neve to get through.

It was nice. So nice to have someone else there, someone like Neve, like her sisters, and better still, who knew who they were, who they had been back then, and understood.

The door in Neve's head hadn't spat out any new memories, but what Danu told her confirmed what she'd seen for herself in the fog: Aodh had gotten restless, gotten angry, and too many of their family agreed with him. Neve, her sisters,

Danu—they had all tried to convince him that the world was changing and humanity needed to be left alone, but he wouldn't listen. As Danu explained, Neve could see fire and smoke behind her eyelids. Nothing solid, just sense memories.

It was hard to reconcile the Aodh that Danu described with the one Neve knew now, the one who'd just wanted to see the world, not destroy it. It made her stomach hurt and her head spin with that same dizzy-sick déjà vu feeling from before.

Aodh hadn't been around since Neve had woken up with her arm in a sling and found Danu in the convent. He hadn't shown up at school to be a pain in the ass either. Not that Neve was worried, or even looking for him, to be honest, but she'd kind of gotten used to him showing up whenever she had her back turned. Probably a holdover from missing Bay and Mercy, which was a little bit pathetic.

"Nemain, do not forget that he's dangerous," Danu said, frowning. "His way is violence, and he already took away your scream in his anger."

Neve startled at that, her hand flying to her throat on impulse. "That's not—" she said. That wasn't right. Getting stabbed hadn't exactly been good for her health, but Neve had felt her warscream build before in the heat of a fight, or when some sparking irritation mimicked the proper anger she couldn't reach anymore. It was psychological, not physical.

Wasn't it?

"Please, I know you want to see the best in him and in every-one, but I can't let you get hurt again," Danu said, looking so sad that Neve wanted to say whatever it took to make that expression go away. "We're not like humans, love. We don't change like they do. He's family, but please still be careful."

Alexandria had said something similar. Neve's stomach swooped but she just nodded, her jaw clenched against the bile suddenly rising in her throat. It was getting worse, the sick feeling in her stomach. Neve wondered if it was just going to be like this until she turned eighteen and the door in her head finally opened properly.

One thing at a time. First Neve needed to get her sisters back, and then she would worry about her memories.

The one snag was that, as much as Neve tried to convince herself otherwise, Danu was weird about Alexandria.

Alexandria had been over to visit almost every day since the Gate had last opened, and she had come once with the rest of the group, though they hadn't done any self-defense training that day. Neve wasn't up to it, for one thing, and for another, the Daughters had their hands full with the siphoning spell, so Clara and Maeve couldn't drop everything to teach them the most effective techniques for throwing a punch.

Danu had been warm and courteous to Neve's friends, so it wasn't a weird human prejudice thing, thankfully. Danu had been away for a long time, so she was bound to have some outdated beliefs, but if her baseline was human-versus-nonhuman, that might have been an issue.

But she was kind to everyone else, which only threw the stiffness with which she regarded Alexandria into even sharper relief.

There had been a tense minute when Neve wondered if it was the gay thing. Wouldn't that be something out of a coming-of-age movie, if Danu didn't have an issue with Neve dating a human but drew the line at that human being a girl. Then Neve remembered that Daughter Clara and Aoife had been married since Neve's first lifetime. Probably by Danu, now that Neve thought about it.

What was it, then? Alexandria's connection to the Gate? That didn't make any sense, and it wasn't as if it was Alexandria's fault anyway. It was just a fluke, some cruel twist of fate or magic or whatever that made her the person able to walk through the Veil. And why would Danu be mad about that, anyway? Danu was part of the reason Alexandria's connection *existed*.

Neve didn't know how to ask, partially because she was afraid of what the answer might be, but she felt the tension grow every time Alexandria stepped into the convent. Alexandria could feel it too; Neve saw the way her mouth tightened whenever Danu made some excuse not to be in the same room as them, or spoke to her with rigid, detached politeness.

In the end, though, it didn't take long for Neve to find the answer.

Neve's arm was healing well. Slowly, but well. It still hurt like hell if she moved too quickly, and she couldn't lift much, but Clara had decided she had enough range of motion to ditch the sling.

"That's looking better," Danu said, drifting into the infirmary as Neve swapped out her sling for a series of bandages.

"Thanks." Neve tied off the bandage, flexing her fingers to make sure she hadn't made it too tight and cut off her circulation. "The teeth on those guys are no joke."

Danu gave a wan smile and Neve immediately wished she hadn't said anything. *Those guys* were still her family, even if she barely remembered them and they didn't remember at all when they came out of the Gate all mushy and murderous.

Neve sighed, wanting to apologize before she remembered all the other times she'd tried and Danu had just shut her down. "Why did we make it like that?" she asked. The question had been swirling around in her brain for a while, but Neve had never been able to come up with a solution that made sense.

"The simulacra?" Danu asked. "The bodies they come through in are durable and resilient, and can't technically be killed. Instead, the spell sends them back. We wanted to keep them safe."

Safe. There was that word again. Neve didn't know how safe it was to be fighting over and over forever, and stuffing the sidhe into monster bodies when they came out of the Gate seemed like a great way to kickstart a perpetual-motion violence machine.

"What changed, then? Why do they come through differently now? They're . . . they're feral." Before, the demons were at least semiorganized. But now they were just mindless monsters trying to kill anything they could reach. It didn't make sense.

Danu hedged, suddenly very interested in reorganizing the different jars of salve and bundles of herbs on the shelf in front of her.

"What?"

"I . . ." Danu sighed. "I don't want to upset you."

Neve held very still. "Why would it upset me?"

"It's just that I know you two are close, is all—"

"Close with who?" Neve demanded before the obvious answer occurred to her. "Alexandria?"

Danu looked away, fiddling with the long stem of some plant Neve didn't know by name. "It's not her fault," she said slowly. "But that doesn't stop me from worrying."

"Worrying about what?" Neve's jaw twitched, and she had to make an effort to unclench it. Danu was fidgeting uncomfortably, casting sad little looks that set Neve even further on edge.

"Your Alexandria can pass through the Veil. She can move through magic, which means that when she came back through the Gate, the spell was damaged."

"But she's not a witch. She can't do magic, how—"

Neve recalled how Alexandria had touched the single remaining monster that had come through the Gate. She remembered the way the spell sloughed off the sidhe with the oozing rotten flesh, stripping them bare before they dissolved into particulate and were gone. She had no way of knowing, of course, but no one thought the sidhe was still alive.

"It's not her fault," Neve said quickly.

Danu raised her hands, looking miserable. "It's not. Of course it's not. How could it be? And I know how close you are, but . . . Nemain, it's a miracle you're still alive."

Wait, what? Neve swayed a little, thoroughly unmoored now. Alexandria's whole deal was a little weird and a lot unfortunate, but she wasn't dangerous. Especially not to Neve.

"Like I said, she can move through the Veil," Danu explained gently, speaking as though Neve were a spooked animal about to bolt, which was equal parts condescending and helpful given that Neve felt very much like a spooked animal about to bolt. "Which means she can pull things through. Pull people through."

"But that . . ." Neve's head was swimming as she tried to force this new information to make some semblance of sense in her mind. "Isn't that a good thing? Wouldn't that mean she can . . . she can get Bay and Mercy?" Neve said. Hope lit in her chest, and it was almost like feeling the connection to her sisters again.

"No, she can't," Danu said, shaking her head. "What she did at the Gate—I know it was in self-defense. I know she was just looking out for you, but the trauma of coming through like that . . . we can't sustain it. All the years catch up at once and—"

"We die," Neve finished when Danu trailed off. The brief glimmer of hope winked out as quickly as it had come, leaving Neve feeling even more cold and desolate than before. Stupid. Neve should know better by now.

She shook her head, trying to dislodge that train of thought. It didn't help.

"Okay, fine, that won't work. But she's only ever done it once and never on purpose. She's not dangerous to any of us."

"That's even worse," Danu said, still fidgeting. "She could hurt you so badly, completely by accident."

That was ridiculous. Danu was being ridiculous and Neve told her so.

"Sweetheart, I just got you back after so long," Danu said, taking Neve's chin in her hand. Her eyes filled with tears. "I don't want to lose you."

"You won't." Neve jerked her face away, taking a step back.

She needed room to breathe, to think. All she had ever known about Alexandria was her connection to the Gate. Then Aodh had added on that the *reason* she was connected to the Gate was some inexplicable ability to pass through the Veil. Neve had thought it was just a quirk of magic, unlucky but localized. Connected to the Gate and nothing else. The Veil was a physical location. Wasn't it?

Neve shook her head. What Danu was saying didn't make sense.

But Neve had seen it.

"I don't want to lose Macha or Badb, either, or any of my other children. The way things are right now, she might be the only thing on this side of the Veil that could kill them permanently."

Neve blinked, watching Danu twist the fabric of her skirt between her fingers.

"She's not going to hurt them, either," Neve snapped. "She hasn't so far and she's not going to, so just drop it, okay?"

Danu's eyes went flinty and hard for a split second, so quick that Neve thought she might have imagined it when Danu spoke again.

"I want them back, Nemain. I want my family back. I want us all together, whole and safe."

"Alexandria is not keeping us from being together," Neve said sharply.

"Maybe not intentionally—"

"Please," Neve said. "I just . . . I don't want to talk about this anymore."

Danu looked like she might argue before she sighed. "Okay," she said, tucking a strand of hair behind Neve's ear. "Just promise me you'll be careful."

CHAPTER TWENTY-THREE

Danu's words were boring a hole in Neve's brain. Neve couldn't get it out of her head—not the idea that she was in danger (that was still asinine), but the thought that Alexandria might somehow affect the Gate before it released Bay and Mercy.

It was ridiculous. Of course it was. Alexandria had been by the Gate the last two times it had opened and nothing had happened. Even when it was dormant, her mere presence wasn't enough to cause any sort of weird chain reaction that Neve could see.

But how could Neve know for sure? Everything about Alexandria's relationship to the Gate, the Veil, was so utterly opaque that Neve had no concept of the shape of it. Until a few months ago, she didn't even know that Alexandria had a connection to the Gate, let alone that she could pass through it. And that didn't even scratch the surface of being able to pull other things out.

The Gate had reacted to Alexandria, and Alexandria could sense the Gate. It had called to her that night during the storm, and she'd known when it was about to open and vomit out goo monsters. Magic was like so many other things in the universe; it tended toward entropy. There was a reason why not just anyone could learn magic, and why maintaining spells long term took a shit-ton of energy. Magic did not want to be channeled, and so it made sense that the spell would seek out a way to break in Alexandria.

Neve was so close to getting her sisters back. By tomorrow, enough of the magic would be siphoned off for Danu to get to Bay and Mercy. After that . . . they would have to see.

It would take a long time to undo the harm Neve and her sisters had done. She knew that. But what else could she do? They had messed up so, so badly. She didn't think that she'd be able to make it right in another dozen lifetimes, but that didn't mean she didn't still have to try.

Whether or not the sidhe would let her try was another matter altogether. Danu had promised she could make the others understand, and Neve had no choice but to believe her. More than that, she wanted to believe her. Not just because she wanted to avoid a conflict that might turn the town into a smoldering crater, but because it would be really nice, actually, to have her family back. To know them again, beyond what she read in stupid mythology books and obscure folklore studies that barely scratched the surface because her family's history was an oral tradition, and writing things down was for suckers, apparently.

They could be together again. All of them. Just like Danu said.

"Okay, what gives?" Alexandria demanded in school the day after Danu's revelation.

Neve snapped back to the present to find Alexandria glaring at her, dark eyes narrowed and unamused. They were in the library, someplace Neve usually took pains to avoid, but today she had made an exception because Alexandria was spending her study hall period here.

It took her a moment to replay the last minute or so and realize that when Alexandria had reached for her hand, Neve had jerked it away before they could touch. Which was a bad look.

"Sorry," Neve said, shaking her head. "I was totally spaced out."

"A memory?"

"No, just thinking," Neve said.

"It's tomorrow, right?" Alexandria said, the sharpness in her gaze softening somewhat. "I know you're worried, but— okay, what the hell, Neve?"

She'd gone to touch Neve's shoulder, a simple, thoughtless gesture she'd done a thousand times before, and Neve had dodged without even thinking about it.

"I'm sorry," Neve said again, cringing.

"What, do I have cooties or something?" Alexandria asked

in a whisper, one eye open for the librarian, who was a real stickler for the volume rule. Normally, that was enough to make Neve want to start yelling out of principle, but right now she was grateful Alexandria couldn't shout at her without getting kicked out for her trouble. "You've been jumpy and weird all day and now you won't let me touch you? What is going on?"

"I'm sorry."

"Yeah, you keep saying that, but you're not saying what you're sorry for."

Neve didn't want to have this conversation right now. Or at all.

"I get that you're worried about Bay and Mercy, but—"

"I am worried about them," Neve said, suddenly feeling very overwhelmed. Her thoughts kept spinning away from her, and every time she tried to herd them into some semblance of order, she ended up more jumbled than when she started. There was a panicky, tight feeling in her chest that had nothing to do with the stab wound for once.

Neve exhaled, trying to force her pulse to slow, but it didn't help, just left her with even less oxygen than before.

"Just . . . if something happens to the Gate or the spell, this might be it. I don't know if we'll get another chance, and last time you—"

"I what?" Alexandria demanded ferociously.

"That's not what I meant," Neve said, trying to backtrack. "I'm just scared because there's so much we don't know about you and the Gate, and the last time you—we—went through it, everything changed and—"

"And you're blaming me for that?" Alexandria's voice rose in pitch, if not volume, making Neve wince again. "You said what happened to the Gate wasn't my fault. You promised."

"No, I—it's not. It's not your fault that all this happened to you. Or that you are connected to the Gate. But when we came back, that's when things changed," Neve finished miserably, looking away.

Alexandria looked like she was about to cry, her mouth twisting. "Do you think I'm going to hurt you or something?"

This was horrible. Neve was horrible. She was a horrible girlfriend and an even worse person.

"No, no, no," Neve said, purposely reaching for Alexandria's hands, but it was Alexandria who pulled away this time. Neve tried not to feel hurt and failed. Shitdamn, she was such a mess. "I don't. I promise I don't. I'm just nervous and Danu said—"

The tearful look crystalized on Alexandria's face. "Danu said?" she repeated, her voice frozen over. "What did Danu say? Did she tell you I'm dangerous? That I'm going to hurt you and mess up the spell?"

Neve's tongue felt like it was stuck to the roof of her mouth. She swallowed hard. That was exactly what Danu had said, and worse, Neve knew that was exactly what Alexandria had feared the most. And now here she was, repeating those fears back like they were facts.

Weren't they, though? Neve hadn't known better when she'd told Alexandria otherwise. She hadn't been lying; she just hadn't known the truth then. That didn't mean Alexandria was any more responsible now than she had been then. What had happened to her—what was happening *to* her—wasn't her fault. Neve just knew the risk now. It wasn't fair for Alexandria to be angry with her just because Neve had updated information.

"She did, didn't she?" Alexandria said when Neve didn't answer, too busy rationalizing herself into a black hole. "God, I didn't want to believe him, but this is exactly what he said—"

"Who?" Now it was Neve's turn to stop Alexandria mid-sentence.

Alexandria huffed, giving her a mulish look. "Aodh. Obviously."

"Oh, so we're listening to Aodh now?"

She didn't know why she was suddenly furious, but the thought of Alexandria and Aodh meeting behind her back made Neve's blood boil. What the hell did they have to talk about? The last time Neve had checked, she'd gotten a pretty harsh lecture for not killing him on sight.

"You're the one who was feeling all bad for him, like, three days ago," Alexandria shot back.

"I don't feel bad for him," Neve protested. "He almost killed me!"

"He's the reason my parents are dead—" Alexandria cut herself off with a growl and shook her head, waving her hands in front of her face. "No, I'm not justifying myself to you. Yes, Aodh came and talked to me. And I didn't believe him." Alexandria gave an utterly humorless laugh. "But he was exactly right. Goddamn."

"Right about what? What did he say about me?"

Alexandria scowled. "Nothing. Absolutely nothing about you, Neve. Because—*shocker!*—not everything is about you."

She picked up her books, sweeping them into her backpack in one movement, and strode away from the table.

"This literally is about me!" Neve shouted after her, pushing up from her chair fast enough that her ribs twinged.

"Ms. Morgan," Mr. Prim, the librarian, scolded, appearing out of the stacks like an uppity, sweater-vest-wearing phantom. "That is entirely too loud. Lower your voice or take your conversation elsewhere."

Neve bared her teeth at him, a sharp spike of anger making the world go red around the edges. She wanted to scream his stupid little library apart. That would show him some real volume.

But the burst of malice vanished as quickly as it came and Neve just sat back down, still glaring at the tweedy little man until he disappeared among the bookshelves to harass someone else.

The day did not improve from there. Alexandria was conspicuously absent from their only other shared class, and when Neve saw the empty desk, she nearly walked out herself. It was a mix of stubbornness and pride that made her grit her teeth and go to her seat anyway, though she regretted it almost immediately.

What she wanted to be doing was hunting Aodh down and demanding to know what he and Alexandria had been talking about. The not knowing was driving her crazy. It was stupid and possessive and it was burning a hole in her brain. She hadn't seen Aodh since Danu reappeared, and he'd been, what? Skulking around like a dickhead and gossiping with her girlfriend? About what? How would Aodh even know Danu said that stuff about Alexandria, and why the hell was Alexandria mad at Neve when Neve had only just found out herself?

And since when would Alexandria trust anything Aodh said? She was the one who had been pissed at Neve for giving him half a chance and for maybe being able to see beyond the objectively atrocious shit he'd pulled to get out of the pocket dimension she'd put him in. Alexandria had been pissed about it *literally* three days ago! And now they were besties?

It wasn't fair. It wasn't fair that Neve had been drowning for weeks and now that she finally had a chance to get her sisters back, Alexandria was acting like she was the asshole. She was doing her best. And it wasn't good enough—it wasn't even close—but Neve was trying. She was trying so hard that it felt like it might actually kill her, but what else was she supposed to do?

Fuck, Neve missed her sisters. She wanted them back so badly. The wanting was an ache in her chest, all empty and hollow where they had been scooped out with a melon baller and Neve had been left to bleed without them.

She wanted them back and she was going to get them back. Alexandria might be mad now, but once Bay and Mercy were home and they were safe, Neve would make it better. Somehow. Danu would deal with the family and Neve would make things right with Alexandria and everything would be okay. They could figure out Alexandria's connection to the Gate once there wasn't the possibility that she'd take Bay and Mercy away from Neve forever, but not before.

One more day. They were coming home soon, so soon. Neve just had to be patient for one more day and pray that nothing bad happened in the next twenty-four hours.

Even as she thought it, Neve had a sinking suspicion she'd jinxed herself. Maybe it was just her feeling bad about fighting with Alexandria—Neve hoped that was all it was—but something in her gut warned that something was coming and Neve had better strap in.

CHAPTER TWENTY-FOUR

Neve didn't hear from Alexandria for the rest of the day. Not that she was waiting for a text or anything, except for the fact that she absolutely was. She didn't know why she refused to reach out first. Some stupid insistence that Neve wasn't the one who was wrong, wasn't the one who needed to apologize.

Except she absolutely did need to apologize, because she'd basically blamed Alexandria for Bay and Mercy being gone, which Neve knew firsthand that Alexandria already blamed herself for.

It wasn't fair. It wasn't fair that Alexandria was connected to the Gate, it wasn't fair that Neve had been so useless that Bay and Mercy had thrown themselves back through it to save her. It wasn't fair that Aodh had almost been acting like a person for a minute there, only to turn around and stab Neve in the back like he hadn't been satisfied with stabbing her in the front and decided to make things symmetrical for some unknown, deeply frustrating reason.

None of this would've happened if she were human. Neve didn't think she'd ever really wanted to be human before, not actually. Yes, meeting Alexandria had made her appreciate her temporary humanity in a way she never had, but Neve had still loved who—*what*—she was. But that was before she found out that she was a monster. Worse than a monster, because at least monsters didn't know any better.

She thought about what Danu had said, about Alexandria being able to pull people through the Veil, stripping them of anything that made them more than human. Would that really be so bad? If Neve were human, she wouldn't have to worry about her life stretching longer than a mortal life span. She wouldn't have to watch her friends die—watch Alexandria die—while Neve kept on going without them, maybe forever.

The idea of eternity used to be comforting. However she messed up, however horrible things became, it was nice to know that there would be another chance. A chance to make things better, to *do* better. But having to just keep on going? No, thank you.

But if she were human . . . would she have met Alexandria in that alternate universe where Neve was just a girl and nothing more? No reincarnation, no memories hanging over her head, no past mistakes trying to make her pay before she even remembered what she'd done wrong, none of it. Probably not, which meant Alexandria would still have her parents and would probably be living a much safer, much more normal life. Maybe that would be better.

No. Neve didn't know where the surge of denial had come from, if it was the remnants of Nemain in her head, or from Neve herself. She loved what she was, because she was part of something. She was one third of a single entity, an aspect of a stronger, better whole. She loved being Morrigan. Didn't she?

Neve didn't know if she wanted to be human, but she couldn't deny that her life would be a hell of a lot easier. Even if it wasn't easy, at least it would be different. Right now, Neve was desperate for things to be different.

She wasn't sure when she managed to fall asleep, after spending several hours in her bedroom staring at her phone screen, trying to decide if she should call Alexandria and feeling desperate for Alexandria to call her. But it felt as if she'd barely closed her eyes when something in her bedroom creaked. She snapped to consciousness between one heartbeat and the next, her eyes flying open, instincts screaming at her to move when a hand pressed down hard on her mouth.

Neve jerked as if she'd been burned, the hand muffling the stream of expletives that lurched out of her throat. She bucked and kicked, but the hand didn't move and neither did the weight suddenly on her chest, pinning the bedclothes to her body. Neve's lungs burned and the pain only worsened when a fist ground down on the knot of scar tissue that had formed over the stab wound on her chest. Neve's whole world went white and then dark again as her body spasmed and her heart kicked into double time. Even if his hand hadn't been over her mouth, there wasn't enough air in her lungs to form words.

"Oh, for the love of—could you *please* be quiet?" pleaded Aodh's voice, because Neve lived in the worst possible world. Of course it was him, why wouldn't it be?

Neve should have known better. Danu had *warned* her about him. Danu had warned her not to let her guard down.

Aodh sighed, blowing out a puff of air. "How about you calm down and we can try this again, hm?"

The hand moved away. Neve spat in his face. Aodh reeled, not moving off her entirely but shifting his weight enough so that it was a little bit easier for her to breathe.

"Disgusting," he complained, wiping the glob of saliva from where it had landed under his left eye.

"Get off me," Neve wheezed.

"Not until you listen to what I have to say," Aodh said.

Neve was going to kill him. She couldn't move—he'd pinned her arms beneath his knees, which was really starting to hurt—but if she could shift her weight a little, she might be able to wiggle free and grab the knife under her pillow.

If she survived this, Neve was going to come up with a way to tape her blades to her hands, because this was absurd.

"What is it?" Neve should be conserving energy, conserving her breath so that she could scream, could call for help, but she was terrified and desperate to seem anything but.

"Worried that the family won't be on your side after all?" she goaded, knowing it would hurt.

"Danu is lying."

Whatever insult she was about to fling at him withered and died on her lips. Aodh wasn't smiling, wasn't rising to the bait. His hands, no longer pressed over her mouth to keep her from shouting, were empty, free of weapons. Neve knew how quickly that could change, however, and didn't trust it for a second.

"Bullshit."

Aodh's gray eyes shone in the light coming through the window—the same window he must have used to get in.

"It didn't happen like she said," Aodh said, deadly serious. "We fought, yes, but there was never going to be a war. We would have . . . I would have . . ." His eyebrows furrowed and he made a low noise of frustration. "It didn't happen like she said."

"I remember it," Neve snarled at him.

"You remember wrong."

He was lying. He had to be lying. Why would Danu go to all the effort of powering the Gate spell and let herself fade away, be in stasis for a thousand years, if it hadn't been completely necessary? If it hadn't been the only way to keep their family from tearing itself apart?

"There was a fire," Neve said, recalling one of the first

memories after Aodh cracked the door in her head. "I remember. You killed everyone." Neve could feel the phantom heat on her skin, the horror of knowing that no one could have survived the blaze and that Aodh was to blame.

Neve's mouth filled with saliva, acid crawling up her throat even faster since she was horizontal. Danu had no reason to lie. Aodh had hated Neve and her sisters since before she remembered that he existed. He'd kidnapped Alexandria and nearly killed Neve. Even before that, he was responsible for Neve and her sisters dying a dozen times over, and he'd been tormenting Alexandria her entire life. No matter how guilty she felt, or the inexplicable soft spot she'd gained for him over the last few weeks, he was still, objectively, the bad guy here.

Aodh's eyes tightened. "It didn't . . . it was an *accident.*" There was so much pain in his voice that Neve almost believed him before she caught herself. "I wasn't supposed to be there, but I wanted to go *somewhere* and . . ." He trailed off, swallowed hard, and when he spoke again, the words were cold. "You remember wrong. I don't know why, but you do."

"What if I don't believe you?" She shouldn't be challenging him. She should be calling for help, doing anything she could to fight him off. Neve searched his face for any indication that he was lying. She came away with nothing.

"Then I'm down one half-useful ally and you can continue to sit on your hands and do nothing."

Neve bared her teeth at him. "Why do you even care?"

"I don't," Aodh said archly. "But you have a lot more to lose than I do, cousin."

Now he *was* lying, though Neve wasn't sure about what part.

It didn't matter. Neve threw her weight to the right and managed to heave Aodh's weight off her. She hit the floor in an ungainly tumble of limbs and bedsheets before lurching to her feet. She felt better standing upright, the knife from under her pillow gripped tight and angled at the soft spot of Aodh's clavicle, just below his throat.

"What did you say to Alexandria?" Neve said, only feeling slightly more in control, but she would take it over nothing. "About me? About Danu?"

It was maybe not the most important question, but it was the one that had been burning a hole in Neve's brain for the last twelve hours, so it came out first.

Aodh looked at her flatly. He still hadn't gone for a weapon—his sword was nowhere to be seen—but Neve didn't let that fool her into thinking that he was unarmed. There were a dozen places on his person where he could stash a knife, all of which were quick to access if and when he decided to use them.

"Why don't you just ask her yourself?"

I did, Neve wanted to snarl, *but because of whatever you said, she wouldn't listen to me, you little bastard.*

"Where is she?" Neve asked instead, fear sparking in her gut. Her eyes narrowed and she pressed the dagger harder into his skin, opening up a shallow cut that welled with blood. "What did you do?"

"Oh, keep your wig on," Aodh sniped, twitching slightly but otherwise not reacting to the bleeding. "She can't exactly scale three stories, can she? I'm just the messenger."

"Why wouldn't she just tell me herself?" Neve demanded. This was a trap; it had to be. It didn't make any sense, and the whole thing was making Neve feel as if gravity had been switched on her while she wasn't looking.

"Well, you see," Aodh said with a patronizing air that made Neve want to cut him again just so he'd stop, "apparently Mummy Dearest has you thinking that your girlfriend might kill you any second."

Neve's mind stuck briefly on "Mummy Dearest" before chugging along again.

"That's not . . ." Neve said, floundering, because that was exactly what had happened. "Why wouldn't she just come and tell me herself? Or pick up the phone and call?"

Aodh snorted, rolling his eyes theatrically. "Right, and come here? She's not stupid. Danu's got you all twisted around. Too big a chance you'd tell her everything."

Neve opened her mouth to protest, to argue that she wouldn't do that, before she shut her mouth again. She probably *would* have gone to Danu, if only to demand an explanation.

Aodh snorted. "Clearly, your human is the smart one."

Neve didn't bother feeling offended, too busy trying to reconcile with the fact that Alexandria didn't feel safe in the convent. That she felt so unsafe, in fact, that she'd sent Aodh, of all people, to fill Neve in.

And fill her in on what, exactly? What was the endgame here? What did Aodh gain—what did Alexandria gain—from making Neve distrust Danu the day before they opened the portal?

"I want to hear this from her," Neve said, forcing her voice to be as even as she could manage.

Aodh shrugged, as if he didn't care in the slightest. "By all means. I'm just the messenger, after all."

"This is so stupid," Neve said, pulling her knife away from Aodh's neck.

He just smiled and gestured to the open window. "After you, cousin."

Given the fact that she was fairly certain he was about to murder her, Neve thought she did an admirable job keeping it together as she and Aodh descended the walls of the convent. Especially considering that Neve was down her good arm. Even so, she took care to strap her sword to her back and grab an extra dagger, just in case. Aodh made a show of rolling his eyes at her when he saw the precautions.

To Neve's surprise, Aodh didn't guide her to the Gate but to the garage. He gestured at Neve to get into the driver's seat, and Neve didn't need any prompting to drive them both to Alexandria's aunt and uncle's house.

Neve drove the familiar route in a daze, trying to process what Aodh had said. What did he mean, that Neve remembered wrong? Was he saying that her memories were tainted somehow? How was that even possible? And what was the point of taking some memories and altering others?

Her stomach roiled, and her head pounded as she tried to sort through it all. She must have made a sound, because Aodh turned to look at her, the blank expression giving way to something that might have almost been concern. But they arrived at the Abbotts' house before he could do something horrible like try to be nice to her.

"Hey, wait," Neve said once she'd parked the car. Aodh was already halfway across the street, not waiting for her to catch up.

Aodh turned around, already rolling his eyes. "What?" he snapped.

Neve hesitated, lingering by the open car door. There was no guarantee that Alexandria had actually sent him. This might be a trap. It was probably a trap.

Aodh made an impatient noise, crossing his arms over his chest. "If you're done second-guessing yourself, could we—" He didn't get a chance to suggest what they could do, because Neve closed the gap between them and punched him in the face.

It felt like hitting a brick wall, and a jolt of pain shot from her knuckles to her elbow, but Aodh's head snapped back.

"What was that for?" he shouted, one hand flying to his mouth. Blood trickled out of his split lip.

"Stabbing me," Neve said. She shook out her fist. "And kidnapping my girlfriend. Don't do it again."

Aodh peered at the blood on his fingertips when he took his hand away from his mouth. Neve noted with satisfaction that there was already a bruise forming. Good. The matching bruise on her knuckles ached, but she thought it was a fair enough trade.

"So are we going to do this, or are you just going to hit me again?" Aodh complained.

"I might still hit you again," Neve replied before taking off across the street. She grabbed on to the ivy that climbed the exterior wall of the Abbotts' house and pulled herself up. She didn't love having Aodh coming up behind her, but she also wasn't about to let him go through Alexandria's window first. Besides, if she fell, there was a nonzero chance she'd take him down with her, which made her smile a little.

Alexandria's room was empty, which wasn't a comforting sign. It was almost three in the morning. Neve had been relatively certain that Alexandria would still be awake—her sleep schedule was a nightmare, to put it lightly—but if Aodh had brought Neve here to kill her, she thought that Alexandria would be present at the very least.

Neve nearly went for her dagger when the bathroom door opened.

"Jesus tap-dancing Christ," Alexandria exclaimed, practically hitting the ceiling when she saw that her room was no longer empty. She clapped her hand over her mouth. There was a moment of tense silence, but nothing stirred.

"What are you *doing* here?" she hissed, closing the door once it became clear that no one else in the house was awake.

Aodh raised one shoulder and then dropped it. "You told me to get Neve."

"I didn't say break into my house in the middle of the night," Alexandria pointed out.

"You should've been more specific, then."

Alexandria looked like she was going to say something before she dragged her hand down her face. "Okay, fine. Whatever."

"Are you okay?" Neve burst out. Alexandria looked fine, but there was still a part of her that was certain this was a trick, because honestly, it was the one explanation that made any sort of sense.

"Yeah, Neve. I'm fine," Alexandria said dully. She hadn't looked at Neve once this whole time, and it was starting to make Neve a little twitchy.

"I'll give you two a minute," Aodh said in a shocking act of grace. Then he ruined it by smirking at them and swinging back out the window. The frame creaked its objection to being used as a jungle gym but held. Pity.

"Okay, what the hell is going on?" Neve demanded. "Are you okay?" she asked again. "Did Aodh—?"

"I think Danu is lying to you," Alexandria said, still not quite looking Neve in the eye. "I don't know why, but I don't think she's trying to get Bay and Mercy back. I think the spell does something else."

"Why?" There was that bottomless, upside-down feeling again, like Neve had jumped from a high height without a parachute or a net. Hearing Alexandria repeat Aodh's words was unnerving. "Because of Aodh? He's a liar, you're the one who—"

"Not just him," Alexandria cut her off. "He and I . . ." She shook her head, refocusing. "I am never—*never*—going to forgive him for what he did. But I don't think he's wrong."

"Wrong about what, exactly?"

"I don't know," Alexandria snapped, crossing her arms defensively over her chest. "But her story doesn't add up, and I . . . I have a feeling."

"You have a feeling," Neve repeated, at a total loss to do anything else. Was that it? All this because Alexandria had gotten a bad vibe?

"Yes, a bad feeling," Alexandria said, doubling down. "It's

the same way I felt right before something bad happened and I had to move again. Something is wrong. Don't you think it's strange that Danu just swoops in and has the answers to all your questions and the solutions to all your problems?"

"Why wouldn't she?" Neve replied. She wasn't trying to fight, she really wasn't, but something in her rankled at hearing Alexandria talk about Danu like that. "She helped us. We needed her help, so why wouldn't she have answers?"

"Helped you with what, though?" Alexandria insisted, sounding even more agitated. "You don't remember why you and your sisters made the Gate, except that there was some vague threat of a war. Weren't you three literally war gods? You couldn't de-escalate?"

"We tried," Neve said, forcing the words out through another bout of nausea.

"No, she *said* you tried. You have no idea!"

"Then what?" Neve demanded, straining to keep her voice down because the last thing she needed was for the Abbotts to wake up and walk in on them in the middle of a fight. "Why would she lie? What does she gain?"

"I don't know, but I think we were right about one thing." Alexandria moved to the desk in the corner and pulled out a scrap of paper. She laid it out flat, revealing a near-perfect replica of the spell diagram that Aoife and Clara had used to figure out that Danu was powering the Gate.

"Danu was a battery, and I don't think she was the only one," Alexandria said, drawing her finger over the lines where they converged in the center. "None of this has made any sense to me, because why would you three choose to forget your family? Why would you design the spell to make them into monsters that you had to fight over and over and over? If you were trying to keep everyone safe, why forget? What good does that do anyone?"

Neve had been asking herself the same questions and coming up with nothing. Hearing Alexandria say everything Neve had been thinking just threw the discrepancies into even sharper relief.

"I think the Gate has been a battery this whole time," Alexandria said, finally looking Neve in the eyes. "I think it's been feeding off all the blood and violence for the last thousand years and storing it somehow."

"For what?" Neve asked, desperation creeping into her voice. It felt true, which was almost too horrible to contemplate. More than that, it felt like a way back to solid ground. Neve had been falling for weeks, flailing around for anything to grab on to. What Alexandria said felt steady in a way nothing had since Bay and Mercy disappeared through the Gate.

But how the hell would Neve know? Danu's explanations felt true too.

Except for when you get sick if you think about them too hard, she thought.

"Why would Danu do any of this?" Neve asked. "If the Gate was meant to store power, what does she need all that power *for?*"

Alexandria's fingers tapped a nervous rhythm against her leg. "I don't know," she admitted after a moment. "But I don't think it's anything good."

CHAPTER TWENTY-FIVE

A feeling of wrongness and a cryptic allegation that Danu was using the Gate to siphon and store energy wasn't a lot to go on. But they didn't have time to figure out the rest.

Neve's head felt like it had been stuffed with cotton, muffling everything except for the Möbius-strip loop of her thoughts.

"Cousin, I can hear you thinking," Aodh said back in Alexandria's bedroom, which was doing nothing for Neve's temper. "Don't hurt yourself."

Neve wanted to hit him again just on principle.

"Kiss my ass," she snapped.

"Classy as ever."

"Both of you shut up," Alexandria interrupted.

After Aodh had returned, they'd decided that the only way to get to the bottom of this was back at the convent. They would need the Daughters' help for anything that came next, much to Neve's chagrin.

"I didn't know if you would believe me," Alexandria said when Neve asked why she hadn't just come to the convent or sent a text or something instead of having Neve go back and forth across town in the middle of the night.

Neve's cheeks burned with shame and she swallowed the scalding remark on her tongue. She wanted to apologize, but the last time she'd tried, it had ended with Alexandria storming out on her. The gulf between them felt so much larger than the scant few inches between the passenger and driver's seats, and Neve didn't know how to forge a way across.

"Okay, so what is the plan here?" Neve asked, throwing the car in park once they were back at the convent.

"Talk to the Daughters, figure out what's really going on," Alexandria replied, taking care to close the door quietly behind her. "Come on," she said in a whisper. "Side door."

Neve felt a little ridiculous as they creeped around the side of the convent. It was the middle of the night; no one would be awake. But she was careful where she stepped anyway.

Alexandria didn't have Neve's uncanny night vision, however, and tripped on an overgrown root as the three of them tiptoed through the garden. Neve righted her before she could fall, taking her hands away as soon as Alexandria had her feet back under her.

"Thanks," Alexandria said without looking.

"No problem," Neve replied. "Is that, uh . . . is that the whole plan, then? Talk to the Daughters?"

Alexandria scowled, any softness in her expression vanishing in a heartbeat. "For the moment, yes. Sorry my planning skills aren't up to par, Your Majesty, but I can't do everything."

Behind them, Aodh snickered.

Neve glowered, turning back to him. "Shut up," she and Alexandria said together. It only made Aodh laugh harder.

His laughter cut off abruptly as they entered the convent to find that it wasn't as dark as it should have been.

"Oh, Nemain, thank goodness," Danu said, appearing from around the corner with her hands clasped as if in prayer. "I've been so worried."

Neve reacted to Alexandria's sharp intake of breath rather than her own sense of danger, angling her body in front of Alexandria's. The movement did not go unnoticed. Danu frowned, eyes flicking between Neve and Alexandria and Aodh and then back to Neve again, as if she was trying to figure out a tricky puzzle.

"Is everything all right?" Danu asked, cocking her head to the side.

"Yes," Neve said way too fast. The nausea from before hadn't abated. In fact, it might have been getting worse.

"You look like you're going to be sick," Danu said, taking a step forward. Neve stepped back, taking Alexandria with her as she maintained the safe distance. Danu's frown only grew. "Sweetheart, what is going on?"

This was wrong. Neve was wrong; she shouldn't be doing this. She shouldn't have left with Aodh and shouldn't have listened to Alexandria. What did Alexandria know? She was only a human and she'd done enough harm already and—

"That"—a light touch accompanied Aodh's voice and the fog of panic lifted as quickly as it had come—"is a nasty little trick."

Neve blinked away the tears that had already begun to trickle down her cheeks. What the—

The concerned look on Danu's face was replaced by something thunderous and dark, and it took Neve way too long to connect her sudden mental clarity to Aodh's arm slung around her shoulders, the tip of one knuckle just barely grazing the bare skin of her neck. A flash of purple curled under the skin of his throat: he was fighting against Aoife's spell.

"Aodh," Danu said, her voice still pleasant and light, completely at odds with the dark look in her eyes. "How good to see you, dear. I've been looking for you."

"That's so funny, because I've been avoiding you," Aodh replied, his voice as airy and false as Danu's.

Neve's head still swam, though the chaos was all her own now. Neve recalled Aodh's ability to crawl into people's heads and whisper compulsions in their ears. She hadn't considered that he could shield the minds of others. Or that other members of their family might have a similar ability, one subtle enough that Neve hadn't even noticed it.

Danu trilled out a humorless little laugh. "Avoiding the consequences of your actions even after all this time. I really expected better." Her gaze fell on Neve, who suddenly felt all of four years old, small and utterly helpless and certain she was about to get in trouble.

There was a shove somewhere deep inside her mind, and the feeling of being a little kid vanished like it had been pushed out by force.

"Stop it," Aodh snarled. His palm was pressed hard against the back of her neck, and Neve understood. It *had* been pushed out by force, and he'd done the pushing.

"You always did insist on causing trouble," Danu said. There was an icy edge to her voice now, a blade hidden beneath the mild tone.

"And you always liked to blame me for things that never happened." Aodh's palm was sweaty against her skin, and Neve could feel him trembling ever so slightly, as if withstanding massive pressure from an invisible source. "That I massacred a village, for one thing. That I was going to start an interspecies war, for another."

"You wouldn't listen—"

This time, Neve felt the slightest pressure on the inside of her skull, skimming over the surface of her mind before it was foisted out again.

"I just wanted to see the world—"

"You were trying to leave!" Danu shrieked. Her composure shattered, violently and all at once, like sand struck by lightning, before she took a deep breath and schooled her expression back to pleasant neutrality.

Neve had seen Aodh do something similar, his mood swinging from furious to scary calm and back again. Apparently, he and Danu had more in common than she thought.

"What is the Gate for?" Before the three sidhe could collect themselves, Alexandria spoke up, lobbing the question at Danu while she was still off-balance.

It was a mistake. Danu, previously focused on Aodh and Neve, turned her attention to Alexandria, who was still mostly hidden behind Neve's body. Mostly hidden was not nearly enough, Neve thought suddenly as the look on Danu's face sharpened into a malicious point. It made Neve want to scoop Alexandria up in her arms and run as fast and as far in the opposite direction as she could possibly get.

"Oh, you," Danu said. Her eyes narrowed into slits. "You've ruined everything, haven't you?"

"Ruined what?" Neve demanded loudly, trying to draw Danu's attention back to her. Distantly, she wondered where the hell the Daughters were, and why they hadn't heard the obvious commotion. "Is it true? Is the Gate powering something?"

Danu listed slightly, her hands coming up to massage her

temples like she was staving off a migraine. "This was supposed to be a nice surprise," she complained, like Alexandria had blown the whistle on a birthday party. "And now it's ruined."

"What is?" Neve demanded, taking a step forward as her temper flared and threatened to snap. It was a weak fire compared to what she was used to, but it was still something. Aodh scrambled to keep his hand on her, swearing under his breath as Neve moved. "What did you do?"

Danu heaved a sigh, looking genuinely disappointed as she regarded the three of them. "I'm doing what I always said I would do. I'm bringing our family back together. I'm going to make us a home, a real home, right here. We'll all be together again, and there won't be any reason to fight at all."

She sounded so happy at the prospect, her expression going faraway and dreamy. Neve thought that might have been the scariest thing. She steeled herself.

"*Shit*," Aodh said before Neve could demand more of an explanation.

"What?" Alexandria asked urgently. "What does that mean?"

"We'll all be together," Danu said again. "No more of this squabbling. Won't that be nice? The family together, just like it used to be."

Neve didn't remember how it used to be; that was the problem. One of many.

Pain split through her skull and Neve hissed, her eyes

squeezing closed. She knew without having to open them that the fog had returned and brought a memory with it. She could still feel the pressure of Aodh's hand on her neck, but either he didn't have the ability to stave it off or didn't want to, because Neve felt the world spin beneath her feet, and when she finally opened her eyes, she was somewhere else.

"Yes," Neve heard Mercy's—no, Macha's—voice saying as Neve dropped into her old body in the middle of a conversation.

Neve recognized the weight of the bronze armor she wore and the feel of long, heavy hair intricately braided down her back. She knew, instinctively, that Badb had done it up for her, even though Nemain was too old for someone to be doing her hair.

"It would be nice," Macha said, sounding bored, as if she'd had this conversation more than once. "But I doubt you'd convince the others to abscond with you."

"Abscond with us," argued Danu, who looked almost exactly the same as she did . . . would—whatever—look in the future, standing in the hallway of the convent, ranting about ruined surprises and trying to poke holes in Neve's head.

Thinking of the present—the future—made Neve's mind spin until she banished that thought and focused on where she was.

"Danu, I understand it's hard, but this will always be our home," Badb said kindly, gesturing at the garden and the settlement built into the rock behind. More and more sidhe had been leaving recently, striking out on their own and going to explore the world as it

271

changed before their very eyes. Humans were young and new, but they worked so quickly. In what felt like no more than a blink of an eye, they'd raised monuments and created cities, marshaled armies and conquered territories, before it all came crashing down and they started over again. Even Nemain had to admit that it was exciting.

Danu didn't think so, clearly, and the more of their family who left, the more she'd begun to talk about making a new home, just for them and theirs, away from humans.

The Morrigan had laughed at first, promising her that humanity was no danger to them.

"If anything," Nemain had said, "we are a danger to them. They're so fragile."

Nemain and her sisters, presiding over battles and skirmishes, had seen firsthand what humans could do to each other. Rumor had it that the humans thought they were an omen. The other sidhe were getting little monikers of their own. Brigid, with her love of wild places, was the spring. Neit, who was usually somewhere on the battlefield when the Morrigan arrived, was war. Humans were fascinating. Nemain didn't begrudge Aodh his eagerness to visit.

"Besides," Badb said gently, laying a hand on Danu's shoulder, "it would take ages to raise enough magic to make a place like that."

Danu didn't look mollified. Nemain let her stew. Danu was just upset that Aodh was preparing to leave; that was all. He'd been looking forward to going off on his own for ages now. Nemain would be sad to see him go too, but she was also eager to reunite with him out in the wide world. She couldn't wait to see what he would do there.

She didn't know yet that she wouldn't get the chance.

Neve blinked back into the present, sucking in a breath through her teeth. She braced, but this memory didn't come with a surge of stomach-turning nausea.

"You were trying to leave," Neve murmured.

"That's what I told you, didn't I?" Aodh snapped back, his voice tight with strain. Neve could feel the tension of his body next to hers as he fought off some onslaught she couldn't see. "Why would I want to wreck a world I hadn't even gotten to see yet?"

Neve thought of the first memory that had broken through, of finding the smoking remains of the human settlement. She recalled the horror at the destruction, the senseless bloodshed. It still felt real to her.

"What was I supposed to think?" Neve swallowed. Her mouth felt dry. "I remembered you killing people . . ." He'd admitted as much when she'd first remembered. "You said that we were better than them, that we loved them enough to abandon you."

Aodh's mouth twisted. He looked almost chagrined. "I was angry," he admitted. "I was angry for a thousand years. You left all of us behind, with a spell that turned us into monsters if we tried to leave. Of course I thought you chose them over us."

"Well, you've seen the world now," Danu interrupted, clapping her hands before Neve could cobble together a reply. "I hope it lived up to your expectations. I really do."

"So that's what this was?" Neve gritted out. "The whole time, all this was so you could split us off from the rest of the world?"

"It's for the best," Danu said, her voice taking on a placating tone that set Neve's teeth on edge. "Don't you see? The humans kept changing things. Too much, too quickly. They were going to ruin everything, take over everything until the world we knew was gone. And you all insisted that they were *interesting*. None of you saw the danger. None of you listened to me." She sighed, flicking an invisible spot of dust off her dress. "I wanted to make something new, something just for us, but obviously, that isn't going to happen." Neve shifted her body weight again as Danu's eyes cut to Alexandria. She couldn't square this Danu with the one in her head.

Or maybe she just hadn't wanted to see it before. Neve had noticed the little flashes when Danu looked at Alexandria. She recalled her own irritation with Danu in the memory, that Danu insisted the family stay together no matter what and refused to acknowledge that their family *was* still together, just a little more spaced out.

Maybe Neve had been so desperate for someone to swoop in and solve everything that she'd chosen not to notice the rest of it.

Also there was the fact that, apparently, Danu had been messing with her head.

"But it's fine," Danu said, shaking out her hands like she could shake off the inconvenience of the Gate opening early. "Plans change. I wanted to make something new. Something just for us. But it's all right. I will work with what I have. We'll still be together. That's the important thing." Abruptly, she brightened. "You'll like that, won't you, Nemain? You like this little town, don't you? You and your sisters. Oh, I didn't think of that. Yes, all right, I feel better now."

Neve's head swam. This was . . . too much. There was too much going on too quickly. She couldn't process it all.

"Here?" Alexandria piped up again, and Neve swallowed a groan, wishing that Alexandria would stop drawing attention to herself. "You can't make Newgrange Harbor your sidhe paradise. There are people here."

Danu leveled a truly nasty smile their way. "That is easily remedied, my dear. I wanted this to be a happier reunion, but my children do have their uses even while . . . warped."

She was going to let them out, Neve realized with a sick thud in her chest. Transformed as they were, the sidhe were mindless, feral. They'd attack anyone. Everyone. They'd kill anyone still in Newgrange Harbor when Danu turned the town into her little paradise apart from the rest of the world.

"Oh no, no, no," Danu said quickly, seeing the horror

dawning on Neve's face. "Don't worry, darling, I'll turn them right again once it's done. This is just easier. Two birds, one stone, and"—her mouth twisted into a frown again—"I won't have to worry about anyone making the wrong choice again."

"The wrong choice." Aodh's voice was soft and so laden with malice that it made Neve shiver. Her eyes darted to him, but he was looking at Danu. His face had gone completely blank, and instinct screamed at Neve to get as far away from him as possible before she got stabbed again.

"Yes, darling," Danu said with exaggerated patience. "I *wanted* to give you a chance to come to the correct conclusion on your own. I thought that after enough time . . ." She trailed off, sighing.

"We have been killing each other for a thousand years," Neve rasped.

Danu waved a careless hand. "We're immortal," she said, as if Neve's horror was something she could just swat out of the air. "And you never did any permanent damage." Danu's eyes alighted on Aodh and Alexandria in turn. "*You two*, on the other hand. I knew the risks when I sealed myself away, but I will not let the deaths of my children go unpunished."

Neve took a step back, bringing Alexandria with her. She didn't even think to fight. She just had to run. They had to get the hell out of there and they needed to do it *now*.

There was a smell like a thunderstorm and Neve saw the

tiniest flash of violet light before the hallway disappeared in a supernova that shook the foundation of the convent.

When the light receded enough for Neve to see again, Danu was still standing, her dress smoking slightly, but she looked otherwise unharmed.

Above her, Daughter Aoife stood on one of the catwalks, wreathed in purple sparks. Magic crawled over her skin and dripped off her fingertips. Her eyes were electric.

"My lady," Aoife said in a voice that would have been completely unruffled if it weren't distorted by the sheer quantity of magic she was channeling. If the rage on her face wasn't lighting her up from the inside. She must have heard everything. "Consider this our resignation."

CHAPTER TWENTY-SIX

L ike, well, like magic, Neve shook off the panic-born paralysis. She grabbed Alexandria's hand and ran, practically dragging Alexandria along as they raced deeper into the convent.

Behind them, Danu screeched with fury, and Neve knew that she wouldn't be forestalled for long.

"Here, in here!"

Neve ran faster toward Clara's voice, still holding Alexandria's hand as she skidded into the workshop with Aodh close behind. Clara closed the door behind them, and Neve felt a buzz in her gut as some sort of spell went off.

"Your mom has *issues*," Alexandria panted, hands on her knees as she tried to catch her breath after being hauled in a full-tilt sprint after Neve.

"She's not my mom."

"And 'issues' is an understatement," Aodh added darkly. He was sweating as well, his breath coming in thin little gasps, though Neve knew it wasn't from the dash to the workshop.

"Are you okay?" Neve asked.

Aodh gave her a sharp smile. "Don't start worrying about me now, cousin. It doesn't suit you."

Neve flipped him off.

"You're okay?" Clara said, hovering over the three of them, her eyes scanning for injuries. She nodded, looking shaken but satisfied when she couldn't find any. Nothing new, in any case.

"Yeah, for now," Alexandria said, shooting a doubtful look at the door.

"She's going to kill everyone," Neve said in a rush. "She's going to open the Gate and use the sidhe to kill everyone."

"And then we get to all be together in a happy, deeply haunted town. Hooray," Aodh chimed in, and Neve wanted to smack him because he was *not helping*.

Clara's face blanched. "That's . . . we thought something was—that is very, very bad."

"How do we stop it?"

"I—"

The air split with a crack. Alexandria shrieked and Neve went for her knives, pulling back her arm to throw before she saw Aoife and Maeve stepping through the hole in reality.

"You can teleport?" Alexandria squeaked.

"Only when absolutely necessary," Aoife replied tightly. If it was possible, there was even more magic coming off her now. The air tasted like burnt sugar on Neve's tongue.

"We didn't know," Maeve said abruptly, looking Neve in the eye. "We didn't know about any of this."

Neve believed her. Without a second thought, she believed that the Daughters had no idea what Danu had done or what she had planned. It was written clearly on every single one of their faces.

For a moment, she tried to find the words to say that she understood. Neve had been wrong—she and her sisters had been so wrong for so long—and worse than that, she'd been horrible to the people who'd raised them over and over again. Who had sacrificed everything, including their mortality, to keep Neve and her sisters safe, and all because of a lie.

Neve had been so awful, had said such awful things, to all of them.

Maeve exhaled softly as Neve launched into her arms, pulling the old woman into a fierce hug.

"I'm sorry," she whispered.

Maeve would have been right to be angry, to push Neve gently but politely away, or to say that she needed time. But instead, she just held Neve tight without a word.

Aodh coughed. "As touching as this is—ow!" he complained loudly when Alexandria smacked him.

Neve broke away with a sniff.

"There's too much magic drained away from the Gate already," Aoife said grimly. "It's going to open." She scowled.

"I should've known better. I should have seen what it was doing. I'm the witch—"

"She lied to all of us," Neve said firmly. She gestured in the direction of her forehead. "She messed with my memories, and probably Bay's and Mercy's." The Daughters', too, Neve realized with a start. The grim look on Maeve's face said that she'd reached the same conclusion.

"I still should have—"

"That, shockingly, is not our biggest problem," Aodh said. "Whether the Gate opens or not, she's trying to rip this town out of existence, with everyone still in it."

The Daughters all went still. Clara, if possible, got even paler. Apparently, they hadn't heard that bit of the villain monologue earlier.

"I think the Veil was just a holding cell," Neve explained quickly. "Someplace to keep everyone while she generated enough power to make something new. Just for us. No humans. But we woke her up too early, so she's trying to use Newgrange Harbor as a template." She didn't want any of them to have the option to leave. No more chances to make the *wrong choice*.

"How do we stop her?" Alexandria asked, shifting from one foot to the other, her gaze flicking between faces too quickly to track.

"We kill her," Aodh said simply. Neve blanched, and he

rolled his eyes. "Fine. *I'll* kill her, since you've taken a vow of nonviolence as of ten seconds ago."

As much as the urge to strangle him returned, Neve also understood that she was being given an out.

"One thing at a time," Maeve said. She pushed her wide sleeves up to her elbows. "We cannot let the Gate open as it is."

"There's no way to . . . I don't know, jam it closed?" Alexandria asked.

"If there was, we would have done it by now," Aoife said. "It would have saved us a lot of heartache."

Aodh made a derisive noise under his breath but wisely kept his thoughts to himself.

"It's not meant to close from this side," Neve said. She was an idiot for not thinking of it sooner. It would've been a piss-poor power source if they were able to put an end to the fighting like that.

But would it have stopped? The question rose unbidden. Would Neve and her sisters have given up what they'd thought was their birthright? Would they have given up fighting?

Bay would have. Neve knew that immediately. Bay had always been the gentlest of the three of them. She would have given it all up in a second if that had meant peace was guaranteed.

Neve wasn't so sure about herself, or Mercy. She wanted to say that they would have, of course they would have, because both of them knew that the best way to keep everyone safe was to not fight in the first place. The irony was not lost on her that trying to prevent a war had led to a thousand years of bloodshed and violence.

"Kind of a shitty battery if you can just remove the energy source," Neve said, shoving those thoughts out of her head. It didn't matter what she would have done if given the chance to close the Gate permanently, because she hadn't been given that chance. She had plenty to beat herself up about without adding hypotheticals to the list.

"So what the hell do we do?" Alexandria asked, looking at the assembled faces for . . . what? A solution to present itself from nowhere?

"We kill her," Aodh said again. "Obviously."

"Will that even help? Will that keep the Gate from opening?"

Aoife's eyes flashed, the white scleras going briefly violet. Clara made a noise of distress and Neve didn't blame her. If Aoife wasn't careful, she was going to burn herself out.

"I don't know," Aoife said, her eyes returning to normal after a second. "It might, but there's no guarantee."

Well, good to know that they were going to continue flying blind.

A massive boom shook the room, giving off a smell like lightning, and Aoife cried out. She staggered, and Neve lurched forward to catch her before she could fall over.

"I'm all right," Aoife protested.

"You're not!" Clara shouted. "You're going to die if you keep this up."

Aoife gave a grim smile. "I think it's a little bit late to worry about that, love."

"Stop!" Neve shouted, her voice cracking over the word. She couldn't stand to hear them talk like this, like their deaths were all but certain. "We can't just . . . there has to be something we can do."

"What if I go back?" Alexandria offered quietly, so quietly that Neve almost didn't hear her.

"What?"

"You came back okay," Alexandria said, twining her fingers together before gesturing at Aodh. "So did he. When I was with you, you both came out as yourselves. If I . . ." She swallowed hard. "If I go back, I can bring them out as themselves."

Neve blinked. So many arguments rose to the top of her mind, so many different ways to explain what a *spectacularly* bad idea that was, that all she could say was *"No."*

"The Gate is opening anyway!" Alexandria argued, digging her heels in, and Neve immediately realized her mistake. "What other choice do we have?" Her face was so pale that her eyes looked pitch-dark in contrast. She clenched her hands by her sides to keep them from shaking, but Neve saw anyway.

"She's going to use them to kill everyone. Neve, she's going to use Bay and Mercy to—"

Another massive crash. Several stacks of books fell from the force, and a fine layer of dust rained down onto their heads. Neve felt the walls begin to press in on her. They were out of time. She didn't know if Alexandria could *get* back through from this side, and if she did, then what? What was the best-case scenario here? Even if they weren't monsters that had gone completely feral, the sidhe still had a thousand years' worth of axes to grind.

But they would have their minds, at least. They could be reasoned with. It wasn't a whole lot, but it was better than the alternative.

Neve very specifically didn't think about the fact that the worst-case scenario would be another member of her family finishing what Aodh had started and killing Alexandria along with her.

Aodh heaved a massive sigh. "I'll take her."

"What?" Neve and Alexandria demanded in unison.

"You're not exactly in peak form, cousin," Aodh said, as if explaining to a child. "And unless you're suggesting she go through alone—"

"*No.*"

"Then I'm your best option." He looked between Neve and

Alexandria expectantly. "We're running out of time."

Neve felt as if she was losing her mind. If he seriously thought she would be stupid enough to—

"Okay," Alexandria said, her face set with grim determination. "He's right." She looked like she wanted to vomit as she said it. "It makes sense."

It absolutely, positively, *did not make sense.*

"A thousand years is a long time to be angry," Aodh said, his eyes cutting to Neve significantly. The wound on her chest throbbed. She knew what he wasn't saying—what neither of them were saying. Aodh was less likely to get killed on sight, if they even managed to get through the Gate at all. He had a better chance of keeping both of them alive.

"You don't have to do this," Neve said, catching Alexandria's gaze and holding it. Alexandria was still pale, but her hands didn't shake.

"Yes, I do." Alexandria shot Aodh a dark, complicated look. "He'll keep me safe. He owes me."

Aodh made a face and rolled his eyes, but he didn't contradict her.

"We'll buy you as much time as we can," Daughter Maeve said, her jaw set. Clara and Aoife nodded. Neve wanted to snarl at them for going along with this, for letting any of this happen in the first place, but she couldn't bring herself to be angry with them anymore. If there was another way, Neve didn't see it, and they were out of time. Despair rose like bile in her throat.

"You're coming back," Neve said roughly, like she could make it true by sheer force of will.

Alexandria nodded, gnawing on the inside of her cheek. This wasn't a goodbye. Neve wasn't saying goodbye; neither of them were. Alexandria was going to be fine; they were all going to be okay. It wasn't goodbye.

Still.

Neve snagged Alexandria by the wrist, reeling her in, and kissed her hard. It was quick, desperate, and Alexandria didn't waste any time kissing her back just as fiercely.

"I love you," Neve rasped.

Alexandria looked like she might cry, but the tears that shone in her dark eyes didn't spill over. Neve's mouth opened and then closed again. She wanted to say that Alexandria was the bravest person she'd ever met and that Neve was so, so sorry that she had to be. She wanted to say thank you. For putting up with all Neve's bullshit and more important, not putting up with it when it mattered most. There were so many things she wanted to say, so many things she hadn't said yet. Neve wanted to make the world stop in its tracks until she found the right words.

"I love you too," Alexandria said. "I'm so glad I met you."

"Take the back way," Aoife advised, nodding at a door that hadn't existed just a moment before. "Quickly."

Alexandria swallowed, bobbing her head in a nod. "Thank you." Then she pulled Neve down into another bruising kiss. "Don't die," she ordered.

"Give her hell," Aodh said instead of goodbye, opening the door that Aoife had conjured. Alexandria gave Neve one final searing look before she strode through the door and was gone.

CHAPTER TWENTY-SEVEN

N eve gazed at the wall where the door had been just a moment before for a few long seconds before looking away. Her heart felt like dead weight in her chest, her stomach knotted tight with worry.

How could she have done that? How could Neve have let Alexandria leave, with Aodh, of all people? How could she even entertain trusting him like that?

It's not about trusting him, she thought in a voice that sounded suspiciously like Nemain, except her self from their first life was rarely helpful. Or kind, for that matter.

Unfortunately, she was also right. It wasn't about trusting Aodh, because despite everything, Neve very much did not; it was about trusting Alexandria. Which she did, even if Neve felt like she was going to vomit at the thought of Alexandria going behind the Veil again.

Now she just had to trust them both to come back alive.

"How much time can you buy them?" Neve asked, exhaling a breath that burned on its way out. She turned to the Daughters and hoped her expression contained more determination and less pants-shitting fear. The Veil needed to *exist* for this to work, and without Danu powering it, there wasn't much time.

"Not long," Aoife said grimly. "There isn't much of the spell left, but . . ." She cast about the room, eyes landing on some of the half dozen spell-infused artifacts that the Daughters usually used during the worst attacks. Neve could see Aoife running the numbers, trying to calculate how much latent magic they might be able to pour into keeping the spell active. "We can give them a little more time than they might have otherwise."

That was not remotely encouraging, but Neve knew it was the best she was going to get. Until about a half hour ago, she'd been desperate to kill the Gate spell, and now she would give anything to keep it going.

"Neve," Maeve said gently, moving as if to catch Neve's hand before she hesitated. Neve waited for the impulse to yank herself out of arm's reach, to snap and snarl and do everything she could to make Maeve and Aoife and Clara feel as horrible as Neve felt. It didn't come.

She was still angry, she realized with a kind of detached surprise. But it was a different kind of anger than she was used to, banked coals in lieu of an inferno. Longer-lasting but less destructive. Warm. Neve had been so cold for so long that the warmth felt good. It felt good to be angry, to hold the heat close to her heart.

Neve looked at them, really looked at the women who had

given up everything they'd ever known to take care of Neve and her sisters. Who had raised them and cared for them and loved them, every version of them, in every lifetime. Who had lost them too, over and over and over again.

Maeve and Aoife and Clara. The Daughters. Her guardians, her teachers. Her mothers, despite all her protests to the contrary. They had done the best they could do. Neve recognized that now, even if their best hadn't been good enough. Even if they had lied. It didn't mean that they loved Neve and her sisters any less.

Maeve made a little *oof* of surprise when Neve pulled the old woman into a fierce hug, careful to moderate her strength. After a moment, Neve reached out and pulled in Aoife and Clara too. It was awkward and too tight, and Clara was definitely crying into Neve's shirt, but she didn't pull away.

"I'm still—" Neve said, her voice coming out a little bit choked.

"We know," Clara sniffed. "It's okay."

"I'm sorry."

This time it was Aoife. "We know that, too."

"We love you," Maeve said, and Neve needed to stare directly into the ceiling lights to keep her own tears from spilling over.

"Yeah, me too," Neve said, swiping at her nose. "Don't let her burn out," she said to Clara. They both knew who Neve meant.

"I am right here," Aoife grumbled.

"I won't," Clara promised, and Neve believed her. Neve chose to believe her, which felt more important.

Purple sparks rained down from the ceiling, and Neve could feel the spell keeping Danu out begin to splinter. Aoife made a low, pained noise, her eyes going briefly violet again.

"I'll keep her occupied," Neve said. The Daughters would try to forestall the Gate spell from ending before Alexandria and Aodh had a chance to bring the sidhe through unscathed—and Neve was trying very hard not to think about every single awful way that could go wrong—which left Danu.

"What are you going to do?" Maeve asked. The lines around her eyes deepened with worry.

That was a good question. Neve only had a dagger on her, and she didn't know if she could fight Danu even if she wanted to. Danu wasn't a warrior, but she *was* old as hell, and that made her strong. She was strong enough to power the Gate spell this whole time without the magic eating her from the inside out, powerful enough to supplant Neve's memories with false ones that affected her even now, before she'd turned eighteen. It wouldn't be a fair fight, and even if it were, Neve didn't like her odds.

Her only advantage was that Neve didn't think Danu wanted to fight her, either. All of this—everything she'd done—was to keep her family together, to keep them close.

Her methods were batshit insane, but Neve thought of the emptiness inside herself without Bay and Mercy. She thought of Aodh's anger and loneliness.

Alexandria and Aodh had both called them codependent, and wasn't that the story of their whole family? Just a bunch of codependent, overpowered idiots clinging to their loved ones as hard as they could, heedless of the damage they caused to a world that was so much more fragile than they were.

"Take this," Aoife said abruptly. She rummaged through stacks of paper and nearly sent a pile of books toppling before returning with a small pendant on a silver chain. Not silver, Neve realized, taking the necklace. The metal was too dark. Iron. "Our lady—Danu can meddle in the mind. It won't stop her, not completely, but . . ."

"Thank you." Neve took the necklace, looping it around her head and tucking the pendant beneath the collar of her shirt. She inhaled deeply, trying to force her churning mind and galloping heart to be calm. "Let me out," Neve said. "I'm going to talk to her." She didn't glance back when the door closed behind her.

Danu was barely ruffled when Neve emerged from the workshop.

"Hello, sweetheart," she said, smiling at Neve with genuine warmth.

Neve found herself smiling too, in spite of the circumstances.

It really was good to see Danu again. She had been gone for so long, and Neve had missed her, even if she hadn't known exactly what she was missing. Danu took care of them; she had always taken care of them. She would take care of Neve now. It was okay.

No. No, it wasn't okay. Neve bit the inside of her cheek hard enough to draw blood. The necklace sat heavy against her skin, hidden beneath her clothing.

"Stop that," Neve snapped, wishing Aodh was here. Wishing to be anywhere *but* here. Wishing for Alexandria. But even though magic and monsters might be real, wishes were bull-shit, so Neve would just have to deal. She sent silent thanks to Aoife for the necklace. If it was this hard to keep her thoughts together with it, Neve shuddered to think of the state she'd be in without it. Beneath the necklace, the banked coals of her anger flared, heat building in her throat.

"I'm not doing anything," Danu said, her smile dimming slightly. "It's okay to want someone to lean on, darling. That's what I'm here for." She extended a hand and Neve took a step back, keeping as much distance between them as she could.

"Don't be foolish," Danu said. Her hand dropped to her side, and the pendant around Neve's neck felt even heavier, like it was being pressed into her skin by a massive, invisible hand. "You are so young and you have been so brave. You and your sisters . . ." Danu made a wounded noise. "You weren't

meant to be separated like this. None of this was supposed
to happen this way. You . . ." She trailed off again. "You have
been so strong. And I'm sorry that I left you like I did, but it's
going to be okay now because I'm back. I'm going to take care
of you."

Neve didn't know what was worse: that Danu was being
honest or how desperately Neve wanted to believe her. How
many times in the last few weeks—hell, how many times since
September, when all this shit started—had Neve yearned for
exactly what Danu was offering? How many times had she
wished for someone to swoop in and magically make things
better? Make them make *sense*. Neve was tired and she was
hurt and she didn't want to fight anymore. She wanted Bay
and Mercy back. She wanted her sisters. She didn't want to
feel like this anymore—hollowed-out and broken.

"Stop it," Neve snarled through the heat in her throat, taking a step back. The pressure of the pendant against her skin
was painful as it slowly, inexorably embedded into her flesh.

"It's okay," Danu said encouragingly. "You don't have to be
strong anymore, Nemain, you—"

"Don't call me that," Neve shouted. The harmonics of her
voice shifted, and her lungs burned as the closest thing to a
warscream she'd felt in months tried to build in her throat.

Danu's eyes went flat, though the smile remained. "It's
your name."

"My name is Neve."

"You're confused," Danu tutted. "I can understand that. But you'll see that I'm right, in time."

Neve shook her head, trying to force herself through the messy jumble of emotions that Danu was pushing into her. Or maybe she was just taking what was already in Neve's own head, bringing it to the forefront. They were Neve's feelings, regardless of where they came from.

But that didn't make them true. Just like her memories. It was like Bay had explained when she'd turned eighteen, two years and a lifetime ago. The people they'd been and the things they had done were a part of them, and there wasn't anything they could do about that. But they could learn from it and do better than before.

Neve chose to do better. To try, at least.

"It's not our world anymore," she gritted out. "It wasn't then, either, and everyone could see that but you."

Darkness fell across Danu's face like thunder. "You're confused," she said again, her voice utterly devoid of emotion in a way that reminded Neve of Aodh. She wondered who would hate that comparison the most, Danu or Aodh? "These lives were a necessity to maintain the spell and keep the cycle going, but they're not who you are. This is not who you are."

Neve backed up another step, never daring to take her eyes off Danu. She didn't know how much time had passed, how much time she'd bought the Daughters, bought Alexandria and Aodh.

She realized her mistake a second too late, watching Danu's eyes narrow into hateful slits the second Neve thought about Alexandria.

"What have you—" Danu demanded.

Pressure burst behind Neve's eyes with the sensation of something foreign probing through her mind, too urgent to bother with subtlety.

"Well," Danu said, calm again in an instant. The pressure behind Neve's eyes didn't withdraw. "I am . . . disappointed."

Neve walked backward, keeping her body angled between Danu and the door. Her distraction hadn't worked nearly as well as she'd wanted it to.

Danu's eyes tracked the movement, and she laughed, a high, bright sound that scraped up and down Neve's spine. "Sweetheart, do you really think I would let my spell be undone by some human?"

The heat in her throat flared again and Neve forced herself to focus. That human was putting herself through hell right now with the person she hated most in the world. Neve just had to keep Danu busy. "No," Neve croaked, trying to keep Danu's focus on her. "You weren't thinking about anyone but yourself. Probably why we all left."

The air stilled so suddenly that for a moment, Neve's lungs

seized, and she was certain that she was suffocating.

Danu crossed the distance between them so quickly that Neve barely saw her move before a hand like iron clamped around her shoulder. "That is enough, Nemain," Danu said, and for the first time, she sounded angry.

Welcome to the club, Neve thought, trying to wrench herself out of Danu's grip.

"I have been patient," Danu said, calming somewhat, but the flinty edge in her voice remained. "And I have been kind. But it is time for you to grow up."

CHAPTER TWENTY-EIGHT

Nemain wasn't sure where she was. The scenery around her was foreign and unfamiliar. How had she gotten here? She couldn't remember. There was a nagging feeling in the back of her mind, some kind of tugging insistence that urged her to pay attention to it, but Nemain was a little preoccupied with the mystery of her surroundings. Her hand went to her waist, where her daggers sat in their belt, as confusion turned to fear.

This wasn't right. She shouldn't be here. This was—

The garden. The realization hit all at once and recognition quickly followed. Of course. Nemain's hand dropped from her waist and she shook her head, feeling foolish. She'd been sparring with her sisters earlier, two-on-one just to keep things interesting. Perhaps one of them had hit her harder than she'd thought. That wasn't a comforting thought, but it had only been a momentary lapse. Nemain remembered now.

"What could you possibly be thinking about?" An unexpected feeling rose in Nemain's chest as she turned to greet her sister. Macha wasn't wearing her armor anymore, but her enormous sword was still strapped to her back, half-plastered to the thin fabric of her undershirt with sweat.

"I miss you." Nemain's mouth formed the words without her consent, as though someone else had said them.

Macha's eyebrows rose. Worry flashed in her eyes, but there was still a smile on her face, which seemed to Nemain to be sharper and colder than it should have been. But it was the same smile Macha usually wore. Nemain didn't know why she'd thought that. She didn't know why she'd said *that.*

"Do you miss me, too?" asked Badb, striding up to Macha. She'd also stripped her armor from earlier, but Nemain couldn't stop looking at her hair, which was perfectly ordinary except for where a long scar cut through her scalp, from her right eyebrow to nearly the top of her head.

"How did . . . ?" Nemain asked, peering closer. Her stomach roiled at the motion, and she had to squeeze her eyes closed until she was sure she wasn't about to be ill. *"This isn't right."*

Macha and Badb exchanged worried looks, except even those were wrong. Concerned, yes, but there was a hardness there too that Nemain was unused to. That couldn't be right, either.

What was going on? Where were these expectations of her sisters coming from? Why didn't she remember how she got to the garden, and why did she feel so sick?

Because it isn't real. *The thought came unbidden, in a rasping voice that she might have recognized as her own if she'd screamed herself hoarse for hours.*

Her sisters were still looking at her oddly, but the dizzy-sick *feeling only got worse the more she looked at them. She felt as though she were glimpsing them through a warped mirror, a hundred slightly distorted reflections.*

"This isn't . . ." Nemain said, taking a step back from them. "You're gone."

"We're right here, sister," Macha said, her head cocked at an angle.

"No, you're not."

Neve rose to the surface of her mind with a gasp that sent shocks of pain through her torso. They weren't in the garden anymore. Danu's garden, she realized after a long beat. The garden she had had before any of this, before the Veil and the Gate and the spell.

They weren't in the convent, either. Neve had just enough time to begin to panic about how long she'd been gone. Was the Gate open? Where were the Daughters? Where was Alexan—

There was a hand on her shoulder and pressure behind her eyes so suddenly that she didn't have time to scream.

The smell of blood hit her first. Nemain blinked as her vision returned to her, unsurprised by what she found. How had she gotten here?

She could spot her sisters, their hair and weapons shining in the weak sunlight that illuminated the battlefield, though the fighting was long since over. She didn't know who had been fighting, or who had won, or even if either faction had won at all. Any survivors had long since left this place; she could tell by the smell and the flies and the lack of pained groans from the dying. The dead didn't make nearly as much noise.

Look what they do to one another.

The scene flickered and changed, shifting into a different battle-field, then another, then another. Each was horribly familiar, a tableau of needless, awful suffering. They whirled past her, one after another, until she couldn't smell anything but the stench of blood and rotting bodies.

This wasn't real; it wasn't real. It was all in her head. They were just memories; this wasn't real. It wasn't—

"Stop it!" Neve cried, crashing back into her own body, into her own time. She clapped her hands over her ears like the memories were something that could be so easily blocked out.

Her eyes opened into pained slits, terrified of what she might see, but instead of another scene of bloodshed and misery, Neve saw the ocean. Her ocean. She had absolutely no memory of how she'd gotten down here, but all things considered, it was the least of her worries.

Danu stood by the Gate, which was seething, spitting out whorls of magic the color of fresh bruises. She frowned, her head cocked to one side in a way that was so like Mercy's had been in Neve's memory that it made her shudder.

If Danu's look of delicate consternation was any indication, the Gate should have opened by now. Whatever the Daughters were doing, it was working. For now.

"Don't you want to stop fighting?" Danu asked, her hands open in a pleading gesture. "You've seen enough, darling. It's okay to want to stop."

Neve's chest was tight as she huffed out a thin, humorless laugh. Danu's presence in her head was lighter than before, like her attention was split. Neve steeled her resolve. She had to keep Danu's focus on her; she couldn't let her try to smash the Gate open before Alexandria and Aodh brought the sidhe through.

"Thanks for the permission." The words spat hot and venomous from her scalding throat. "But you don't get to swoop in with a solution to a problem *you* caused."

The pressure behind Neve's eyes exploded, and she flinched, pressing her hands tighter against her temples. There was something coppery and wet on her lips. Blood. Her nose was bleeding. Not a good sign.

"I don't appreciate your tone," Danu said primly.

Neve snorted, which only aggravated the nosebleed. "I don't appreciate getting killed every hundred years just because you couldn't cope with being an empty nester. No *shit* I'm tired of fighting."

Danu made an outraged noise under her breath, and this time Neve anticipated the touch that would sink her back beneath a tide of memories. Neve jerked out of her way, her knife slashing wildly at whatever she could reach.

And then she was dying. As herself this time. There was no fog of confusion, no dizziness as her mind tried to trick itself into thinking that what she was seeing was real. Neve knew that it was a memory. She knew that Danu was messing with her. That didn't make it any less horrible.

She'd been stabbed. The feeling was intimately familiar, though this time the object that had punched through her torso, spearing her lungs and heart in the process, wasn't a sword. It was a claw, a great big serrated thing nearly the length of Neve's short-sword but twice as wide.

She tried to open her mouth to scream, but all that came out were a wet gurgle and a spray of blood. She knew that if she could crane her head to look, she would see the bloody mess of her intestines spilling out of the ruined shell of her body. Already, the pain was fading, taking the world along with it.

Huh, Neve found herself thinking, an echo of her dying thoughts at the time. *I guess I'm the first to go in this life.*

She didn't come back to herself at the beach. Well, she did, but not in her own body or her own time.

Neve's body adapted before she did, falling into the familiar rhythm of a fight just long enough for an enormous set of jaws to clamp down and rip her throat out.

It kept going like that. Neve had always known that she would remember how she'd died in her previous lifetimes, and that none of it would be pretty. But she had expected to remember in the safety of her own home, with her sisters by her side. Not being shoved through her own deaths as if she was experiencing them for the first time all over again.

You'll be safe, Danu's voice intoned, as Neve died over and over again. When she ran out of deaths, Neve watched the same thing happen to Bay and Mercy. Sometimes both, sometimes one or the other, but the feeling that she'd lost something integral, that a part of herself was missing and she was incomplete without it, was always the same. As horrible as it was, that was almost easier, because Neve had been living with that feeling since Bay and Mercy went back through the Gate.

Bay and Mercy had gone back through to give Neve a chance to live. They knew as well as she did that this was their last life. That the chain was broken and if they died, they wouldn't come back. But they'd gone through anyway.

It didn't need to be like this.

Even half-senseless with pain, the grief of a thousand years pouring through her until Neve wanted to rip her own heart out to make it stop, Neve felt a spark flicker to light in the cold, empty cavern of her chest.

"You did this to us!" Neve shouted at the sky for lack of a better place to direct her words. It might have been her imagination that the air shimmered as the harmonics of her voice pitched toward a scream.

"Everything I did, I did for my family," Danu's voice echoed, coming from every direction.

"Bullshit!"

"We aren't like them," Danu said gently. "It's not our world anymore, remember?"

"That's not—" That wasn't what she'd meant.

"Won't it be better when you don't have to hide?"

Neve thought of the relief she always felt when she came back to the convent, when she could be as strong and as fast as she wanted, without having to pretend. She thought of the effort it took to blend in, hot resentment flooding forward because why should she? Why should she pretend? She was better than they were. She was—

"God or monster doesn't matter. You're not like them and they will hate you for it."

Neve saw the looks on her friends' faces the night they helped her open the Gate the first time. The fear and the trepidation. She saw Alexandria's dark eyes shining as she woke up from a nightmare, both of them knowing that Neve was the same kind of monster that stalked her in her dreams.

"Don't you want someplace you can be yourself?" Danu asked gently, so gently. "Where we can all be together? Haven't you missed your family, Nemain?"

Somewhere, Neve felt her knees give out and the grit of the sand through her clothes. She felt tears sliding hot down her cheeks. She was so tired. Tired of fighting, tired of hiding, tired of trying to force herself into shapes that didn't fit. She wasn't strong enough—she wasn't human enough. She remembered too much and not nearly enough, and no matter how hard she tried, she just kept making things worse.

This wasn't her world. It didn't want her and it never had. She didn't want it either, not until recently. Could she go back to that? Could she go back to reveling in standing apart, to having no one but her sisters?

Wouldn't it be easier to be somewhere else? Somewhere just for them? Somewhere they didn't have to hide?

Neve thought of the way Tameka laughed when Neve was being an idiot, the dopey smile Tameka got on her face when she talked about her little sister. She thought of Puck and Ilma, who were so crazy about each other that it was obvious even to Neve. She thought about Simon's jokes and how Michael believed the town legend of the creepy witches in the convent on the hill and the weird girls who lived there, and was her friend anyway.

Neve thought about her friends and how they'd chosen her, even when she was prickly and mean. Even when they learned what she was.

Neve thought of Alexandria, who'd known what Neve

was from the beginning and hadn't let Neve push her away. Alexandria, who was smart and brave and kind, when she had every excuse to turn her back on everything and everyone. Who talked too much and spent too much time on Wikipedia and never let Neve get away with anything.

Her humans. Her friends and the girl she loved. This was their world, and over and over again, they had offered Neve a place in it. That made it her world too.

Something caught, deep in the heart of her. Her throat burned so hot, Neve thought it must be visible through her skin. The fire in her belly spread, licking into her lungs, through her veins. It didn't fill the part of her that belonged to her sisters, but instead of putting it out, their absence gave the fire room to grow.

Around her, the world—the memory—began to shudder, losing some of its shape. Heat built inside her until it was unbearable, burning at the base of her throat until Neve had no choice but to open her mouth and scream.

CHAPTER TWENTY-NINE

T he world crashed back into focus as the cage of memory shattered apart.

In front of the seething Gate, Danu took a single step back. Outrage flashed on her face at having made even that much of a concession. The pendant around Neve's neck pressed hard into her flesh, finally biting through the skin, and Neve could feel Danu's presence in her mind, trying to calm her down again. Neve felt the swell of grief and fear and confusion, but she knew that they weren't hers. Not right now, not in this moment. Even if she'd felt those things before, even if some of the thoughts Danu was trying to shove into her head were her own, that didn't make them right and it didn't make them true and it sure as hell didn't mean that Neve was going to let Danu wipe Newgrange Harbor off the map.

Danu's eyes glittered, and Neve could feel the power being exerted over her. But it didn't break through. Neve had her own power back, and everything Danu tried to push into her head was turned to ash before it could take root. The heat at the base of her throat, which had for so long been snuffed out by the loss of her sisters, was as hot as it had ever been.

Neve was still alone. Her sisters were still gone; Aodh and Alexandria hadn't returned; her human friends were hopefully far away from here, where they might be safe. Neve was on her own. And she was fucking *pissed*.

Danu sneered as Neve pulled out her dagger. It was the only weapon still on her, and it wasn't as if she could use her sword with her bum shoulder anyway.

A flash of déjà vu—one from this life, for once, and without the accompanying burst of nausea. Neve, down to one arm, on her own in front of the Gate with no idea what the hell was coming next.

This time, at least, Neve knew she was in for a fight. She didn't like her odds, but if Danu wanted to get in her head again, she was going to have to work for it.

"Really, Nemain?" Danu's voice was cajoling despite the pitted darkness in her eyes. "Are you going to try to kill me?"

"I don't want to," Neve replied. Despite her meddling, Danu had been right about one thing when she cracked Neve's head open like an egg: Neve had missed her. She'd missed them all, their entire family. She'd spent so long wondering what had happened to the rest of the pantheon and why they had disappeared, leaving only the Morrigan behind.

"You're weak, then," Danu said. "And I shoulder some of the blame. I should have known that leaving you three with humans for too long would have adverse effects." She sighed delicately, like she was about to say something else. Maybe she was. Maybe it was just a misdirect. Either way, Neve was beyond listening. Instead, she screamed.

The air, heavy with salt water, shimmered as the sound wrenched from Neve's throat, making her scream a tangible thing. Tangible or not, it was one hell of a way to block out any more of Danu's bullshit.

Danu was forced back another step, even closer to the Gate.

"Dear, sweet Nemain," Danu said before she moved too quickly for Neve to brace herself. She didn't have time to suck in a breath before Danu's hand wrapped around her throat and *squeezed*. Neve's voice choked off, leaving her ears ringing.

No. Please, not this. Not again.

Panic and pain narrowed her world down to nothing except for desperation for oxygen to replace the air she'd spent screaming.

Neve's left hand grabbed at Danu's wrist, trying to pry her off, but it was like she'd been caught in the grip of an iron statue. Black spots were starting to filter into her vision. The thin breaths she managed to suck in burned like she was inhaling fire instead of air.

"It didn't have to be like this," Danu said kindly, repeating Neve's own words back to her. Her voice was fading in and out, soft and so damnably sincere, it made Neve feel ill. She didn't think she was going to have to feel it for very long.

Something pulled at Neve's attention, managing to keep her conscious for a few seconds longer. Her name, she realized. Someone was calling her name.

Danu's grip slackened slightly, just enough for Neve to manage a few desperate sips of air. Her awareness expanded, and she could see that the cliff had finally given way to the Gate beneath. It was open.

Neve's stomach leaped into her throat as she prepared to see the mindless monsters charge through. She'd failed. She hadn't bought Alexandria and Aodh enough time. Danu had won.

So it came as something of a shock when a small hand landed on Danu's arm, right above where Neve was still weakly trying to pull herself away.

Danu's eyes narrowed. "That was foolish."

Neve managed to turn her head a fraction, her swimming vision resolving enough to see a pale, determined face, dark eyes blazing. Alexandria. Relief made Neve's knees go weak, and she might have collapsed if not for the iron grip on her windpipe.

Behind them, the Gate was still spitting and churning. Neve could see the shadows of figures within the Gate, moments from passing through.

"Let go," Alexandria said.

"You." Any trace of kindness, pretend or otherwise, vanished from Danu's face, leaving an empty mask behind.

"They know," Alexandria said. She didn't let go of Danu's arm, holding firm even though her hand shook. "We told them everything. You won't be able to use them. They know."

Neve's ears popped like a thunderstorm had suddenly rolled in, as Danu's face twisted with rage. "You . . ." Her mouth opened and closed as if she was so angry, she couldn't speak. "You *horrible girl.*"

Neve felt Danu's weight shift, a split second of warning before Danu released her and lunged for Alexandria. Neve was moving the second Danu's grip slackened, fighting through the haze of pain and oxygen deprivation that seized her muscles. Neve didn't know what her plan was. She didn't have a plan. Her mouth opened like she might try to scream, but her throat was raw and her lungs ached, so all that came out was a croak. She went for her dagger with her good arm to . . . what? Was she really going to kill Danu? *Could* she even kill Danu?

She didn't get a chance to find out. Alexandria scrambled, somehow managing to keep her grip on Danu's arm as she fell backward onto the sand.

Neve didn't know if it was some kind of instinctive second sight, the same way she sensed magic or her connection to her sisters, or if it was just a response from her oxygen-deprived brain. But in that moment she saw Danu, and she saw something shimmer between her and Alexandria. A veil. *The* Veil. Not just the magic of the Gate, but magic itself. The intangible, impervious thing that had separated the worlds for so long. And then she saw Alexandria pull Danu through it.

Neve reached Alexandria and hauled her away, out of Danu's reach. But Danu didn't follow. She made a tiny noise of surprise, pressing a shaking hand against her own cheek.

She looked like she might say something, but then Danu's eyes caught on something behind Neve and Alexandria. Neve felt the pang in her gut that accompanied the Gate opening and without looking, she knew what Danu was seeing.

With her eyes shining, Danu's mouth curved into a gentle smile. "My beautiful family."

Wait! Pain shot from her shoulder all the way to her wrist as Neve reached out with her injured arm. She didn't know what she was trying to do, or even what she *would* do if she caught Danu in time. It didn't matter anyway. There was nothing to catch.

It was probably a testament to her age and strength that it took so long for the years to catch up to her. But with the inevitability of a natural disaster, magic crashed through the air, so searingly bright that Neve had to close her eyes. She pulled Alexandria close to her chest.

"I'm sorry," Alexandria said when the light finally receded, hanging on to Neve like a lifeline. Neve clung back as tightly as she dared. "I'm sorry," Alexandria said again.

When Neve opened her eyes, she didn't look at the spot

where Danu had been. She knew what she would see.

I'm sorry too, Neve didn't say. She didn't trust herself to speak. Tears gathered on her eyelashes and Neve didn't try to dash them away. She didn't want to look at where Danu wasn't, certain that the roiling mess of emotions in her stomach would bubble over. It was too much.

Instead, Neve turned her head to look at the Gate. A crowd—that was both larger and smaller than Neve had expected, or maybe feared—had materialized a few steps from the portal. She thought she recognized a few of them, before Neve saw two figures shove their way to the front, and the empty place in her chest burst back to brilliant life.

The sound that ripped from her lips wasn't a scream but a strangled sob as the frayed thread of Neve's composure snapped. She didn't know who moved first, if Neve ran to them or if Bay and Mercy ran to her. All Neve knew was the savage, desperate relief as Bay and Mercy collided with Neve and Alexandria hard enough to send all four of them tumbling back onto the sand. Her throat burned and her eyes stung and Danu was dead. Neve was crying openly now, with anger and grief and *relief.* Mercy's grip was so tight that it almost hurt, and Neve could feel Bay's fingers petting her hair, and for the first time in weeks, Neve thought that things might actually be okay. She had her sisters again. They were alive. They were together.

CHAPTER THIRTY

What came next was . . . tense. The Gate was gone. They'd been right about that much, at least. The cliff beneath the convent was just another unassuming bit of stone now, as if it had never held a portal at all.

What had come through the portal—*who* had come through the portal—was not so unaffected. The sidhe, Neve's family, the remaining pantheon, *were* angry, just like she'd feared. Aodh had been right: they wouldn't have listened to Neve and even if they had, they wouldn't have trusted her. But despite what he'd done, Aodh had gotten them to listen long enough for Alexandria to offer a way home.

Neve hadn't gotten the full story from either of them. Aodh had made some cavalier comments that made Neve want to strangle him, and Alexandria just shook her head the one and only time Neve asked. That was okay. Neve could take the hint, and in the meantime, she would be there if and when Alexandria decided she *did* want to talk about it.

Bay and Mercy had been likewise tight-lipped about their experience behind the Veil, keeping their answers succinct and impersonal when they did have to talk about it. But that didn't keep the echoes of their emotions from reverberating in Neve's chest. During the few hours a night they managed to sleep—usually all three of them piled in Bay's bed, because none of them was willing to be more than an arm's length away from one another right now—Bay and Mercy were ravaged by nightmares. Terror and regret tore at them, so potent that it sometimes took until dawn for Neve to wash the fear away again. Twice she'd woken up already humming, reacting to a nightmare before she was even fully awake.

It wasn't as if they had a whole lot of time to talk anyway. There hadn't been a lot of downtime in the days after, and for the most part, Neve was grateful. If she was busy, she didn't have to think. She didn't have to remember that Danu was gone, and didn't have to deal with the fact that, in spite of everything, Neve was sorry. She'd have to deal with that eventually, she knew, but in the meantime, Neve was happy to kick that can down the road.

Practically, Aodh and Alexandria's intervention might have kept the long-awaited reunion from devolving into a bloodbath, but that didn't mean the Daughters were any more prepared for several dozen new residents in the convent. Or, you know, what to do with them.

Aoife took care of the space issues with relative ease. Neve worried that she was overextending herself, but Aoife just made a blithe comment that she was "using less magic than she ever had in her life and would not be coddled, thank you."

Even with the strain of tripling the space inside the convent, Aoife looked better than she had in weeks. Months, even. All the Daughters did. Clara was smiling again, and Maeve looked lighter, the weight of centuries a little easier to bear with her family intact once more. That didn't make it perfect. Sometimes, Neve was still so angry with them that she didn't trust herself to be in the same room, and Bay and Mercy had their own issues with the Daughters to process. But every time Neve got angry, or Mercy got that icy glint in her eyes, or Bay went quiet like she might never speak again, it wasn't forever. They weren't going to repeat the mistakes of the past. There weren't any more lifetimes or do-overs. There was just moving forward and trying to do better.

Their little family drama—the one between the Morgans and the Daughters, at least—wasn't the biggest problem. The biggest problem wasn't even the fact that half the sidhe— whose names and faces Neve was starting to remember more frequently, and without the sickness that accompanied a tainted memory—refused to be in the same room as her or either of her sisters. The biggest problem was also the simplest: what the hell to do next. It had been Aodh, surprisingly, alongside the Daughters, who made the argument that the best thing to do was stay.

"It's a big world," Aodh had said. "And a lot has changed."

It wasn't a perfect solution. It *wasn't* a solution, not really. It was a Band-Aid until they figured out something better. And it didn't keep a handful of sidhe from disappearing anyway. No one chased them. If there were reports of tall, mostly ginger people with super strength and no idea how to exist in the modern world, well . . . they'd cross that bridge when they came to it. Until then, Neve and her family had enough on their plates with the sidhe who chose to stay.

Including Aodh. Neve kept waiting for him to vanish, to wake up and learn that he'd left without saying goodbye. But he stayed.

"So eager to get rid of me, cousin?" Aodh said frostily when Neve finally asked him about it. He prickled like an irritated cat before letting out a sigh. "Our family is here. And . . ." He made a show of examining his fingernails, not looking Neve in the eye. "And I don't think you would last a day without me. I didn't go through all that effort just to watch you mess it up."

Neve bit the inside of her lip to suppress her smile at the obvious attempt to save face. Aodh had plenty to make up for, and it seemed like he was going to stick around long enough to try.

"What are they going to do?" Neve asked one night, still awake despite the late hour and the exhaustion tugging at her bones.

Alexandria, who was sprawled across Neve's stomach with a book, looked up. "What do you mean?"

"They don't know how to live in this world," Neve said, trying to articulate the big, unwieldy feeling that had been sitting in her stomach since the Gate had closed, once it became clear that there wouldn't be a fight after all. "It's not . . . it's not ours anymore. It's yours."

"Hell yeah," Alexandria said, punching a fist in the air. "Score one for humans."

Neve snorted. "I'm serious. They don't know how to be human. What are they going to do?"

"They'll learn," Alexandria said, like it was that simple.

"Could you do it?" Neve didn't mean to ask the question, but she was too tired for her filter to kick in before the words were out of her mouth.

"Do what?" Alexandria shifted, putting her book down and sitting cross-legged on the mattress.

"Make us human." Neve didn't look at her. Her eyes were fixed on a loose thread on her bedspread. Neve and her sisters were on their last life, but they were still irreconcilably inhuman. Too strong, too fast, and Neve still didn't know if she should just . . . expect to live forever. She hadn't asked, because the prospect made her nauseous. "What if there was a way to bring us through? Without killing us, I mean."

Neve could sense Alexandria's hesitation and looked up to see her gnawing on the inside of her cheek. "I don't know."

"Would you?" Neve asked, so suddenly that it took them

both by surprise. "If you could? Would you . . ." She trailed off, unable to make herself say the rest. Thankfully, Alexandria was smart enough to fill in the blanks.

Neve's heart kicked painfully when Alexandria took a long time to reply. She didn't know which answer she was more worried about. She didn't know which one she wanted.

"No," Alexandria said after the pause had dragged on for so long that Neve had started to fidget.

Neve's breath felt like it had been punched out of her. *No.* Just like that. She didn't even know if it was possible, so why did she feel disappointed?

"Not right now," Alexandria continued quickly. "Even if I could, it's too . . . it's too soon. There's been too much. I just—" She sighed. "That's not something you should decide when you're grieving. And I don't want to be the thing that takes you away from your sisters."

Neve's heart thudded painfully at the thought, even as she opened her mouth to argue. "I'm not—"

"Yes, you are," Alexandria contradicted immediately. "I would know. I did a lot of stupid shit when I . . . when I first lost my parents."

Too soon. Neve rolled that around in her head for a moment, biting back the immediate impulse to protest, to make her case.

"Okay," Neve said after a long moment.

Alexandria let out a relieved breath, looking up at her hopefully. "Really?"

Neve nodded. Alexandria was right. She was grieving. Grieving Danu, despite everything. Grieving herself, too, sort of. Who she had been. Who she'd thought she was. There was too much mess all bound together for her to make any kind of rational decision right now.

Neve held out her hand and pulled Alexandria onto her chest when Alexandria took it. She held her close, feeling Alexandria's heart against hers. Neve pressed her cheek against Alexandria's hair. She smelled like pomegranate shampoo. Neve liked it.

"I love you," Neve said into Alexandria's hair, the words smushed and barely audible. She felt Alexandria's chest hitch.

"I love you too."

Maybe one day—one day that was a long, long way away— Neve would ask Alexandria to make her mortal. Maybe Alexandria would say yes. Then what? Neve didn't know.

There was so much left to do. Help rebuild, for one thing. Mourn. Actually, properly mourn for everything they'd gone through in this life and all the others. Alexandria would probably stay, but maybe she'd leave for a while too, go to college or something. The thought made Neve's stomach clench, but there was something undeniably light about thinking of a future that didn't have a bloody sword hanging over it. There was nothing coming, nothing to brace for. There was just . . . life. This life. Her life.

Their life, maybe. Neve hoped so.

She almost opened her mouth to ask, to voice some of the churning insecurities that pinged inside her brain, before opting against it. Instead, she just held Alexandria close. They had time. A whole lifetime of it.

EPILOGUE

Neve turned eighteen. The day she'd been looking forward to for as long as she could remember
finally came. It was . . . complicated, to say the least.
Birthdays had always been muted in the convent, none
more so than the day they each manifested, because of the
onslaught of memories that would follow. But Neve had sort
of crossed that bridge already. Still, it was nice to have her
sisters there with her to sort out the rest of it. Despite what
had filtered in through the cracks, a thousand years was a long
time, and Neve didn't think she would have been able to manage it without them.

The day concluded with Neve, dehydrated from crying and
dizzy from the press of memories, blubbering into her slice of
cake as Bay and Mercy, along with Alexandria, Tameka, Puck,
Ilma, Simon, and Michael, sang a horribly out-of-tune rendi-
tion of "Happy Birthday." At the end of the song, Bay got her
a new slice of cake.

And that was it. Neve was eighteen. She'd made it.

ACKNOWLEDGMENTS

Well, well, well. We made it. Hello again, people who read the acknowledgments.

In publishing, much is made about second-book syndrome and the so-called "book two blues," which are just cute ways to say that, for most people, writing the second book is much, much harder than the first. I'd love to say that this book was the exception to the rule, but honestly, there were a couple of times in the last year where I wasn't sure it would get written at all.

Every book is a labor of love, and nothing gets published without a team of amazing people behind it. I'd like to extend special thanks to Steven Salpeter and Nicole Ellul, without whom this book definitely would not exist. Steven, thank you for your guidance and advocacy on my behalf. Nicole, you have the patience of a saint, and if the pope ever answers my emails, you will be canonized for it someday. (I'm pretty sure that's how sainthood works.)

To the team at Simon & Schuster, especially Sarah Creech, Sara Berko, Amanda Brenner, Nicole Valdez, Alyza Liu, Kendra Levin, and Justin Chanda: thank you for all your hard work.

I consider myself extremely lucky to be surrounded by friends and family who have supported me through the wild ups and downs of writing this book. Courtney, Erica, Cat, Lucy, Iz, and Alechia, thank you for always fielding my panicked calls, DMs, and emails at 2:00 a.m. with the subject line "Is This Anything?" Kelsey, thank you for helping me workshop it when I wanted to walk into the river.

Mom, Dad, Lauren, and Eamon: thank you for having my back and being there for cheerleading and reality checks as needed.

I'd also like to extend my solemn thanks and also apologies to my roommates, Sean and Kristen, who never threatened to break the lease once, not even in June, when I was fully losing my mind. Y'all are the best.

Finally, thanks to you, reader. From the bottom of my heart, thank you for coming on this journey with me, Neve, and everyone in Newgrange Harbor. We hope you enjoyed the ride.

ABOUT THE AUTHOR

Cayla Fay is a coastal New England local, D&D enthusiast, and believer in the power of black lipstick. They have a JD from Suffolk University and a BA from Fordham University. When not writing, she spends her days walking her shih tzu, Charlie; listening to way too many podcasts; and exploring the defiantly tangled streets of Boston.